ALSO BY ERIC KRAFT

Little Follies

Herb 'n' Lorna

Reservations Recommended

Where Do You Stop?

What a Piece of Work I Am

At Home with the Glynns

Leaving Small's Hotel

Inflating a Dog

PASSIONATE
SPECTATOR

PASSIONATE
SPECTATOR

ERIC KRAFT

St. Martin's Press   New York

www.stmartins.com

Portions of this book first appeared in *Exquisite Corpse,* the *East Hampton Star,* and *Ninth Letter.*

Author's notes: I am indebted to Alan Wachtel for correcting my mistaken memory of John R. Philpots's *Oysters and All About Them,* and to him and Sandra Wilde for their generous gift of a copy of that pioneering work. The map on page 143 is an adaptation of the U.S. Geological Survey AST81-2 Trackline Map; it should not be used for navigational purposes. The information about the horseshoe crab in Chapter 18 came from the *Funk & Wagnalls Encyclopedia,* the *Encyclopedia Britannica,* and John R. Philpots's lesser-known sequel to *Oysters and All About Them, Arthropods and All About Them.*

www.erickraft.com/peterleroy

Library of Congress Cataloging-in-Publication Data

Kraft, Eric.
    Passionate spectator / Eric Kraft.— 1st ed.
    p. cm.
  ISBN 0-312-31882-0
  EAN 978-0312-31882-6
    1. Manhattan (New York, N.Y.)—Fiction. 2. Autobiography—Authorship—Fiction. 3. Male friendship—Fiction. 4. Self-employed—Fiction. 5. Ghostwriters—Fiction. I. Title.

PS3561.R22P37 2004
813'.54—dc322
                           2004040548

First Edition: July 2004

10 9 8 7 6 5 4 3 2 1

For Mad

For the perfect flâneur, for the passionate spectator, it is an immense joy to set up house in the heart of the multitude, amid the ebb and flow of movement, in the midst of the fugitive and the infinite. To be away from home and yet feel oneself everywhere at home; to see the world, to be at the center of the world, and yet remain hidden from the world—such are a few of the slightest pleasures of those independent, passionate, impartial natures which the tongue can but clumsily define. The spectator is a prince who everywhere rejoices in his incognito. The lover of life makes the whole world his family, just like the lover of the fair sex who builds up his family from all the beautiful women that he has ever found, or that are—or are not—to be found.

—Charles Baudelaire, "The Painter of Modern Life"

Multitude, solitude: equal and convertible terms for the active and fecund poet. He who does not know how to people his solitude will not know either how to be alone in a bustling crowd.

—Baudelaire, *Paris Spleen,* "Crowds"

The man who trips would be the last to laugh at his own fall, unless he happened to be a philosopher, one who had acquired by habit a power of rapid self-division and thus of assisting as a disinterested spectator at the phenomena of his own ego. But such cases are rare.

—Baudelaire, "On the Essence of Laughter"

PASSIONATE
SPECTATOR

Preface

The Groundwork of This Well-Meaning Book

Reader, lo here [is] a well-meaning Book. . . . I desire therein to be delineated in mine own genuine, simple and ordinary fashion, without contention, art or study; for it is myself I portray. . . . Thus, gentle Reader, myself am the groundwork of my book.

—Montaigne,
"That We Should Not Judge of Our
Happiness Until After Our Death"

I AM A CROWD. If you see me on the street, strolling, I may seem to be alone, but I'm not. If you are watching me from the building across the street with your binoculars while I am sitting at home in the little room where I do my work, the business of reminiscence, you may think that I am alone, but I am not. I am never really alone. All the people who have played parts in my past, and all the people whom I have invented to fill the gaps in my past, are with me, wherever I am, wherever I go. Their constant presence has made me one of the people one passes on a New York street who hear inner voices, and among those I am one of the ones who listen to them. I walk to the unpredictable rhythms of a shifting internal confabulation, the chatter of a cocktail party of the mind, with everyone at that party vying for my attention, each in a singular way, but each—regardless of what he says or how she says it or how any one of them finds a way to be heard for a while above the others—asking, pleading, or demanding that I tell his story next, or, at the very least, that I find a way to tell her story, even a bit of their story, while I'm telling mine. I'm a memoirist.

As a memoirist, my intention is to tell my own story, of course, and to tell it in a way that keeps my good side toward the camera, but those other people have their parts to play in the story that I intend to tell. They deserve my attention, those people from my past, not only the ones who were really there, but also and especially the ones I have inserted into my past who never asked the favor. I try to pay them the attention they deserve, but I can't pay them all the attention they desire. I just don't have the time, for one thing. I live in the world, as you do, and I have my needs and duties.

For very many years now, I have set aside an hour and a half every morning, early in the morning, when I sit in the little room that I mentioned, a stuffy little room in a small New York apartment, and invite the whole crowd to jabber away as much as they like. Having given them that time, I should be allowed to ignore them until the next morning. I don't owe them any more attention than I have already given them. I should be free for many hours to go about my business and think my thoughts, without interruption. That's what I think. They don't agree.

Instead, they intrude throughout the day. I never quite know when one of them—or a gang of them—will intervene in one of the simple negotiations of everyday social intercourse, but I have come to expect that the intervention will occur, and I've become (I think, I hope) adept at disguising the fact that when they interrupt, when they clamor for my attention, I step for a while out of life and into my memory, or my imagination. If, for example, you were the woman in the delicatessen a block and a half from my apartment from whom I buy a large cardboard container of coffee when I find myself flagging during the part of the day when I try to earn enough money to pay the rent and buy the coffee, you would never know how populous a mind I bring into the store when I come through the door. I'm sure you wouldn't. I'm sure she has never noticed.

"Good morning," I typically say when I enter the establishment.

"Hello, how you doing?" she invariably replies.

"Okay."

This is a perfectly fine exchange. Perfectly normal. I'm sure she has no idea that one of the most persistent time-travelers from my past is standing right beside me, wringing his hands. His name is Matthew, and I will explain him in a moment.

"Time is running out," he's telling me, as if I didn't know. "A terrible fit of desperation has come over me, as I suppose it comes over all of us when we see that we're coming to the end of—the end of—of—"

"The trail?" I offer impatiently. "Our wits? The days of our lives? Our sojourn in this vale of tears?"

"You can say that again—it's gonna be a cold one!" says the woman. "You don't need a bag, right?"

"No, no bag. Thanks. Stay warm." I smile. I've gotten away with it again. Out the door I go, apparently as normal as the next guy.

In the street, Matthew won't let up, even though walking fast and talking faster are making him short of breath. "We come down to these questions," he says. "What are we after? Where are we going? What do we want? How will we spend the time that remains?"

"On a beach, with an oiled beauty by our side," suggests another of them. His name is Bertram W. Beath, BW to his intimates, and I will explain him after I have explained Matthew. Please be patient.

I turn down the street, toward the river, instead of taking the most direct route home, so that I can confront them without being seen.

"Listen, Matthew," I say, setting my jaw, "I've got a lot to do this afternoon. For the Eager Readers series, I've got to write a history of the construction of the transcontinental railroad in words of two syllables or less—"

"What are you going to do about *transcontinental*?" he asks, his brow furrowed with genuine concern.

"I'll call it 'a railroad that would go all the way across the country,'" I say.

"He's good at that," says BW.

"For Mrs. da Silva and the Friends of the Sun Society, I've got to ghostwrite a dozen irate letters to the editor about the administration's misguided energy policies; I have to chip away at this month's newsletter for the proctology group; and I've got to look for new clients for my memoir-assistance service; and none of that is paying me enough to allow me the luxury to listen to you. Save it for tomorrow morning."

"That's telling him," says BW. "Not that it will work, of course."

I turn left, abruptly, and begin walking briskly toward home. After half a block, I glance over my shoulder. They've fallen behind, arguing about something, to judge from the gestures they're making. I quicken my pace. I've escaped them for a while.

They will almost certainly be back at bedtime. I am a twenty-four-hour memoirist. I never sleep. Literally, that is not true, of course, but I think that it is true and accurate to say that the memoirist in me never sleeps, that the memoirist is at work even during sleep, certainly during dreams.

FOR THE OBSESSIVE MEMOIRIST, the actual living of life is a blessing and a curse. Diurnal existence, with its quotidian comings-and-goings, provides the raw stuff, the basic and essential substance of the memoir, and that fact, the utility of life as lived in providing the ingredients for the memoir-baker, if only at the daily-bread level, makes life worth living, but the mind is not content to eat life raw, so the stuff of daily life is just grist for its mill, and the mind requires some time to do its grinding. The memoirist requires some time to do the writing, and the revising, and the re-revising, and on and on until the life in the memoir, the life on the page, has found and memorialized what wasn't evident—perhaps wasn't even there—in the chaff of the lived day. I guess that's not quite right. I suppose the mind does eat life raw, but in the manner of a ruminant, cycling the stuff round and round again, chewing its cud until the mash is digestible.

For the memoirist who invents as much as he records, living life is only half the fun. Life is a rough draft. The mind remakes it, revises it, and rewrites it, unwittingly through memory, deliberately through the imagination. To what we have actually experienced, we add our thoughts about those experiences, and we transform them in the process: the unexamined life is not worth living. We also transform our actual experiences by including in our accounts of them not only the facts but also the possibilities: the unimagined life is not worth living.

———

WRITING MY MEMOIRS does not pay the bills. For that, I have a number of day jobs. Perhaps I should explain my habits. I get up early. I spend an hour and a half in my little room working on my memoirs, listening to my crowded mind. Then I go to a gym while Albertine takes a brisk walk around the reservoir in Central Park. We eat a little breakfast together and read the *Times* for a while. I shower and dress and go to work; that is, I return to the same little room, but I go there to write for other people, doing contract work, writing of many kinds, whatever comes along, whatever I can find, the hackwork of the freelance writer. That is my day job. It makes for an uncertain life, and for the last three years it has been—how shall I put this—unrewarding. I've found enough work to fill my days, six or seven days a week, but it hasn't paid enough to pay the bills. Though the last three years have been particularly disappointing, the pattern was established as soon as we moved to Manhattan: too much work for too little money. Before we moved, we ran a small hotel, Small's Hotel, on a small island, Small's Island, in Bolotomy Bay, off Babbington, on the South Shore of Long Island, where we lost a little money every year for decades. We sold the place and escaped with a bit of cash, but since then we just keep slipping downward, and little by little we have spent the money we took from the hotel (the sweat equity we had accumulated over all those years) and slid into debt, running up balances on credit cards with cash advances to pay our rent and other basic expenses, and even taking a loan from the Relief Fund of the Memoirists Guild, which feels humiliating to me. For the past several months, we have done very little after working hours. We just stay at home and watch rented movies. We've developed these stay-at-home habits partly because we don't want to spend money, and partly because I finish the day so discouraged that I don't want to show myself among my fellow creatures. I don't want to be noticed. I know that my failure shows on my face. Lately, I've begun to think of getting out of town. I've thought about the possibility of our moving to Punta Cachazuda, Florida, where my grandparents retired many years ago. I haven't visited the place since they died, but I know that the living was easy there—and cheap.

However, that may not be necessary. I have some hope for a new business venture, Memoirs While You Wait, which I initiated while we still lived on Small's Island. I've had some interesting clients. Actually, I've had two clients, and when they came to me, independently, they barely had one interesting life between them. That is to say, if I had skimmed the cream from both their lives, I could have served up one interesting life. Of course, I urged them to exaggerate, embellish, and, when opportunity knocked, steal to make their lives more interesting on the page than they ever had been in fact, so you may be sure that the lives that I sent my two clients home with were far more robust than the feeble things they brought me. I'm good at this memoir-assistance business, and I really do think that I can make a go of it.

Lately, however, business has been slow. That is, slower. Even slower than that. As I write these words, I have no clients. I can't explain it. I'm using the same methods to advertise my services and solicit clients, but I'm not getting any. Perhaps people are no longer interested in writing their memoirs? Perhaps only a small percentage of the population is at any one time interested in writing their memoirs, and those people have already written them, and so the well is dry? Nonsense. The fault must be mine somehow.

NO MORE THAN FIFTEEN MINUTES AGO, while I was beating myself up in the foregoing manner, I decided that a large container of coffee was probably just what I needed to help me get into fighting trim for the working day.

"I'm going to get the Big Coffee," I said to Al, grabbing my keys and wallet.

So much depends on chance. Once upon a time, during another period when I was feeling the weight of debt, Albertine told me that I shouldn't worry because I had what she called "Leroy Luck." I'd never heard of Leroy Luck before, and I accused her of inventing it to cheer me up. "It's the same sort of luck that Jack had in 'Jack and the Beanstalk,'" she said, "the luck of the dreamer, a boy's luck, the sort of luck that works in the background while a boy is sitting on the sand and his thoughts are sailing out to sea." There have been times when I've thought that she might be right.

At the corner where I turn left to go to the delicatessen where the Big Coffee is brewed and purveyed, an enterprising homeless man named

Henry sets up a card table every Tuesday and offers for sale anything he has found in the neighborhood trash that seems salable to him. On other days he sets himself up at other locations. I know that because I have sometimes seen him set up elsewhere, and because I asked him. I mentioned to Albertine, laughing as I did so, that I could probably sell a few copies of my memoirs from a folding table in a good location. "Don't you dare," was, if I remember correctly, her advice. This was a Tuesday. The card table was up, and it was covered with salvaged goods. I slowed as I passed, running my eye over Henry's wares, but not making eye contact with him because I was embarrassed to be on so tight a budget that I couldn't buy anything from a homeless guy doing business from a shaky card table. That quick, hangdog glance was enough, though. There, right in the center of the table, was a book, a book that, if its title could be believed, held just the information I needed. It was called *Creative Self-Promotion*. I had been shy about self-promotion. I knew it, and I was ashamed of myself for it. The man who does not ride the tide of his times is out of step, as I think someone said. Perhaps, with a handbook to follow, I could overcome my reticence and start touting myself and my services as shamelessly as all my friends and neighbors. I had the coffee money. I could buy the book instead of the coffee.

"How much?" I asked. Henry shrugged. I gave him the coffee money.

When I returned home, Albertine, canny observer that she is, noticed that I wasn't carrying a container of coffee.

"Didn't you get the Big Coffee?"

"No," I said. "Henry was set up at the corner, and—"

"You bought a bag of beans."

"What?"

"You traded the cow for a bag of beans."

"Oh," I said. "Maybe. I bought a book." I displayed it.

"You're branching out?"

"Hm?"

"Going into taxidermy, are you?"

"Taxidermy?"

"Creative Self-Promotion for Taxidermists?"

"For taxidermists?" I turned the book around and looked at the cover.

There, below the bold title that had caught my eye, was the continuation of it, in smaller type, in italics. "I didn't notice that part," I said.

"You didn't notice it?"

"I was a bit bedazzled, struck by the coincidence of my finding just what I think I need on Henry's table."

"So you didn't notice the illustration?"

I did now. A man looked fondly at a table lamp with a base that seemed to be made from a stuffed squirrel, his handiwork, evidently.

"I told you, I was—" I began in my defense.

"—bedazzled," she said, and because she loves me she hugged me.

BECAUSE I AM THE MEMOIRIST, I am the principal player in the comedy that follows this preface, its groundwork, as Montaigne put it, but I am supported—if the groundwork of a book may be said to be supported—by an able and eccentric cast. Foremost among them are Albertine Gaudet, Matthew Barber, and B. W. Beath.

ALBERTINE GAUDET is my wife. I have heard her referred to as my long-suffering wife. She is sleeping beside me while I compose this paragraph in my head. We met while we were in high school, shortly after I returned from a summer in New Mexico, winging back to Babbington in a small plane that I had built in the family garage. She did not fall in love with me at first sight, though I was already in love with her before I met her, having seen her image in a drawing, admired her from afar, and listened to the praise of a friend who also loved her. When we met, she was being pursued by a number of eager boys and young men who are all now, I venture, captains of industry and finance, assiduously plundering their employees' retirement funds. To make her mine, to get her to accept me as hers, I had to woo and win her, had to seduce and convince her. I told her that I would take care of her, promised her a rich life, attempted to stand on my head to make her laugh, and told her that when we were together she would always have a piano.

MATTHEW BARBER was my high-school classmate. I sometimes claim to have known him since we were boys in grammar school, but that's not true. Matthew was an enigma. If I had been asked when I knew him whether he was the saddest boy I had ever known, I would have said that he was. He seemed uniformly and predictably miserable, so much the very type of the pessimist that he would willingly endure being satirized as such. To the humorous exchanges within our group he would even contribute an exaggerated note of gloom that never failed to get a laugh. Not only has Matthew occupied me during my recent morning memoir hours, but he awakened me recently, in the middle of the night, as a player in a nightmare. In the nightmare, I seemed to be a livery car driver or a taxi driver—

"Taxi. A taxi driver."

"Okay. A taxi driver."

In the dream—nightmare—I was driving an unruly group of kids, rich and arrogant kids, and one middle-aged man who resembled Matthew.

"Resembled Matthew? Was Matthew. This happened to me. You were not the driver. Believe me, you were not the driver. Let me tell it—"

"All right, I will let you tell it."

"Oh, thank you very much. Will you please get that tone out of your voice?"

"Tone?"

"That tone of compassionate understanding."

"I'm sorry. It's just that I feel—"

"Sorry for me?"

"Yes."

"Why? I don't ask for it. I don't want it. Why do you have to feel sorry for me?"

"Because—"

"Yes?"

"Because I think that you are what I might have become if I hadn't met Albertine, hadn't wooed her, hadn't won her."

BERTRAM W. BEATH is what Matthew might have become if he hadn't had a conscience.

"That, I think, is not entirely fair."

"Be my guest."

"It is not that I haven't a conscience; it is simply that I own the secret to striding through the world as its master—I take that back—as if I were its master, which is enough—the master of its knocks and slights, the disappointments and offenses that eventually get the best of most of the people I see, turning them into fearful cowards who no longer think to master the world but only hope to make it through the next day without looking too foolish, suffering too greatly, or losing too badly."

"And what is that secret?"

"Watch."

STRUCTURALLY, this book is arranged to mimic a mistaken memory. Many years ago, I found in a library a book called *Oysters and All About Them.* I was fascinated by the information in the book, but its organization intrigued me even more. The author, John R. Philpots, had first produced a slim volume with its title making the extravagant claim of completeness. Not long after the book had been released into the world, its readers hastened to point out to Philpots how very far short of "all about them" his book fell. No slacker, Philpots got to work on a second revised edition. In it, he included the entire first edition, unaltered, but he wrapped that edition between an extensive preface describing the responses of readers and an extensive set of appendices in which he corrected errors and expanded the information he had originally provided. He sent the second revised edition into the world, and it met a fate like that of its precursor. Readers flooded Philpots with letters correcting and enlarging what they had found in the second edition. So, Philpots produced a third, assembling it in the same way he had assembled the second. At its center was the entire second edition (and at the center of that was the entire first edition, remember) wrapped within a preface and appendices. The edition I found in the library was, as I recall, the fourth or fifth. It was a fat volume, the result of Philpots's adding successive layers of text in each edition, as an oyster adds layers and layers of nacre on the irritating grain of sand that is the inspiration for its pearl. The full title of this edition was *Oysters and All About Them: being a complete history of the titular subject, exhaustive on all points of necessary and curious information from the earliest writers to those of the present time, with numerous additions, facts, and notes.*

I was so fascinated by the book and its organization that I asked a librarian whether I might buy it.

"Buy it?" she squeaked.

"Yes," I replied brightly.

"Sir," she said, her voice icy, "this is a library, not a bookstore. We do not sell books; we lend them."

"Of course," I said, "but if you look at the slip in the back of the book you will see that I am the first person to have borrowed it since 1911."

"That is of no consequence," she said, "no consequence at all."

I didn't ask again, nor did I steal the book, though I should have. A few months later, I felt the need to consult it again, and found that it was not on the shelf where I expected to find it. Had someone else taken it out? Astonishing. I asked to have it put on reserve for me. A librarian, not the one who had been so offended by my offer to buy it, looked it up in the newly computerized card catalog.

"Oops," he said, "you're a couple of days too late."

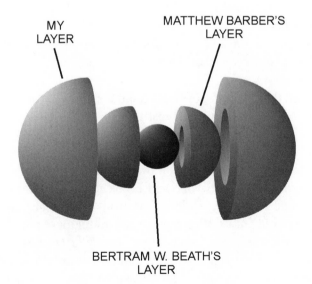

FIGURE 1: This book is arranged in concentric layers, like a pearl, but not quite like *Oysters and All About Them.*

"Too late?"

"It was de-accessioned last week."

"De-accessioned?"

"Removed from the shelves. Removed from the library's holdings. Sold."

"Sold?"

"Yes, at our Big Book Bargain Bonanza sale, last weekend."

"But—this is a library, not a bookstore."

"It's a new idea of our head librarian's—cull the collection and raise some money for new purchases by selling some of the deadwood."

"Deadwood?"

"Nothing important. Old books that hardly anyone ever borrows. Out-of-date reference works. That sort of thing."

"Are you sure someone bought it?"

"Absolutely."

"How can you be so sure?"

"Because at the end of the sale a decorator bought everything that was left."

"A decorator?"

"A guy named Bagshaw. Specializes in filling empty shelves with books. They give a room that lived-in look, you know."

"Right. I know."

I assumed that I would never see the book again. From time to time I recalled it, fondly, and with the wistfulness we feel for the things we've lost, and I ruminated on its unusual organization, at least as I remembered it.

Then, one rainy afternoon not more than a few months before I began working on this book, Albertine and I took refuge in a bar in our neighborhood called Books 'n' Booze. The walls of this bar are lined with shelves full of old books. With a pastis in hand, I toured the shelves, and, as you've already guessed, I came upon a copy of *Oysters and All About Them*. It was the fourth edition, in two enormous volumes, totaling more than thirteen hundred pages, but it wasn't organized as I had remembered it, in layers, like a pearl. I suppose that, over the years, my memory of the organization of Philpots's book became distorted by my anticipation of my own: this one, in which the text is in three layers. Thus, within the mind at least, the future can alter the past.

Peter Leroy
New York City
December 6, 2003

Chapter 1

I Am Among the Many Called

There always seems to be something else to do. There is the work at hand. Perhaps you have a challenging project in your shop at the moment. You tell yourself that mounting Mrs. Weaverbird's Standard Poodle is your focus. You should put everything else aside and concentrate only on that. But a small voice keeps nagging at you, saying, "If you don't do something to promote your services, there will be no more Mrs. Weaverbirds in your future, and no more Standard Poodles, either." Learn to listen to the voices you hear in your head. They may come from some part of your brain where wisdom resides.

—Darryl O'Farrell, *Creative Self-Promotion for Taxidermists*

I WAS ASSIDUOUSLY TRYING to think of promotional schemes for Memoirs While You Wait, but it wasn't going well. You know how it is when you put your mind to the solution of a problem. As often as not, your mind refuses to be put, or at any rate to stay put. It may allow itself to be put, but in a bit it has strayed from the place or problem to which it was supposed to have stayed put and has begun to wonder what you'll be having for lunch. When I find my mind disobeying orders like that, I ask myself what Balzac would have done, and I get up and go to the delicatessen for "the Big Coffee," which, in the breezy idiom Albertine and I playfully affect when we are alone, means a large container of coffee from the delicatessen a block and a half away, no other.

I got my coffee, and on the return trip I stopped at the bank of mail-boxes in our building to pick up our mail. You never know when the wizards of Serendip are going to send you a good idea in the mail. In this case, the good idea was distributed throughout the mail, it was all over the mail, it was the mail, and apparently all the mail. The mail that filled the box was advertising. I was going through it in a desultory manner when—bingo! The fistful of mail all but screamed at me, "Direct mail, you dolt!" Of course. I could market Memoirs While You Wait with a clever and compelling direct-mail campaign. I would study the pieces that I held in my hand, gifts from the masters of the genre, sent to me absolutely free, and I would profit from them instead of dropping them unread into the trash as I normally did.

What was in this treasure trove? Oh, you know. This and that. I was bored by the time I got through three of them. None of them was compelling enough to convince me to buy or give, and I am ordinarily more susceptible than most to the seductive call of advertising. What is it Albertine calls me—"credulous rube"—or is it "gullible bumpkin"? Both, to tell the truth. Of the two, I think I prefer "gullible bumpkin." It comes off the tongue nicely. Assessing the samples of direct-mail advertising while I made my way up the stairs, I decided to abandon the idea while it was still young. The simple truth was that it wouldn't work. If the Institute of 'Pataphysics hadn't succeeded through their lavish mailing in convincing me to donate to their building fund, how could a necessarily far more modest package from me ever convince anyone to employ me to assist in the writing of, or undertake the entire ghostwriting of, a memoir? I might just as well stand on a street corner and hand out fliers while chanting "Memoirs—memoirs written while you wait—your story told by you—or your story told by me—whichever you like," which Albertine has absolutely forbidden me to do.

The final letter, however, really was compelling. (I lie. This letter wasn't the final one. Placing it last in the telling, though it was third in the browsing, seemed to me more dramatic. So I have.) The envelope was printed in a clever attention-grabbing way. It bore the single word SUMMONS cunningly made to appear as if it had been stamped on the envelope by hand. The letter came, if the return address could be believed, from the office of the Under Secretary of the Department of Juror

Selection and Notification of the Department of Justice of the State of New York.

"Al," I said, entering the apartment, and I meant to follow that with "what do you make of this?" but she came tripping forward and threw herself into my arms, scattering the mail.

"I got a gig!" she cried.

"Good for you!" I said, swinging her round in a circle. "Good for us! What is it?"

"It's a retirement party."

"Oh."

"It's a job."

"That it is."

"I answered an ad. The head of the cardiac catheter lab at Carl Shurz Hospital is retiring, and the staff is throwing him a party."

"Jolly."

"Five of them are going to sing old pop, rock, and country songs, but they don't trust themselves to sing a capella, so they hired me to carry them over the rough spots."

"You're good at that."

"They call themselves the Five Statins."

"The Five Statins?"

"Atorva, Lova, Simva, Prava, and Fluva."

"Just off the boat from the old country, I take it."

"Theirs is a heartwarming story—"

"My heart is ready. Warm it."

"There's a theme to the playlist: 'Your Cheating Heart,' 'Heart Breaker,' 'Hearts Made of Stone' . . ."

"Got it," I said.

"Any suggestions?"

" 'I Left My Heart in San Francisco'? 'My Heart Belongs to Daddy'? 'My Heart Skips a Beat Whenever I Read the Word *Summons* on an Envelope Addressed to Me'?"

"I don't know that last one."

I bent to pick up the mail. I handed her the letter marked SUMMONS and said, "What do you make of this?"

She took one look at it and said, "You've been called for jury duty."
I opened it. She was right.

ON THE MORNING when I had been summoned to appear at the court-house I found, after I got out of the shower and dressed, that Albertine had prepared a package for me.

"I tried to get all of this into one case, but it didn't fit," she said. "So, you've got the black briefcase and this canvas bag from the Museum of American Slogans."

"I'm going to look like a dork."

"Does that matter?"

"I guess not."

"In the outside pocket of the briefcase, you've got a subway map. I've marked the best route in red. I also jotted the route on this little card that you can slip into your wallet or just carry in your pocket. It won't be as obvious as unfolding the whole map."

"Al, I've been living in this city for nearly five years. I think I can—"

"Oh, I know that you can find your way home—if you don't get distracted—but you are so easily distracted."

"That's true."

"If you find yourself in unfamiliar territory, use the map."

"Check."

"You've also got a notebook . . . a camera . . . your little microcas-sette recorder . . . a container of hummus and some pita . . . an apple . . . a bottle of seltzer . . . a bag of low-fat pretzel nuggets . . . don't go buy-ing hot dogs on the street . . ."

"*Creative Self-Promotion for Taxidermists*?"

"What?"

"Did you put the book in? I thought I might get some ideas, some ways to find work, promote the business, bring home the bacon."

"Okay. I'll get it." She did, and she slipped it into the briefcase. "Are you ready?"

"Yes, I think so," I said, wondering whether to tell her now what I felt it was my duty to tell her sooner or later, or wait until the evening, when she had a martini in her.

"But?" she asked with an eyebrow elevated.

" 'But' what?"

"There is a but in the room. I hear it scuttling along the baseboards."

"There is something, my darling. I—uh—I'm not going to be reporting for jury duty alone."

"You're never alone. You're a memoirist."

"Yes—well—this is not my favorite company. Matt and Bert are back."

"Matthew and BW?"

"Yes. They've been on my mind more and more for the past few days."

"I thought you seemed more than usually distracted."

"I think I'm going to have to find out what BW is up to. Matthew, too, but it's BW I'm particularly curious about."

"That's going to mean a lot of sex, isn't it?"

"I wouldn't be surprised."

"Should I go shopping for gear of some kind while you're out?" she asked, with a sparkling eye and a winning smile.

"No, no, no," I said, as if I didn't want to trouble her. "You recall that Thoreau counseled against any undertaking that required the purchase of new clothes."

"Did that include shoes?"

"I suppose it did."

"It couldn't have. New shoes are the oxygen of the soul."

"Thoreau said that?"

"I said that."

"What I mean is, if we can take this seriously for a moment—"

"Peter, I know what you mean, and I hope you don't intend to take it all that seriously."

"I just mean—"

"You mean that you intend to have BW bedding a lot of women, probably girls, too."

"That is what I mean, and—"

"—and that will require your bedding a matching set of women—"

"Well—"

"—in your imagination."

"Yes."

"Just make sure that you do not allow the inhabitants of your imagi-nation to invade your real life."

"I'll try."

"They frown on that down at the courthouse."

"Right."

"It's a just-the-facts kind of place."

"Mm."

"And don't let Matthew and BW annoy you." She hugged me, kissed me, and whispered in my ear, "Do you hear me in there, gentlemen? Don't mess with my honey's mind. He's given you room to roam in this head of his, but don't abuse his hospitality. I want him coming back to me tonight, not either of you two."

I TOOK THE ROUTE that Albertine had recommended and arrived at the City Hall stop well in advance of the specified assembly time. The way to the courthouse lay to my right as I emerged from the subway—

"We're early," said BW. "Let's spend some time sitting on a bench in the park across the street and watching the women on their way to work."

"I wouldn't do that," cautioned Matthew. "I think we'd better get to the courthouse, find the Jury Assembly Room, and report in."

"We have time to kill."

"One of the things I learned in elementary school was that it is not a good idea to upset the teacher on the first day."

"He does have a point there," BW conceded.

"Yeah," I said. "Let's go."

Chapter 2

My Mind, Left to Its Own Devices, Wanders

Perhaps you think it is "beneath the dignity of the profession" to market yourself and your services aggressively. Perhaps you think that the quality of your work alone will bring customers to your shop. Perhaps you think that the world will beat a path to your door if you build a better mousetrap. Perhaps you think that a jolly fat man in a red suit will bring you customers in a sleigh pulled by reindeer.

Start living in the real world! You're on your own here, pal. You're adrift in a dark sea, and nobody lucky enough to have a life raft is going to invite you aboard to share the hardtack. If you don't start swimming now, you're going to sink.

When you think of the highly competitive world of taxidermy in those terms, do you still think it is more dignified to drift (and sink) than it is to swim (and survive)?

Of course not.

Think of your loved ones! If you don't make the effort, if you allow yourself to sink, think of their tears, their shattered hearts, when your bloated body washes ashore, the hideous remains of one too vain to sweat, too proud to swim.

But wait! It need not be so!

Think of the smiles on those very same faces if you stride, unharmed, from the waves to the shore, bearing the plunder of the world. "Home is the sailor, home from sea!" Think of the tears of joy. Savor the kisses, the warm embraces. Start now. Start now.

Take that first stroke.
—Darryl O'Farrell, *Creative Self-Promotion for Taxidermists*

THOSE OF US who had been called and had dutifully answered the call sat. We were sitting in a large, dusty room identified by a sign to the right of the entry as the Jury Assembly Room. We were left sitting. We were left to sit. We looked around at one another. We studied the walls, the doors, the floor. We noted the absence of windows. Each of us began to understand, individually and idiosyncratically, based on the web of experiences that formed our individual neural networks of life-learning, that sitting would be a major part of the jury-duty experience and, for those called but not chosen, the dominant memory of it.

I was determined to put my time to good use. I opened *Creative Self-Promotion for Taxidermists* and read the inspiring passage that I have placed as headnote to this chapter. You can imagine the zeal that it aroused in me, and perhaps you can also imagine the shame that it made me feel when I recognized myself in the portrait of the drifter too proud to swim, the dreamer waiting for the world to beat that path to his door. "By golly," I said to myself, clenching my teeth and my fists, "I will swim. I will overcome my natural reticence and force myself to pitch my business services to the first likely client I see."

I looked around the room. "There must be two hundred people here," I told myself. "If I can get just one percent of them as new clients, that will be—well—two. Maybe I can get two percent. That would be four. If I got five, that would be all I'd need—all I could handle, really. Five clients. Two-and-a-half percent of the assembled. That's my goal. Two-and-a-half percent. Just a notch above low-fat milk. I can do that."

A silver-haired clerk took his place at a desk at the front of the room, welcomed us, and explained how we were to comport ourselves for the next few days, while we were in the jury pool, waiting to see whether we would be chosen to serve, beginning with the issue of smoking.

"If you smoke, you must leave the building to do so," he began. Actually, where I have written *you,* the clerk said "youse," but I didn't think that you would believe me if I quoted him exactly, since *youse* seems, on the page, like a limp attempt to make him a "colorful character."

"Smoking is not permitted anywhere in the building," he continued. "If you are caught smoking in the building, you will be issued a summons and you will be fined. Folks, you are in the criminal court building. It is chock-full of law-enforcement personnel. The chances of you smoking here and not getting caught are very slim.

"While you are waiting to be chosen for a jury, you can remain here in the Jury Assembly Room, or if you want, you can wait in the room across the hall behind me where there are desks and cubicles if you need to work. Do not use a laptop in the Jury Assembly Room. Use the room across the hall. You also have the option of waiting in the room out the door and to your immediate left, where there is food service. If you have to use your cell phone, you must use it in the men's room or the ladies' room, depending on whether you are a gentleman or a lady. On your seat you will find a Juror Information Packet. Kindly peruse it at your leisure. Thank you and enjoy your service."

MOST OF MY POTENTIAL CLIENTS were sitting with me in the Jury Assembly Room, but a smaller pool of potential clients might have settled in the room across the hall, and if I didn't inspect that room, I might miss the best prospects. I would also be underestimating the total size of the assembled multitude. Perhaps, with those in the room across the hall counted, it would prove to be sufficiently large for me to need as little as two percent of it. I also had the thought that I might use that room as a practice pool, take my first few strokes there before a smaller audience than the Jury Assembly Room held.

I examined the room across the hall. It was a small dusty room with study carrels.

"It reminds me of college," said Matthew, with a shudder.

"On the whole, I enjoyed college—more than enjoyed it," said BW.

"To tell the truth, I loved it," I said. This really was the truth. I took great pleasure from learning something new, and at college, if one kept one's ears open, it was possible to learn something new nearly every day.

"I learned a lot," I said. "I met some interesting people, made some lasting friendships."

"I had memorable sexual experiences and intellectual encounters," said BW. "Formative, really."

"I even liked the food," I said. "I've never had better fried flounder."

"Yes, yes, yes," said Matthew. "Seafood and sex. Rah-rah. Two cheers for dear old college days, but, when I reminisce about college, or when a memory of college happens to return to me, as it did when I peered around the door frame into this dusty room with its carrels, those pleasant things are not what dominate my memories."

BW and I waited a moment.

"Well?" BW asked impatiently after the moment had passed. "What does?"

"Exams," said Matthew. My heart raced, shuddered, skipped a beat. He was right. I saw it. I felt it. The little room, with those people bent over their laptops, tapping at their reports and correspondence, made me feel that there was probably an exam coming up, just around the corner, probably tomorrow morning, in a course that I had forgotten enrolling in, on a subject that I knew nothing about.

"You know," I said, turning from the room and beginning to walk away, "the people there look like the sort who claim to be too busy to write their memoirs. We will reject this room, 'the room across the hall.' "

Outside the Jury Assembly Room and to the left, there was the third room, "the room with food service." In it there was a cafeteria table, and along one wall were several vending machines that seemed not to have been used in a long time, since they were stocked with candies that I hadn't seen since I was a child. There were bars of Smiling Dentist brand Turkish Taffy, the sticky stuff that threatened the incisors when you bit off a chew from its slatelike slab and threatened all the fillings in your mouth when you worked to soften and masticate the stuff; Dandy Disks, flat wafers of tinted sugar that you could put on your tongue and allow to soak up the saliva till they melted in sweet subtlety, if you had the patience; Lonely Cowpoke candy chewing tobacco; Coffin Nails candy cigarettes; Jolly Gangster bubble gum cigars; and Ty-Nee-Tippler Nips, wax bottles of colored syrup that resembled nip bottles of liquor and made a fine match with the candy cigarettes and cigars. Arranged around the room were television sets on articulated metal supports that reached out from the walls like the arms of menacing robots in a bad dream. One displayed all sports, all the time; a second displayed all money, all the time; and a third, fourth, and fifth played domestic dramas, one in English, one in Spanish, one in Cantonese.

On the first screen, an anguished man of forty or so said in English to his heavily made-up wife, "I've been keeping something from you and I can't keep this locked up within me any longer." The sound was lowered on the other sets, since English is the official language of the justice system in New York, but sound wasn't required. The man's anguished look and the woman's makeup were much the same on all the screens. The dialogue must have been close enough not to need translation.

I rejected the food-service room, too. The faces I saw there were too blank. I like to think that memoirists tend to look interesting. The people I saw were allowing the television to write their memoirs for them.

"You could use the television angle, though," suggested Matthew. "You could pitch your memoir ghostwriting services to these people along the lines of 'Don't let a television soap opera write your life story for you. If you write your own life story, you can star in your own soap opera.'"

"Clumsy, Matthew. Very clumsy," said BW.

"But it has promise," I said. "It's something to fall back on if all else fails."

"Thank you," said Matthew. He looked as if he might stick his tongue out at BW.

"You're thinking the way a self-promoter should think," I said. "Darryl O'Farrell would be proud of you."

There was one other place to check. The men's room, where potential clients would repair to use their cell phones. I had a cellular phone, but I was a bit reluctant to use it in a public place because it was an outdated model reinforced by a supplementary battery in a color different from the body and—

"The truth," said Matthew.

Oh, hell—to be truthful about it I had cobbled the phone together myself out of pieces of cast-off phones I'd found at yard sales and stoop sales and other trash heaps and instead of trying to cram the working bits back into a decent shell I had laid them out in a plain black box with the extra battery taped to it. It functioned just fine—most of the time—but whenever I suggested using it to make a call, Albertine would say to me,

"You're not going to whip that thing out in public, are you?" I wasn't going to use it now. I had no need to call anyone. If I had called anyone, I would have called Albertine, just to let her know that I was still alive. (The desire to let someone, anyone, know that one is still alive is the motive behind most of the cell phone conversations I hear on city buses. It is the deepest meaning of the "hey" that bus-riding cell-phone users use to start their conversations.) Such a call would be pointless—not because Albertine wouldn't be interested in knowing whether I was still alive or not, but because she wasn't expecting to hear from me and would be practicing the piano with her headphones on, preparing for her gig at the retirement party for the head of the cardiac catheter lab at Carl Shurz Hospital. She wouldn't pick up the phone.

The men's and ladies' rooms were side by side, and they were labeled MEN and LADIES, not MEN and WOMEN. A young lady was on her way into the ladies' room, already employing her cell phone. "Hey," she said. "I know it's early for you, but I just wanted to share something with you. You know that stamp they use at the bar, the way they stamp your hand? Well, this morning I looked in the mirror and that stamp was on my forehead! I was like, 'What *happened* last night?' " She disappeared into the ladies' room, and I went into the men's room. There was no one there who would have made a suitable client. The place was full of men shouting into cell phones, their voices echoing off the tile, the volume level rising as they strained to make themselves heard above the others and their own echoes.

I RETURNED to the enormous room. Dutifully, I scanned it for potential clients. There were nominees, but they would all need work. Life is like that. It gives us, at best, sketches of what we want. Everything requires improvement.

"How about the silver-haired clerk at the front of the room?" said Matthew. "He seems a likely candidate."

"Oh, please," said BW.

"He probably has many an anecdote to tell," I said.

"Oh, I'm certain he does," said BW, "and he probably considers himself a raconteur. He has undoubtedly said, after telling one of his stories to an appreciative circle of bar buddies, 'I tell you, if you put that in a book, nobody'd believe it.' Ask yourself how many of those stories you would have to listen to, and ask yourself how many he would be willing to write down. Are you going to have to spend long hours nursing beers and taking dictation?"

"However boring he may turn out to be—" said Matthew.

I was beginning to fear that he might turn out to be very boring indeed.

"—he really does seem like the obvious choice."

"On the other hand," said BW, in a lowered voice, "there is the woman sitting beside us." She was young, with long, dark hair, laughing eyes, and the sculpted body of an aerobics instructor. "All you would have to do is lean a bit to your right and say—"

"Excuse me—are you a taxidermist?"

"What?" I said, as surprised as if she had asked me whether I had ever thought of writing my memoirs.

"Forgive me, but I couldn't help noticing the book you were reading earlier—something about taxidermists?"

"Oh—yeah—that." With apologies to the taxidermists in the audience, I must admit that I was embarrassed to have been mistaken for a taxidermist, and I was about to dismiss the profession with cavalier disdain when I saw in her eyes an eagerness that made me temper my reply. "I'm afraid I've misled you," I said, urging a twinkle into my eyes. "I'm not actually a taxidermist, despite the book. I'm a memoirist."

"Oh," she said, with an unmistakable note of disappointment.

"I also help other people write their memoirs—which is why I have the book for taxidermists." Here I hesitated for the brief moment that the conscientious person inserts before a lie. "One of my clients—is—um—a taxidermist."

"Oh," she said, brightening. "Maybe you could put me in touch with him."

"Put you in touch with him?"

"I have a cat," she said, frowning. "Mojito. He's pretty old—and—I'm going to have to—you know—put him to sleep."

"I see," I said.

"This is the moment when you could get away with throwing a comforting arm across her shoulders," whispered BW.

"Don't," said Matthew.

"I was thinking," she said, "that maybe—after—I could have him—um—"

"Um—" I said, while desperately seeking an alternative to *stuffed* or *mounted*. "Ah—preserved?"

"Yes. Exactly. For all time."

"I see," I said. What next? I could imagine many segues from the desire to stuff a cat to the decision to write one's memoirs, but which would work?

"The silence threatens to grow awkward," said BW. "Say something. Anything."

"Mojito," I said.

"Yeah," she said.

"It's a cute name."

"Thanks."

"Is it too early for a mojito?"

"It's always cocktail time somewhere," she said.

With a shrug toward the front of the room, I said, "The boss didn't say where the bar is."

"If you're after a mojito, it's on Ocean Drive," she said.

"El Zoo?" I asked.

"You know it?"

"I do," I said.

"Wait a minute, wait a minute," said BW. "Do not say what you are about to say."

"Leave him alone," said Matthew. "He's in the middle of a delicate negotiation."

"But he is about to tell this delectable creature that he was at El Zoo with his wife, during a Floridian excursion to visit his mother-in-law," BW said to Matthew. "Omit that," he said to me.

"I've had a mojito there," I said, neglecting to mention Albertine or her mother. "Several, actually."

"Believe it or not, I used to work there," she said. "It feels like another life."

"That is fascinating," I claimed. I let a moment pass, a pause during which I might have seemed to be considering whether the question I was

about to ask might offend her, and then asked, "Have you ever considered writing your memoirs?"

"My memoirs? I'm only twenty-four."

"But you've probably seen a lot."

"What do you mean by that?"

"I mean—working at the Zoo—you must have interesting stories."

"Some—but—I don't know—"

Chapter 3

I Am Amazed (Again) by Albertine's Acute Perspicacity

When evening quickens in the street, comes a pause in the day's occupation that is known as the cocktail hour. It marks the lifeward turn. The heart wakens from coma and its dyspnea ends. Its strengthening pulse is to cross over into campground, to believe that the world has not been altogether lost or, if lost, then not altogether in vain.

—Bernard De Voto, *The Hour*

I SHOOK THE SHAKER vigorously—it was a night for shaking, not stirring—and poured the martinis. I handed Albertine's to her, and we touched the rims of our glasses.

"Our negotiations had reached a critical moment," I said.

"Oh, I can see that."

"She may have thought that she was not interested in writing her memoirs, but actually, below the level of thought, down where our yearnings seethe and bubble, she was asking to be convinced, to be sold on the idea that she should write her memoirs."

"At such an early age."

"Exactly. My mind was racing. What was going to work? Fortunately, there was an entire chapter on this critical moment in *Creative Self-Promotion for Taxidermists*."

"Don't we thank our stars that you happened upon that invaluable volume."

"'Deed we do. If you promise not to make use of the secrets I am about to reveal for personal gain, I will tell you that, essentially, the delicate art of selling a mark on a stuffed squirrel—or, by extension, an assisted memoir—comes down to the same two areas of inquiry that keep me awake at night: money and mortality."

"As simple as that, is it?"

"You've promised not to exploit this knowledge."

"My word is my bondage, but are you sure there are no other motives to consider?"

"The lust for fame?"

"For example."

"The desires and fears that vanity inspires?"

"For another."

"They come under the fear of mortality and the desire to outwit it."

"Okay, I can see that."

"Everything else is about money."

"Okay, I can see that, too."

"However, it does not do, in most cases, to say, 'Writing a memoir is a way of cheating death,' or 'You can make big money writing your memoirs.'"

"No, no, no."

"As Darryl O'Farrell puts it—"

"Darryl O'Farrell?"

"The author of *Creative Self-Promotion for Taxidermists*."

"Darryl O'Farrell."

"You know him?"

"No."

"Perhaps you've read some of his other works?"

"No, it's just that—never mind."

"Don't leave me hanging."

"'Darryl O'Farrell' sounds like a name pulled out of a hat—two hats."

"I happen to consider Darryl O'Farrell a friend."

"What?"

"He is more than generous with the knowledge he has acquired, doubtless through bitter experience, and I'm grateful for that."

"My martini has evaporated."

Taking her glass, I said, "As Mr. O'Farrell puts it, people are 'spooked' by that approach."

"I've forgotten what approach we're talking about."

"The direct one. Cheat death. Make big money."

"It all comes back to me now."

"They get the feeling that you can see right down into the depths of their souls (which, if O'Farrell's assessment of the essentially two-horned nature of human motivation is correct, it would not be unfair to say that you can) and they begin to wonder if you are the prince of darkness himself."

"Scary."

"Most shy away then, according to O'Farrell, though there are some few who try to strike a different sort of bargain—sell their souls for a mess of pottage, for instance."

"And the aerobics instructor?"

"Aerobics instructor? I didn't say anything about—"

"The bartender with the sculpted body of an aerobics instructor."

"I didn't say anything about—"

"Behind the gleam in your eye I could detect the sculpted body of an aerobics instructor."

"Oh."

"I'm uncanny."

"You are. You certainly are. We didn't strike any sort of bargain at all—the bartender and I. I wasn't sure what to say next, so I thought it best to say nothing until tomorrow."

"Wise man." I handed her the half martini that brought her to her self-imposed limit. "Thank you," she said.

"I—um—actually thought you might have an idea," I admitted.

"If you promise to make use of what I am about to say for personal gain," she continued, "I will tell you the secret word that will bring your negotiations to a successful conclusion."

"I promise."
"Mojito."
"Mojito?"
"That's the title. The subtitle is *A Memoir of My Cat.*"

Chapter 4

I Plant a Seed

As you begin each day, repeat this simple formula while you are looking yourself in the eye in the bathroom mirror: "I will not allow the sun to set without bringing to my business at least one new customer or at least bringing one person who previously had not considered an investment in a taxidermy product to the point of considering such an investment or at the *very* least planting in the mind of someone who previously probably had not been considering an investment in a taxidermy product the seed of the possibility of at some future time considering it, possibly."

—Darryl O'Farrell, *Creative Self-Promotion for Taxidermists*

MEMOIRS OF PETS. It was a brilliant idea. Albertine amazes me. *Mojito: A Memoir of My Cat.* She had seen at once not only how to eliminate the reticence of the bartender (I nearly wrote "aerobics instructor") but also how I could persuade legions of people who would be reluctant to write their own memoirs to hire me to help them write at least something. People are crazy about their pets. Pet care and pet pampering are enormous industries, and enormously profitable. Why shouldn't I cash in? If Albertine had been on the subway with me, I would have kissed her. She wasn't, of course, though we are always together in spirit, and—

"Have you noticed the blonde with the legs?" muttered BW.

Across the aisle was a blonde reading a magazine and taking notes.

"I noticed her legs first," he went on, "so astonishingly long, crossed as they are, taking more than their share of the available space."

"A bit rude, really," grumbled Matthew.

"It's a rudeness that beauty must be forgiven," BW asserted.

She was quite tall, slim but shapely. She wore tiny sturdy black jean shorts and a thin pale purple short-sleeved top that stopped short of the shorts, so that her midriff was just barely exposed. The straps of her white bra showed a bit at the scoop neck of the top. I wondered whether she might have a pet. She glanced up and caught me looking at her.

"Give her that grin," said BW.

I grinned my endearing you-caught-me grin, and she returned it with one of those I-don't-mind-in-the-least smiles that so improve a moment in a crowded subway car. The train pulled into a station, not mine. She stood to go.

"Oh, spectacular," sighed BW. "Those legs! She knows she's a beauty. Look at the way she tosses that long blond hair, strawberry blond, I'd call it, though not quite. If she looks back at you over her shoulder as she goes—"

The doors opened. She stepped forward. She glanced back over her shoulder and smiled again.

"That was for me," said BW. "A cynosure's smile of gratitude for the eyes in the audience."

The doors slid closed and the train rolled on. I wondered when, that evening, the sun would set.

BRIMMING with vigor and determination, having informed myself of the hour of sunset, I strode into the Jury Assembly Room and scanned the assembled multitude in search of the bartender. I spotted her at the center of a ring of admirers and made my way thither without hesitation, armed as I was with the secret that would make her mine, in the client sense. I elbowed my way through the knot of insignificant others.

"Good morning," I said brightly.

"Oh, hi," she said. "You're the taxidermist."

"Not exactly," I reminded her, "but I would like to talk to you about preserving Mojito."

"Oh, that's sweet," she said. Tears welled in her eyes and she laid a hand on my arm.

"All right, listen up, people," boomed the silver-haired clerk from his station at the front of the room. "We've got a lot happening today and I'm going to call the first group of jurors for a voir dire in the courtroom of Judge Verhoven. Those of you who have read the informative material in the Juror Information Packet are, I'm sure, fully cognizant of the fact that a voir dire is a bit of an examination that you will undergo before you are assigned to a jury."

"I'd like to suggest a way—" I whispered to the bartender, fully cognizant of the fact that sunset does not wait for any man.

"Silence!" roared the clerk. "This means you!"

A glance around the room made it apparent that "you" meant me. I grinned the disarming grin I grin when I want to show that I meant no harm even though all the cans of peaches that a moment ago had made a handsome ziggurat are lying at my feet, and I put a finger to my lips to indicate that I was prepared to do as I'd been told. Then I opened my case and took out a pad and pen so that I could make my pitch to the firm-bodied bartender through the silent medium of the written word.

The clerk, meanwhile, roared on. "If I call your name, I want you to gather your belongings and go out into the hall where an officer of the court will arrange you into two straight lines preparatory to leading you to Judge Verhoven's courtroom." He paused. The sound of my roller-ball pen echoed in the enormous room. He frowned in my direction. "Angelina Carucci," he bellowed, and before I could slide the pad and pitch into the bartender's lap she had answered "Here," gathered her belongings, and departed for the hallway and the chaperonage of an officer of the court. She hadn't reached the door, however, before the silver-haired clerk said, in a tone that aimed to bring the maximum embarrassment down upon her handsome head, "Miss Carucci, you seem to have forgotten your Juror Information Packet."

Juror Information Packet? That must be what I was sitting on. I rose slightly and pulled it out from under me. Juror Information Packet indeed it was, if the inch-high letters on the front were accurate. I glanced at the seat where the bartender had been sitting. There was another Juror Information Packet, delightfully dimpled. I have my faults, but failing to seize the moment is not, I dare to say, among them. It was the work of less than an instant to tear the pitch from the pad, snatch the Juror Information Packet from the bartender's seat, leap to my feet, carry the packet and pitch to the blushing Miss Carucci, and hand it to her with a flourish and a wink.

"I'm sure we all remember junior high school fondly," said the clerk, sliding his glasses to the end of his nose and peering at me over their rims.

Miss Carucci rewarded me with a smile, though, and I felt that I had at the very least planted a seed.

The clerk continued to call names, but mine was not among them. When he had finished, he left us with the recommendation that if we had not already done so we "pruse" the contents of the Juror Information Packet and disappeared through the low door in the wall behind his desk.

The packet included a guide to restaurants and delicatessens within walking distance; a brief history of modern Western law, beginning with the Twelve Tables of the Law of ancient Rome, a code written at the insistence of the plebeians, who threatened revolution if something wasn't done to protect them from the patrician judges who claimed that in unjustly applying the previously unwritten law to discriminate against the plebeian class they were merely interpreting the "will of the gods"; and a booklet entitled *On the Reliability of Witnesses,* by Sullivan Sullivan. A glance at the small chalkboard behind the silver-haired clerk's desk, where the name Sullivan Sullivan was printed in white chalk, led me to believe that the author of the booklet and the silver-haired clerk were one and the same, and yet, I told myself, a prospective juror should keep an open mind and not jump to conclusions.

I opened the booklet.

Chapter 5

On the Reliability of Witnesses

By Sullivan Sullivan

ABOUT THE AUTHOR

For more years than he cares to count, Sullivan "Sully" Sullivan has been a clerk in the Justice Department of the State of New York. In that capacity, he has "heard it all" and "seen it all." Among his colleagues in the Justice Department he is highly regarded as a raconteur, and can hold an audience spellbound with his anecdotes illustrating the credulity of jurors or his hilarious repertoire of bogus excuses for avoiding jury duty.

"IS IT, IN YOUR OPINION as an expert on the reliability of witnesses and the credulity of jurors, Senior Clerk Sullivan, true that one reason jurors fail to detect the false note in a witness's account is that all testimony, from any witness, however duplicitous or devious or deluded that witness may be, comes cloaked in a deceptive verisimilitude because it has its origins in the reality of events that actually occurred, and is, therefore, at least in some sense and to some degree, in the mind of the witness if not in the strictest objective sense, 'true'?"

How many times have perplexed jurors asked me that question!

The answer is, yes, all the things a witness claims to have seen, heard, touched, smelled, or tasted have their origins in what the witness takes to be the real world, that is in the region that the witness perceives as being outside the witness, that vast part of all that is that is not the witness.

Please note that I mean exactly what I wrote in the preceding sentence and only what I wrote, that all the witness's claims have their origins there, but I do not mean that we could find there precisely what the witness claims to have seen (and for convenience let's confine our discussion to visual evidence, and let's call the witness Joe), and I do not even mean that we will necessarily find immediate causes or precursors to what Joe thinks he saw out there, even though everything he says or thinks he saw ultimately originates from events out there.

Some of what Joe claims to have seen may have arisen from other things, to wit, from the human tendency to want to see patterns in the world and to want to extend the familiar to the unfamiliar. So, a melody suggests a singer; moonlight seems to call for a pair of lovers; and even a vacancy toward which people seem to turn implies a missing someone. Now that I have qualified it, I will repeat it: all of what Joe says he saw originated outside Joe. Every piece of testimony begins as a perception; that is, something from the region outside that was taken into the region of the witness. (I employ the passive voice here because so many perceptions are accidental, unwilled. For example, just a few days ago, while I was enjoying a rare hour of relaxation, lying in the sun on a lounge chair, reading a "potboiler" called *The Vampire's Vacation,* I was, apparently, bitten by some insect of which I was at the time unaware, but which seems to have injected me with a toxin to which I have had an allergic reaction, leaving my right side and an area of my lower back just above my right buttock covered with red welts that are sore enough to make sleeping uncomfortable, giving rise, as you might expect, to uneasy dreams. From such an experience might a particularly lurid bit of eyewitness testimony be born.)

The following diagram illustrates in schematic form the situation of the witness (Joe) within the world and of the worlds within Joe's brain, including Joe's imagination. (Perhaps it is even a schematic diagram of what we might call the "witness function.")

The area outside the outermost ring represents the ambient reality through which we all move and from which we get everything we know of everything there is. This is what Emerson called "the actual world—the painful kingdom of time and place."

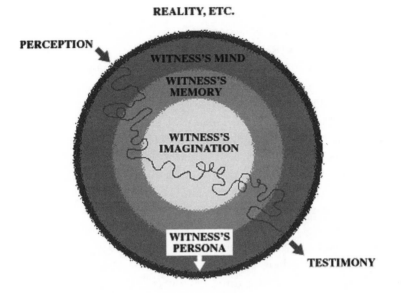

FIGURE 2: Schematic diagram of a witness (from *On the Reliability of Witnesses*).

The first ring is Joe's persona, Joe-to-the-world, a thin protective membrane that surrounds the essential Joeness within. Notice, however, that the ring of persona is gray and fuzzy, as are all the areas in the diagram. These qualities in the schematic, grayness and fuzziness, are meant to indicate (1) permeability, the fact that information can pass through an area (in both directions) and (2) imprecision, the fact that the boundaries of the regions are ill-defined, not sharp and precise. So, the persona is a kind of semipermeable membrane, through which information about the real world can pass into the region of Joe and through which Joe's interpretations can pass into the real world, becoming the statements that you will hear if you are chosen as a juror and Joe is a witness.

So, every eyewitness account begins as a perception.

However, all perceptions are misperceptions.

Why? Because our senses simplify and distort what we perceive, and, an instant after something has been perceived, the intellect has further distorted and simplified the already simplified and distorted perception and categorized it and filed it for reference in the memory, so that it is now only a recollection of a perception, a shadow of its former self, and—by some mysterious process still poorly understood despite the best efforts of students of the brain and mind—these memories begin an apparently inevitable drift toward the region of the imagination, where they are massaged and amplified and bent and twisted until they are scarcely recognizable as the offspring of the bits of the outside world that gave rise to them. (Actually, it's probably a mistake to think of the imagination as lying in a certain region of the brain, though it is convenient to represent it so schematically; more likely the faculty of imagination is distributed throughout the brain and is in large part just the grandiose name we give to noise—random interactions among memories old and new.) Thus, Scrooge's undigested bit of mutton becomes the Ghost of Christmas Past, and thus there is no such thing as an immediate experience, and thus there never is, never can be, a witness-box account of what Joe saw that is drawn directly from life. Every witness's account, every one of them, is conceived somewhere in memory; that is to say, somewhere along the path from the real world to the imagination.

The great Spanish filmmaker Luis Buñuel said much the same thing in far fewer words in his autobiography, *My Last Sigh*:

> Our imagination, and our dreams, are forever invading our memories; and since we are all apt to believe in the reality of our fantasies, we end up transforming our lies into truths. Of course, fantasy and reality are equally personal, and equally felt, so their confusion is a matter of only relative importance. . . . I am the sum of my errors and doubts as well as my certainties.

"A matter of only relative importance"? That's all good and well for Luis Buñuel, but the relative importance of the confusion may be extremely high for the defendant, may even be a matter of life and death, and because it may be that important for the defendant, it must be equally important for you, the juror.

Let me point out the obvious: this confusion of fantasy and reality may not be passive; it may be willful. There are witnesses, many of them regular Joes, who use their time on the stand to tell stories in the limelight.

Their stories may have their roots in what they have witnessed, but they have grown from that thin soil, watered by ambition and fertilized by vanity.

Everyone who tells a story about himself tells it to impress someone. Remember that. It's why there are no honest memoirs. Everyone who tells a story about something that he has experienced—what he has witnessed, for example—is telling a story about himself. Remember that. Everyone who has had an experience has found it more or less unsatisfactory; given the opportunity, he will alter the experience in the telling to make it a story about himself in which he plays a more impressive part than he played in "the actual world—the painful kingdom of time and place." Remember that. If you are sitting in the jury box listening to Joe the witness tell a story about what he saw, then the person Joe wants to impress may be you. Remember that.

I hope you will forgive me for including a personal anecdote here, but it seems to me the best way to make a point about memory and the distortion of memory. I want to demonstrate how a memory can be returned to consciousness by a single stimulus and also point out two sources of distortion in memories that lead to a witness's alterations of the data of experience.

Have you ever seen sweet autumn clematis growing on a wall? Have you ever heard a guy at a bar talking about the amorous exploits of his youth? Well, listen up.

My parents used to think that it was somehow unhealthy for a kid to spend the summer in the city, so every summer I was packed up and shipped off on the Long Island Rail Road to a town that I'll call Dullsville, where I had to spend several weeks with my aunt Wrinkly, my uncle Grumpy, and my cousins, Dopey and Vicious. I was given all of Cinderella's chores to do, and their idea of a good time when the chores were done was a rousing game of anagrams. You will probably not be surprised to learn that whenever I had any free time to myself I used to wander the town in search of some diversion from my boredom and bitterness. One day I came upon a local landmark, the ruins of an old mansion. Once I had found the place, I returned to it as often as I could. There I could remove myself from Dullsville and imagine myself the lord of the manor, the man of the mansion. One summer, early in my exile, I was sitting in the ruins at night, brooding on my fate, when I heard the sound of approaching laughter. Nothing so quickly deepens a mood already dark as the evidence of others' gaiety. I dropped deeper into the shadows and waited for whoever it was to pass in front of the mansion where I might see them without being seen myself. In a moment, two identical blond girls, about my age, passed, walking with their arms linked, talking about a movie they had seen. I didn't need to think about what to do. I knew what I wanted to do, and I did it. I took my shoes off so that I wouldn't make any noise, and I followed them. I needed no skill to follow undetected, since they were engrossed in reviewing the movie they had seen, rehearsing its lines and episodes for each other. Following closely, I heard their conversation as well as if I had been a party to it. From what I heard and what I inferred I came to understand that the movie had been a romance set in the time of the French Revolution. A pair of lovers, doomed by the politics of the times, the strife of the times, nonetheless contrived to meet, even under the most infelicitous circumstances. It was the unlikelihood of their meetings, the preposterous dangers skirted, the uncanny way that they eluded guards and patrols and spies, that had made the girls laugh, though they admitted to each other that they admired the lovers' daring, and they were as apt to sigh with longing as to giggle at the trysts that they recounted. The lovers in the movie had had a signal, the cooing call of a dove, that the girls repeated often as they walked along. Silently, I tried it myself.

Suddenly—that is to say, with a suddenness that I had not anticipated and therefore at first interpreted as caprice—the girls turned from the road and into the yard of a house. Their home, of course. They had crossed a border into a land from which I was excluded. I was dejected. A sense of loss fell on me like a great weight. I turned to go, but then a boldness came over me, inspired by desire and by the example of the indomitable lovers in the movie that the girls had seen, despite my not having seen it myself. I loped across the lawn and quickly made a circuit of the house, which was a kind of carriage house, almost certainly the carriage house for the mansion that had burned. Like a thief or a lover, I hid in a dark corner of the garden, where the overhanging trees blocked the moonlight. Waiting and watching, I was rewarded by a light in an upstairs window and glimpses of the girls in the lighted room, preparing for bed. I climbed the garden wall and waited there, in a crouch, watching the house for signs of wakefulness in any room other than theirs, listening for any sound from a watchdog or a watchful father, and then I scuttled along the wall until I reached the point where it met the house just below the lighted window. What next? Would I dare to do what I wanted to do, or would I just wait there, wishing, and stupidly wondering about the delights that lay within that little room, until the light went out, and then slink home, an unsatisfied coward? I took a deep breath and cooed like a dove. For a moment, nothing. Then the window slid up. I heard the girls whispering, and then I heard an answering coo.

The best summer of my life followed that cooing call.

On the last night of that summer, my last night in the Paradise I had once called Dullsville, a night at the start of September, I was making my way around the carriage house to the back, where I would climb the rope ladder that the girls had made for me, when, in the brilliant moonlight, I caught sight of a vine covered with tiny flowers growing on the garden wall. I didn't know the name of the vine then, but I learned later that it was sweet autumn clematis. It was so startling and so beautiful in the moonlight, damp with dew, that I stood for a while transfixed. I think I knew even then that in the future whenever I chanced to see sweet autumn clematis growing on a wall I would remember it all, every wonderful moment of the summer I spent as the inexperienced fledgling lover of those beautiful twins, everything, right on down to the sight of the sweet autumn clematis that last night of the summer.

Stop.

It didn't happen that way.

I was not the lucky lad in the story. When the girls passed the ruins of the mansion that first night, they were not alone. There was a boy with them. He was the lucky lad in the story. I was just a witness. I followed them that first night. I watched from the shadows while he climbed the ladder to their bedroom. Yet I have told you the story as if I were in it. In fact, I have always told that story to myself as if I were in it. I wanted to be that lucky boy, and so I made myself that lucky boy. If I were called to the stand now, as a witness, and questioned about those summer nights in Dullsville, I would not lie. I am an honorable man. I would not tell on the stand the story that I would tell you in the bar across the street. However, I think it is very likely that my testimony would be colored by what I wished had transpired between the girls and me within their room, by my desires, my longings, and by my envy. If that boy—that lucky, lucky boy—were accused of something, I would want to think him guilty, I would want him to be guilty. He was guilty, after all, guilty of not being me.

So. You see.

The seed of falsehood, fraudulence, and duplicity is recollection, but recollection altered by revision and by wishful thinking: two sources of distortion in memory that lead a witness down the path to error and mendacity.

Chapter 6

Stunned, I Make My Way Home

I FINISHED READING THE BOOKLET with the feeling that it must be some sort of test. Warily, without raising my head from the page, as if I were still reading Sullivan's treatise, I turned my glance to the right and left, and then rolled my eyes in the direction of the clerk's station at the front of the room. Everyone seemed to be involved in private pursuits. None of them seemed to be watching me for a reaction to Sullivan's confession. None of them *seemed* to be watching me, but perhaps they were very good at concealing their surveillance. Perhaps they had been trained. Perhaps someone behind me had been appointed witness for the group so that the rest of them could act the disinterested part. I would not give them what I felt sure that they, or at least some among them, wanted. I would not react. That is, I would not betray my reaction, because I was already, unavoidably, reacting to what I had read. You see,

Reader, I was the lucky boy in Sullivan's story. The girls were Margot and Martha Glynn, and that summer had been the best in my life, to that time.

Could Sullivan Sullivan really have been there, as a witness, an interested observer, a passionate spectator? If so, then my past had not been quite what I had thought it was, because I had never made a place for Sullivan in it. He had, if he could be believed, been there, if only as a spy. Was he there? Was he lying even about being an observer? Had he been in another place altogether? Was the Dullsville where he spent his summers not my hometown of Babbington but some other Long Island town, with a different set of picturesque ruins and a different pair of sandy-haired twins?

"This is making my head spin," I muttered.

"Mine, too," said Matthew.

"Hmm?" said BW. "Sorry. I wasn't paying attention. What's up?"

AT 4:30 OR SO, Sully informed those of us who had not been called for a voir dire that we could go home for the day, to return the next day at nine.

On the subway, I read the booklet again, and when I began to feel the same creeping sensation that I was being watched to see how I would react to it, I slipped it into my bag and took out *Creative Self-Promotion for Taxidermists*. I hadn't been reading for more than a couple of minutes when a petite woman in a smart suit, who was standing across from me, holding the same pole, said, "Excuse me—"

I glanced up, saw the eager look she directed toward me, and said, with the grin I employ to indicate that I am sorry to have to disappoint a person who is about to ask me a question that I feel sure I cannot answer, "I'm not a taxidermist."

"But you are interested in creative self-promotion," she said. All heads turned in our direction. Who, among those riding a New York subway at five in the evening, is not interested in creative self-promotion?

"I am," I admitted.

"Have you thought about a publicist?" she asked.

I said, and I think I'm remembering this correctly, "I—well—uh—" With the population of the car paying such close attention, even if they were doing their best to pretend that they weren't paying any attention at all, I didn't want to admit that I was pretty certain that a publicist would cost more than I could afford, or more than Albertine would be willing to let me pay.

"You're probably thinking that a publicist is a luxury you can't afford," she said with a smile and a wink.

"Well—"

"Any publicist worth her salt will pay for herself several times over."

"Hmm—" I said, in the manner of one who has just heard for the first time that a mysterious dark force is working against gravity to drive the expansion of the universe at an accelerating rate.

"I'm not going to try to convince you now," she said, raising an eyebrow and inclining her head slightly to one side to indicate that she was as aware as I that the entire car was hanging on her every word. "Here's my card." With the prestidigitation of a riverboat gambler she produced a card from who-knows-where:

> *Candi Lee Manning*
> *Nonpareil Publicist*

"Give me a call," she said.

"It doesn't say—"

"Clever, isn't it?" she said, producing a pen. She held out her hand for the card, and I returned it to her. "I made you ask for my phone number. Now I get to personalize the card. We already have a relationship. A trick of the trade"—she handed the card back to me—"that I offer you gratis."

The riders buzzed with murmurous admiration as the car slowed for a station.

"Getting off, please," she said, and she went out the door, followed by a dozen eager unknowns begging her for her card.

"A pro," said BW, in reverent admiration. "A real pro."

Chapter 7

I Attempt to Make My Mind a Blank, and Fail

STIRRING, NOT SHAKING, seemed the order of the evening. I had been shaken enough by the experiences of the day. The shaken martini has a bit of a cloud on the surface, while the stirred martini is, if stirred gently enough, pellucid and crystalline, and I needed clarity.

"You seem a bit distracted," Albertine noticed, "even a bit distrait."

"I've had an unsettling experience."

"With the aerobics instructor?"

"Bartender. No, not with her, though that didn't go so well, either."

"She didn't bite when you dangled the cat's memoir idea?"

"I never got to find out. She was called for a voir dire before I got to make my pitch. I slipped her a note as she left, but I don't even know if she was aware of it."

"That's a shame," she said, and I could see that she really was disappointed.

"The idea is brilliant, though," I said. "I'm going to start promoting it heavily tomorrow."

"No other possibilities today?"

"I—uh—we—the jurors—had to devote most of the day to reading a booklet on the reliability of witnesses."

"That took all day?"

"No. A few minutes. But then I spent a lot of time thinking about it."

She raised an eyebrow. She always knows when there is something unsaid, something waiting to be said, something that I'm hesitant about saying, something that I'm shaping, revising, before I say it.

"Spit it out."

"It was about me."

"The booklet?"

"Yes."

"The solipsism of the juror," she said, with a nod of the head, as if stating the obvious. "The luck of the draw has put you in a position where you are permitted, even encouraged, to think of yourself as important, essential even, and so you succumb to that encouragement, you begin by thinking of yourself as *important* to the juridical proceedings—not you and all the other jurors, not you as typical of any juror, not you as a singular manifestation of the concept of juror, but you, you alone—and then you start to think of yourself as *essential* to the proceedings. Without you, without your presence there, what point would there be in having a justice system at all? It all depends on you. You are the sine qua non. Therefore, it's all about you."

"You seem very familiar with this phenomenon."

She came as near as she comes to blushing. She took a sip of her drink, looked down, and thought for a moment before speaking.

"I am—in a way—because I'm familiar with the solipsism of the reader." She paused. She blinked. She said, "I've felt it since I was a little girl. It has never left me, even though I know now, as an adult, that it is nothing more than a little girl's wish that she were a person more important than she feels herself to be, as a little girl, the wish to be someone essential. This reader's solipsism is—it's—well—very often—when I read a book—actually—every time I read a book—I have the feeling, at some point in my reading, that the book has been written for me." She paused again. "I don't mean for me among other readers, or for me as an example of the type of reader that the book was intended for; I mean for me, alone. I mean that my reading the book is all the author expected, all the author hoped for. I can imagine—and if you laugh at me for this I'll burst into tears or throw something at you—that when I'm at the library there are writers watching me to see if I'll select their books from the 'new' shelf, lurking around the corner, slouch hats hiding their eyes, collars turned up. I never see them when I turn around, no matter how suddenly. It must be that I announce my intention to turn through some subtle shift of the shoulders or a cant of the hip that I'm not quite able to control. They see it, and they hide, or they assume attitudes of indifference. If I'm reading in a public place—on the subway, in the park, at the beach—I think that the author may be nearby, having followed me, watching me for my reactions, and that others, anyone, everyone, may be watching for my reaction, too, to decide whether the book is worth reading. The solipsism of the reader, you see. *The* reader. I am not *a* reader. I am *the* reader. I am the reader addressed as Reader. If I don't read a book—"

She broke off. I saw that she was embarrassed.

"Would you like your additional half?" I asked.

"Please."

"If I don't read a book," she said again with a sigh, "it doesn't quite exist."

WE ATE, straightened up, and went directly to bed. We woke thirty-five minutes before midnight, as we had trained ourselves to do. We rose, a little foggily, and dressed for Albertine's midnight show at Madeleine's. Getting the Madeleine's gig had been a lucky break, and the charming boîte could not be more convenient. It's just a few blocks from our apartment. We can walk to it. There is no need for a limousine, which is a savings, and when one is having trouble finding clients for one's memoir-writing service, one has to cut back somewhere. The hired limousine is almost the first thing to go.

Albertine got herself up with sexy simplicity: a thin but not quite sheer top, a long knit skirt, strappy sandals with very high heels (which I carried in a little canvas bag for her to put on before she took her place at the piano; for walking she wore less painful shoes), all in black, of course; this is New York.

Madeleine's is the dream room for a midnight pianist. It has all the marks of a place that some young couple dreamed about for years before they finally managed to open it, because it is just that. I don't know whether that charming couple is making money. I hope they are. It has been said that in New York it is impossible to go broke running a bar. I hope that's so, because I would hate to see this place fold. The owners have wide-ranging tastes in music, and their programming is equally varied. The flavor of Madeleine's changes from day to day and even from hour to hour, depending on the music. At lunchtime, you're likely to find a lone guitarist, a harpsichordist, or even a harpist, playing classical music. You could do business to the accompaniment. At brunch on Saturday and Sunday, it's always accurate re-creations of pop and rock tunes, which invariably ends in a sing-along. At midnight on Fridays, Saturdays, and Sundays, it's dance music, and the tiny dance floor is hip to hip with flaming youth. At midnight on Tuesdays, Wednesdays, and Thursdays, it's Albertine. The owners have a small budget, so by necessity as well as inclination they give breaks to lesser-known and even unknown musicians. Albertine had never played professionally before she got the midnight gig. She had played semiprofessionally, one could say. When we owned Small's Hotel, she played in the lounge there, but her audience was a captive audience, since there was no other entertainment and there was no way off the island except by hotel launch. I was the captain of the hotel launch, and as the captain I would certainly never have ferried anyone whose only reason for leaving was a desire to hear another piano player. Still, Albertine listed Small's Hotel on her résumé, got an audition, and got the job.

She was wonderful. I love the way she plays. Her sets are always a surprise to me, because I never hear her practice. She has an electronic piano at home, and if she's practicing while I'm in the apartment, she wears headphones. She would be the first to say, and in fact usually is the first to say, "What I lack in talent, skill, and technique, I make up

for in passion, and I try not to take the edge off with too much practice."

WE RETURNED HOME in the small hours and slipped into bed happy
and fulfilled. Albertine drifted off to sleep with a smile on her face.

I was happy, too, but still I couldn't sleep, because even when I go to
bed happy, my mind drifts to thoughts of money, the way Matthew's
drifts to thoughts of mortality, and I begin worrying. I spend many of the
hours when I am in bed, and ought to be making love or sleeping, worrying. This time has not been wasted over the years, not all of it. I have
learned many things. Actually, I guess it would be more accurate to say
that I have discovered relationships among things that I already knew.
That is, I knew the things, but not the relationships among them. I'm getting all twisted here. That's the way thoughts go in a sleepless time of
night. Here's an example of the sort of thing I've discovered. I have
found that all questions about money fit under one umbrella question:
How the hell are we going to make ends meet?

"Have you considered a job? Conventional employment? Going off
to an office and doing some work for which someone would pay you, instead of pursuing one foolish idea after another—" said Matthew, who
can ask some stinging questions late at night.

"Stop twitching," said Albertine, stirred into wakefulness.

"Sorry," I said.

I lay as still as I could.

"In the mortality department," said Matthew, after a while, "the questions are more various, but now that you've prompted me to think about
it, I find that they, too, are huddling under a single umbrella: What can I
do to redeem myself in the time left to me?"

"You could start by going out and getting laid," said BW.

"You could start by growing up," said Matthew. "You could show
some concern for the serious problems that humankind is facing—"

"Oh, look who's talking," said BW. "What have you ever done to help
anyone other than yourself?"

"I've often thought—" protested Matthew.

"And stop thinking," said Albertine.

"I'll try," I said.

There was sense in her advice. I recognized that, but it was advice that I found very hard to follow. At night, when I was trying to fall asleep, I tried to distract myself from thinking about our problems by thinking about other things, but whenever I encouraged my mind to wander, it insisted on returning to that dark area. I needed a distraction.

"Just lie still and listen to the ticking of the clock."

"The clock stopped."

"Wind it up and listen to it."

"I'm sorry I bought you that clock."

"It's beautiful."

"But it doesn't work."

"It works long enough to put you to sleep."

"It just upsets me—another mistake—another—"

"Listen to the beating of your heart, then."

"Okay. I'll try that. Goodnight."

"Goodnight, my darling."

I listened to the beating of my heart. Lub-dub. Lub-dub. Lub-dub. Lub-a-dub-dub. Rub-a-dub-dub. Three men in a tub.

"Lub-a-dub-dub?" said Matthew, alarmed. "That's too many dubs."

Lub-dub. Lub-dub.

"That's better."

Lub-dub. Lub.

"What? Where's dub?"

Lub-dub. Lub-dub. Lub.

"Again?" he said. "This is not good. Your heart is giving out. You're running down. Running down like an old clock—"

"That's it," I said, subvocally. "Get out of here. Go away. I banish you. You're infecting me with your frets and miseries. It's bad enough that I have to worry about money and marketing, but now you're going to have me wringing my hands over mortality and self-worth. Go!"

"Where?"

"I don't care. Anywhere. Back. Go back wherever you were before you showed up here. And go now. Go."

"And good riddance," said BW.

"You, too," I said. "You're going with him."

"Oh, no, not that. If you're going to send me away, send me some-where warm—"

"Go. Both of you. I'm making my mind a blank. I'm thinking of nothing but an endless white expanse."

I thought fiercely, and I did manage to fill my mind with blankness, but after a while some flaws in the blankness, some noise, some random threads of denser blankness, began to assert themselves as faint features, and nowhere began to become somewhere, and I began to wonder where I would have gone . . . as Matthew.

Chapter 8

As Matthew, I Am Admitted

The past has no existence except as it is recorded in the present.

—John Archibald Wheeler, in "Beyond the Black Hole,"
quoting himself in *Frontiers of Time*

I SEEMED TO BE NOWHERE. I seemed to be in no place, and I seemed to be in no time. From my earliest memory of it, this adventure is characterized by a feeling of detachment, separation from my self and from my past, and separation from everything else. There was a sense of imminence, too, the feeling that something was about to happen. Whatever was to happen would come from no context. I wasn't asleep, but I wasn't awake. I had the very odd feeling that I was not quite myself. I had the even odder feeling that a piece of myself was missing, had left me, but had been replaced, as if I had undergone a transplant. Then I became aware of someone near me, not far from me, became aware that I was on a bed, that the person was beside the bed. I was looking at a television set—not a television set—a monitor. The person beside the bed was looking at the monitor with me. How had that person come to be there? How did that happen? I hadn't been aware of anyone there a moment earlier. I think that I had been elsewhere a moment earlier, somewhere I would rather have been, dreaming. I had been dwelling in my dream so completely that I hadn't noticed anyone until she had been there for some time.

It was a nurse—a young and pretty nurse—holding a clipboard. I was in a hospital.

"Mr. Barber?" she asked.

"Yes," I said, "Matthew."

"You sound surprised."

"I am. A moment ago—I think that if you had asked me my name a moment ago—I wouldn't have known what to say." I wondered how I looked, and how I looked to her.

"Matthew," she said, and she smiled, and it seemed to me a kindly smile, genuine, not merely professional, not a part of her uniform. "I'd like to ask you some questions. Okay? Are you feeling up to it?"

"Yes. Yes, I'm feeling fine. Well, not fine—but I'm up to some questions." I read her name tag, pinned above her left breast, and added, "Cerise."

"How old are you?" she asked.

"Oh." I hesitated, and for the first time in my life since I was too young to buy a drink, I thought of lying.

"Come on now," she said. "I'm sworn to secrecy."

"I'm forty-six," I said.

She wrote it on the form on her clipboard. "You sound surprised again," she said.

"I am."

"You wouldn't have known that a moment ago?"

"No. I wouldn't. But not only that—"

"Mm?"

"I think—I think I might have given you a different answer."

"You look very good for forty-six," she said, leaning toward me and playing at being conspiratorial.

"I think I would have told you I was older," I said.

"Are you?" She was poised to change the entry on her form.

"No," I said. "I'm forty-six. But a moment ago, I felt older. And to tell you the truth, I still do, in a way. All of this—even you, Cerise—feels like a memory, not like something I'm experiencing right now."

"Déjà vu?"

"Yes, but on a larger scale—and—even though I feel that this is something I've done before—I have the feeling that a couple of strips of time have been clipped from my life."

"Clipped? As in stolen?"

"As in snipped. Like pieces of a film that end up on the cutting-room floor."

"There is a theory," she said, not looking at me, looking instead at the monitor, where my heartbeat slithered from left to right, "that time does not unfold that way, like a movie, running on, from start to finish."

"Really?"

"Yeah," she said. "According to this theory, time is nothing more than an arbitrary system of organization in a neural network—our brains, in other words. Past and future are just as tangled and interconnected in the universe as memory and imagination are in our brains."

"Really?" I said again, and regretted the likelihood that it made me sound either very stupid or very surprised that a pretty nurse should be offering me a theory of time.

"Really? Well, I don't know about 'really.' It's a theory. But it's an interesting one. According to this theory, everything that is, or has been, or will be, or might be, is now, always was, and always will be. There is something like what we call now, but nothing like what we call then. Instead of thinking of time as a ribbon, or a strip of film, or a winding road, think of it as one way of setting up the interconnections and cross-references in a network, the network of neurons in your brain."

"I see it now," I claimed, smiling at her animation. For an instant I realized that I was glad to be there, outside time in a way, in the limbo of the hospital, somewhere between birth and death with, for the time being, nowhere to go, no reason to go anywhere.

"The basic idea is that time is just one of the ways we organize the universe. Of course, we don't actually organize the universe. We organize our impressions of the universe. The universe is as it is. We try to make sense of it. That is, we try to get our brains around it, you know?"

"I know. I'm having a tough time just now trying to get my brain around who I am."

She bestowed upon me a sweet smile of sympathy, but she had a lecture to deliver and wasn't going to stop. "We try to comprehend it, all of it, hold it all in our little brains. Well, we can't do it. The universe is bigger than the human brain, right?"

"Right," I said, but I asked myself whether I hadn't read somewhere that the number of potential states of the brain—the number of unique arrangements of temporary electrochemical interconnections—that is to say, I suppose, the number of thoughts—was many, many times greater than the number of particles in the known universe. If I had read such a thing, I couldn't remember when or where, or even who I might have been at the time, so I didn't bring it up.

"So we simplify," she said. "We find ways to organize the information so that we can understand it a bit better. We find ways to make the universe fit in our brains—or at least a version of the universe. We analyze it. We categorize it. We analogize it. We temporize it. And time is nothing more than one of those systems of organization that we have imposed on the universe."

She raised an eyebrow, asking for an indication of comprehension.

"Got it," I said.

"It's another product of the solipsism of the species, really. We assume that we are the reason for the universe, so it must be as we think it is."

"You got that right," I said, and immediately wondered what had made me say something so unlike what I would ordinarily have said.

"What we call the past," she said, in a summarizing tone, "is really nothing more than the extension of what we call memory to the entire universe. What we call the future is nothing but imagination stretched about as far as it will go. What we call the present is slipperiest of all, because it may be a complete illusion, nothing more than a fleeting infinitesimal cacophony of perceptions that become inextricably tangled with memories and dreams before you can snap your fingers."

"What a liberating idea," I said. "The rent is never overdue, then. Never even due, I guess."

"Well," she said, checking her watch, "unfortunately we order our affairs according to our illusions." She winked, but not in a flirtatious way, and said, in a different voice, all business and professionalism, turning to her clipboard, "Now—have you had any of the following diseases," and she interrogated me about my medical history, my eating habits—nearly all my habits, actually—my job, the stresses in my life—or stressors, as she called them—and when she had finished with those of her official duties that concerned me, Mr. Barber, Matthew, she squeezed my foot by way of goodbye, turned and left me lying there. I watched her walk away. She had a beautifully rounded bottom.

I WAS ASKING MYSELF how I had known the answers to Cerise's questions, since I did not have any memory of any of the things I had listed for her, not even my job or my stressors, when a small gray woman, primly dressed, with a name tag that didn't offer her name but only her status, VOLUNTEER, wheeled a cart into the room, a bookshelf on wheels, and began offering books from the hospital library to her captive audience. By the time she got to me, I was eager, and I realized only then that I had been worried that the other inmates would take the best stuff before I got my chance, just as my younger self would have. Just as my younger self would have? Did I remember my younger self? No. I did remember the feeling, though, the feeling that I might miss out, that everything good might be gone by the time the authorities got around to me.

"Would you care to read a book?" she asked mechanically.

"I think I would," I answered cheerily. "What have you—"

"These books are provided by the Charlesbank Hospital Library, an affiliate of the Boston Public Library system."

"Great—"

"They are yours to read while you are here in Charlesbank Hospital, but we ask that you not remove them from the hospital premises."

"All right—"

"Please observe the two-week borrowing limit on all titles."

"I'm hoping that I'll be gone by—"

"And please be kind to these books: do not fold pages to mark your place, do not write in them, do not take them to the beach, and please do not take them to the sanitary facilities with you."

"I promise. Honest. What have you got?"

"I have just a few left."

"I was afraid of that."

"*As I Lay Dying,* by William Faulkner."

"Are you joking?"

"*Death Comes for the Archbishop,* by Willa Cather."

"Good grief."

"*As a Man Grows Older,* by Italo Svevo. *More Die of Heartbreak,* by Saul Bellow. *The End of the Road,* by John Barth."

"Who sent you?"

"I am a volunteer. A candy striper."

"A candy striper? I thought candy stripers were—"

"Young girls with perky breasts and tight buttocks?"

"What?"

"I said—"

"I heard what you said. I mean what are you trying to do?"

"I am trying to bring you solace."

"Solace?"

"Yes. I am a certified solace provider."

"Certified?"

"By the Solace Society."

"The Solace Society."

"Yes. May I speak to you for a moment?"

"Yes—for a moment."

She came to the bedside and put her hand on my shoulder.

"Have you thought about putting your affairs in order?" she asked.

"You call this solace?" I said.

"Have you thought about admitting your mistakes, owning up to the things you've done, and the things you've left undone?"

"Please—"

"Have you thought about telling your loved ones how wrong you've been?"

"I have no 'loved ones.' "

"Oh, yes you do," she said, in the manner of a grandmother giving the kind of comforting reassurance that parents never can, the comfort of a longer view of life. "You know you do. You owe it to them to admit your mistakes. You owe it to yourself. You owe it to the image of yourself that will endure beyond that self."

"You're serious about this, aren't you?"

"Think about it, won't you, dear? Don't put it off. Time is running out. The clock is ticking. Start now." She patted my shoulder, leaned over and kissed my cheek, turned, and shuffled off.

HAVE I THOUGHT about admitting my mistakes? Daily. I admit my mistakes daily, if only to myself. A man can err in many ways. It's all about letting someone down, I think. He can let himself down. Set the wrong goals for himself. Fail to set any goals at all. Fail to act. Just go along. See what is wrong and do nothing. Should I make a list? Is she going to be back, asking for my list of mistakes? Probably not today. I can return to the pleasant feeling that being here in this bed induces, that feeling of being outside time, safe, and inside here, safe. But why is that feeling so appealing? Why do I feel the need for safety? Why am I so pleased to be tucked away here? Is it an essential part of my personality? Am I reclusive by nature? Am I asocial, potentially sociopathic?

I SLEPT FOR A WHILE, but in the night a nurse woke me to draw blood from my arm. I think that I may have awakened while she was already in the act of drawing blood from my arm. She was gentle, astonishingly gentle, as gentle as a mother, as an angel. She murmured, cooing, comforting me, and I was comforted. When she had finished, when she withdrew the needle from my arm, I thanked her. She ran her hand along my arm. It was a caress. It was that caress that made me understand that I had thanked her for comforting me, and that she understood why I had thanked her. After she left, I told myself that it had been a professional caress, nothing singular about it, nothing personal, that the caring I felt in it was all technique, one of the healing arts, but only my mind believed that, not my ailing heart.

AWAKE NOW, I tried to think of nothing, to return to sleep, but all I could think of was my body. Everything seemed to be in bad shape, like a cheap used car. I performed a self-examination. What, exactly, was wrong? I had the feeling that I wasn't breathing as well as I used to. I didn't seem to be able to draw as deep a breath as I had been able to. My skin felt thick and insensitive, numb. If I touched myself, I hardly felt my own fingertips. I felt vaguely nauseated, light-headed, faint. I felt a numbness in my left armpit, in my left elbow, down my forearm, and in my little finger. All my joints ached. Most of all, and somehow most frightening, I felt a pervasive emptiness. Earlier I had felt that something was missing, some part of me, missing or replaced, but now it was more than that. Now I felt that everything was missing, that there was no me left in me, that everything I had formerly taken to be me amounted to nothing.

Much of what I had hoped for from life had eluded me, I realized. I felt the lack of many things.

Pleasure, for one.

A sense of purpose, for another, and not just meeting a goal or making a deadline, but a higher purpose, something transcendent.

"Meeting a goal or making a deadline"? I must be an executive of some kind, then. I was usually very busy. What did I do? What made me so busy? I had the feeling that I made toys. Could that possibly be? It sounded more elf than executive. I didn't like it. I didn't know why I didn't like it— it sounded like fun, in a way—but I didn't like it. I resolved to change jobs—when I got out of there.

I was going to change many things when I got out of there—assuming that I did get out of there. Everything that had happened to me in my life so far would be stamped "before I went into the hospital," and everything that was to come would be stamped "after I got out of the hospital"— assuming that I did get out of the hospital. While I was there I would make myself come to some kind of understanding.

I would decide what had been missing from my life, everything, and I'd find out how to get it, how to make it part of me.

I felt a power growing within me, even though I was exhausted and trembling. I knew that I was right about what I ought to do, how I ought to spend my time in the hospital, and that knowledge gave me power.

Knowing that, having discovered that, I felt that I had made more than a start. I felt that I had passed through a door into a part of my life and my self that I had been avoiding for a long time. I had admitted myself into the place where I really belonged. I had acknowledged that a place in my heart was vacant and waiting. With that acknowledgment, most of my work was done. I smiled in the dark, and I returned to sleep happy.

Chapter 9

As Matthew, I Begin to Change My Life

There is no place that does not see you. You must change your life.

—Rainer Maria Rilke, "Archaic Torso of Apollo"

YOU'RE ASKING YOURSELF, 'How do I start to change my life?' "
said a voice that seemed to come from directly beside my ear, a soft
voice, purring. "I can practically hear you. Come here. Lean over here.
I'm going to tell you the secret, the secret of how to begin."

The voice was so alluring that I did as I was told, rolled to the side toward the voice, and opened my eyes slowly, and found the little gray
woman from the Solace Society there, beside my bed, well within my
personal space, purring her message in my ear.

"You're here already?" I said.

"I've got a busy day. Lots of visits to make."

"But I'm not really ready—"

"You didn't list your mistakes," she said, and her disappointment was so evident that I felt the burden of having pained her, felt it as another mistake that I would have to redress.

"I made a mental list," I said. "I can recite it—"

"But I have to have something to show—to my superiors."

"You're a volunteer."

"Yes, but we have our procedures, our duties—"

"I wouldn't worry about that too much. You can always volunteer for something else. You can build housing for the homeless—"

"We have our ranks and privileges, too, just like everyone else."

"Oh. Of course. I see. You've got to meet your quota. Okay. I understand. I'll make a list after breakfast."

She pouted.

"Okay, during breakfast."

"Thank you. Now where was I? 'Step Two: How Do I Start?' "

"Listen—since we haven't finished Step One, do you think we could postpone—"

She pouted again.

"Go ahead," I said. "But I warn you that I've got to urinate soon, so please try to make it fast."

"Oh, dear." She glanced at the table beside the bed, picked up a plastic bottle with a large, oddly bent neck, and held it toward me. "Do you want to use this? I'll turn my head."

"Is that what that's for?" I said. "I thought it was some sports water bottle that another inmate had left behind."

She proffered it again.

"No thanks," I said. "I'd really rather wait till you're gone. Just give me Step Two in a nutshell and move on to your next victim."

"All right. Begin where you are."

"That's it?"

"That's it."

"Okay—"

"Don't try to begin at the beginning and clean up all the messes you made along the way."

"Good—"

"After all, if you were going to do a really thorough job, wouldn't you have to repair the damage your parents did first?"

"My parents?"

"And what about the errors of their parents? And theirs? How far back are you willing to go? Are you going to try to correct the errors of all your forebears?"

"Definitely not," I said. "Would you mind handing me that bottle?"

"Not at all. Here you are."

"Thanks," I said. I slid the bottle beneath the bedcovers and maneuvered it between my legs. For some crazy reason I had thought that she would leave when I did this, but the gray ladies of the Solace Society are determined and not easily embarrassed.

"And if you were going to try to undo all the ills that they have done, you would soon be all the way back to our ancestral African mother. But why stop there? You have prehuman precursors as well."

"I really think I get the point," I said. I stuffed my penis into the neck of the bottle and relaxed. I heard the urine, my urine, rushing into the bottle, panicked for a moment, worried that it might be leaking from the bottle or missing it, felt around it and reassured myself that all was as it ought to be, then relaxed again and felt the relief of release, and all the while she went on explaining that it wasn't my responsibility to correct all the errors that preceded my own.

"Although most of the harm you've done can be attributed to the wiring of the human brain that has evolved over the course of who-knows-how-many generations of humans and near-humans who were trying to twist the world to their design, some can be attributed to your animal underpinnings—"

"I've seen the light," I said, comfortable at last. "The big bang was not my fault. I don't have to correct that original error."

She giggled like a girl. "You've got a great sense of humor," she said.

"I'll try to correct that," I said. "I'll start there."

She didn't see the humor in that. She pouted. I brought the urine bottle out from under the covers and held it out toward her.

"You can just leave it on the table," she said. "A nurse or orderly will whisk it away without a word."

WITH THE GRAY LADY OF SOLACE GONE, I took a look around. Above me was a monitor, a crude thing, out of date, like something from a flickering movie, on which I could see a luminous dancing snakeline, an analog of the beating of my heart. Seeing it, and recognizing it, I immediately recovered one of the missing bits of my life: the episode of my entering the hospital. In memory, I found myself sitting in the admitting area, about to be patched with nitroglycerine. I remembered having been outside, and having walked toward the doors, but then there was another gap, just a short one that felt no longer than a hiccup, and the next thing I remembered was my sitting in an admitting area, on a molded plastic chair the color of poached salmon. Fluorescent lights buzzed above me. I was having a difficult time focusing my attention on anything around me, though I was exaggeratedly aware of the beating of my heart. It gave a flutter now and then, and that was followed by a flinty feeling, as if some part of me had turned to stone.

A nurse bent over me. She had the sculpted body of an aerobics instructor. I very nearly laughed at myself for even noticing her body, appreciating it, enjoying it, lusting after it, at such a time, then congratulated myself on this bit of evidence of my vitality, perhaps even my viability. She unbuttoned my shirt (and I told myself, joking with myself, not to get my hopes up). She peeled the backing from a circular bandage and pressed it on me, slapped it on me, saying as she did so, "Nitroglycerin patch. For the angina."

"Thank you," I said, and then, guessing, *"Gracias."*

"De nada," she said, with what I allowed myself to interpret as a twinkle in her eye.

I felt again the flutter of my heart, the flintiness, and it was then, watching her as she bent over the next case, that I first became aware of the other strip of missing time, the one that preceded my arrival at the hospital. I had been awake and aware when I had arrived at the door to the emergency entrance, and I could remember the automatic doors sliding open to admit me, and then there was a brief blank, nothing important, probably just a fainting spell, but what was missing before I had arrived at the emergency entrance felt like a bigger and more important vacancy, something I had to recover to be whole. When I tried to recover that time, made a deliberate effort to backtrack from the emergency entrance, I felt an odd and dizzying sensation of motion, like being in a speeding car, a sensation strong enough to make me put a steadying hand on the edge of the bed. The effort made me feel hungry, and for reasons that I can't begin to explain, I was hungry for crab cakes, but the thought of eating crab cakes made me feel nauseated, and I abandoned the effort to recall.

The heart monitor, and the sensors taped to my chest, had brought that bit of time back to me, with the line on the monitor acting as an aid to memory. Of course, if Cerise's theory, or the theory that Cerise had expounded, was correct, then my past was nothing but my memories, a construct of my own mind, just one of many ways of organizing the electromechanical chaos in my brain, and a heart monitor was as good an aid to recollection as any other. I watched it for a while. Whenever I felt the irregular flutter of my heart and the flintiness that followed it, a moment later I would see the pale green line twitch and spike and go jagged. That lag, that brief hiatus between the cardiac event that I detected and the monitor's version of it, made me feel some superiority to my situation, to my being there on my back, to all the hookups and connections, to the hospital and all its staff. I could feel the fault in my heart before their equipment could detect it. I was still a superior device, still vital, possibly viable, despite my aching heart and faulty memory.

I was in a ward with eight beds. The bed to my immediate left was empty. In the bed beyond that one, an eager inmate was talking on his cell phone, delivering instructions to a subordinate, keeping his business healthy. The bed beyond the eager one's was occupied, but I couldn't see the person in it. That is, I couldn't see the person without making a deliberate effort to do so, which would have required my leaning forward and twisting in that direction, a maneuver that might have marked me as a man too curious for his own good. In the first bed across the broad aisle that ran from door to window there was a young man who was lolling on his bed in the attitude of an idle aesthete, flipping the pages of a glossy magazine. He was wearing tight and tiny red briefs, and he had his bed sheet flung aside so that everyone could get a good view of him. In the next bed was a still body. It was a man with slate-gray hair, lying on his back, with his hands at his sides, apparently asleep or, it occurred to me, dead, awaiting with the patience of the dead the arrival of a crew to cart him off. The next bed was vacant. The last bed, the one nearest the window and directly across from mine, was occupied by a large man of a congenial disposition who, when my eye fell on him, said, "Good morning—and welcome to the cardiac care unit."

"Thanks," I said. I felt that I ought to say more, and I wanted to say more, but I found that after attempting to return the big man's bonhomie all jollity had drained from me, and I was profoundly depressed to be greeting the morning from the cardiac care unit.

"She'll be back," he said.

"Who?"

"Sister Solace."

"Oh. Yeah. She will, won't she?"

"She's going to want that list."

I sighed. "You're right. I'd better—"

"Hold on," he said, and rolled himself out of bed. He drew a terrycloth robe around himself and shuffled across to the side of my bed. He was breathing hard by the time he reached me. "Here," he said, pulling a folded piece of lined paper from his pocket and handing it to me with a stealthy gesture. "You can use these."

I unfolded the paper partially, hiding it beneath my sheets, and scanned what was there. It was a list of errors and faults, apparently quite a long list, since the paper seemed to be covered on both sides. "Are these all yours?" I asked.

"Nah. I hardly made any mistakes at all—if you don't count eating beef every day for sixty-two years. But she won't settle for that—as I found out the first time I was in here."

"The first time?"

"Yeah. I'm a cardiac recidivist. This is my third bypass."

"Ye gods."

" 'And little fishes.' My mama used to say that."

"My grandmother," I said. Did she? I didn't remember her having said that. Where did that come from?

"Anyway," he said, wheezing a bit and, I thought, probably eager to get back into bed, "a guy gave me that list and said just pick and choose enough to make her satisfied. So I did, and it worked just fine. That list's been passed around for years now, I'll bet. You just pick what you want to admit to, and copy it out, and you're off the hook—without having to admit to anything that you actually did."

"Well, I haven't really done anything wrong, either, except—" Except? The word stopped my tongue. Except? I had the feeling that I *had* done something wrong, something that I did not want to admit. Not only something that I didn't want to admit, but something that I had to hide.

"Except?" he said, smiling, waiting for a revelation or a joke.

"Except that I forgot to bring a pen when I stumbled into the emergency ward," I said. "That's because I never take notes." Never take notes? Now where did that come from? I never take notes in a restaurant. I'm a restaurant reviewer. That's it. "I'm a restaurant reviewer," I said, because I was glad to know something about myself.

"Ooh, that must bring some occupational hazards," said the big man.

"Yes," I said. "It does." Something like a memory, just a patch of one, an image in a fog, of someone striking at me, and then of running, my running, and then the difficulty breathing, and the wheezing.

"I'd better go horizontal," said the big man, wheezing sympathetically.

"Sure," I said. "Thanks."

He held up a hand to say that no thanks were necessary among the brethren of the cardiac care unit.

"My name is Matthew," I said. "Matthew Barber." I didn't believe it, but I said it.

"Charles Lee," he said. "But I will answer to Charlie or Stagger. Here comes a pencil." He nodded in the direction of the breakfast cart, which was being wheeled into the ward not by some scowling underling but by the sweet nurse Cerise.

She arrived at my bedside wearing an apologetic look (and, of course, the full complement of nurse attire; I don't want to give you the impression that the cardiac care unit was all fun and games). She served my breakfast on a tray.

"You haven't filled out one of these preference sheets," said Cerise, indicating a form on my tray with a stub of pencil placed beside it, "so you've got just the basic cereal breakfast, I'm afraid. But let us know what you like and we'll do better tomorrow. Okay?" She added a smile to the apology.

"Okay. Thanks. Is it possible for me to take a shower?"

"Unfortunately not. You have to stay on the monitor. But I'll give you a sponge bath when I come back around in a few minutes."

I hope you will forgive me the pleasant anticipation of that sponge bath. I watched Cerise go about delivering breakfast to the others, admired her body, noticed the way the synthetic fabric of her pants stretched over her buttocks as she moved, noticed the line of her panties, and savored the thought that she would be bathing me in a few minutes. Things could have been so much worse. It occurred to me that most people—and perhaps I was among them—tended to see a bad situation as entirely bad, failing to see any hint of a silver lining, yet here I was in a cardiac care unit, in mortal danger, happily anticipating a sponge bath at the hands of an attractive nurse. I had some kind of gift, apparently, some sort of dumb luck. Where it came from, I had no idea.

I looked at the food on the tray and found that I had no appetite. I drank the orange juice. I poured the contents of a packet of powdered coffee creamer into the cup of coffee and raised the Meal Preference Sheet, thinking that I would give it a thorough reading and fill it out slowly, filling the time, for I felt no lack of time, no sense that time was running out, no feeling of impending deadline, or death. I was beginning to like the cardiac care unit, and I was aware that I was beginning to like it. I felt safe there.

"Matthew?"

It was a doctor, to judge from his outfit and attitude.

"Yes?"

"This afternoon we'll be sending you down to the cath lab for an angiogram. You've—never had one before—am I right?"

"Never. Never been in a cath lab, either."

"Cardiac catheter lab," he said.

I tried not to look medically ignorant, but I really had no idea what he was talking about.

"This booklet explains it," he said, without that kindly manner that actors portraying doctors like to use. He handed me a booklet with a drawing of a heart on the cover, grinned in the manner of a person with gas, and headed for the door.

"Sheila gone already?" Stagger Lee asked Cerise.

"She's gone, gone, gone," said Cerise, flapping her hands in the air to simulate flight. "Gone for four days and three nights."

"Where'd she go again?"

"Miami. She and Didi won the trip from the radio. You should have seen them leave for the airport. Right after work, a limo came for them a block long." She turned her cart to deliver breakfast to the beds on the other side of the ward, but over her shoulder she said to me, "I'll be back."

I RETURNED TO WORK on the Meal Preference Sheet. To my surprise, it included dishes that I would have thought a heart patient ought to avoid, though in most respects it resembled the monthly menu for school lunches that used to be published in my hometown newspaper on the third Thursday of the month preceding the month to which it referred. I found myself evaluating it in a professional manner, and it was the discovery of that manner and the automatic way in which I began employing it that convinced me that I was indeed a restaurant reviewer. Yes. A restaurant reviewer. With detached satisfaction I observed myself as I checked off my preferences and noted that I was half-consciously making menus for meals. I was doing the best that could be done given the choices available to me, but became concerned that the kitchen would not necessarily interpret my check marks as anything more than preferences, without recognizing the implied suggestion that they be combined in appetizing ways. Some way to indicate my pairings and groupings was required. Color coding would have been ideal, but I had only the stub of a number two pencil that Cerise had given me. I began drawing lines to link complementary dishes, with arrowheads at either end of the lines. As I drew more of them, they wound up, down, and around the page, from food group to food group. I was checking my handiwork when a voice from the side of my bed said, "That's quite a piece of work you've made there." Sister Solace had returned.

"Yes," I chuckled, proud of what I'd done but trying not to show it. I was, I will admit to you, particularly proud of my arrowheads, childishly proud of them, and hoped that she might comment on them, so that I could shrug off my talent for drawing them as an insignificant accomplishment.

"Have you prepared your list of errors?" she asked, as gently, I suppose, as she could.

"The list," I said. "I haven't quite—"

That pout of hers again. Who had taught her that unnerving pout? Was it part of the Solace Society's training, a weapon in the arsenal of all the Solace Sisters?

"Okay," I said, bringing the master list from under the covers. "I've made a start, but I really have to go through it, make a few changes—"

"That's all right," she said, quivering at the sight of such a long list, a sheet so full of error, "I can interpret it."

I glanced at the list. I thought for a moment of just handing it to her and sending her on her way, but a glance was enough to convince me that I couldn't do that. "I killed a man in the heat of argument," read the first entry.

"If you would just let me copy it neatly—" I said.

"Please?" she said. It was a real plea. She wanted that list. It would be the trophy of her volunteer career.

"Let me just—ah—" I scanned the list and saw at a glance that someone, in the course of the list's evolution, must have categorized and re-copied it. Perhaps that had happened several times. From murder, it descended through lesser crimes, and seemed to be heading toward things I might be willing to claim as errors of my own.

"I'm waiting."

"Well, I've repeated myself a bit," I said, tearing the sheet across the middle. "The bottom half is all you need. It's neater and—more accurate."

She accepted it and scanned it eagerly. "Hmm," she said, and "Ah," and "Interesting," and even "Very interesting." I was beginning to feel an odd sort of pride in my misfeasance when she folded the list, slipped it into a pocket of her uniform, and said with brisk efficiency, "Well, there's nothing so terrible here. We'll get started tomorrow, and we should be able to patch things up in a few days."

She left without even saying goodbye, without consoling me. I felt insulted. "Nothing so terrible?" If that were so, why did I feel the weight of guilt? I must have done something to earn it, to earn the burden of that weight.

Chapter 10

As Matthew, I Have a Close Shave

NURSE MILLS: *(Matter-of-fact)* Sorry. But I shall have to lift your penis now to grease around it.
Marlow's face is suddenly a cinema poster, so to speak, for *The Agony and the Ecstasy.*

—Dennis Potter, *The Singing Detective*

MR. BARBER?" It was Cerise, back with her bathing kit, smiling.

"Matthew," I said. "Please call me Matthew."

"Matthew," she said.

She drew a curtain around the bed, and we were, to the degree that it was possible for us to be so within the ward, alone.

"If you can arrange yourself so that you're a little bit on an angle and let your head rest in the indentation in the side of this pan, I'll wash your hair first," she said. I made the adjustment, and she went to work on my hair, with warm water and shampoo that smelled like almonds.

"I saw that you were visited by Sister Solace," she said.

"Yes. She wanted me to compile a list of my mistakes in life."

"Never made any?"

"Oh, many. A lifetime's worth, I'm sure." Was I sure? What mistakes

had I made? I didn't really know. Everybody makes mistakes. I'm somebody. Therefore, I must have made mistakes. But what had they been? I
couldn't recover the memory of them.

"Didn't anybody offer you the big list?"

"Yes. Stagger Lee did. I had to tear off part of it and give that to her.
So I owe the list half a page of mistakes. Do you think you could get me
a pad and a decent pen or pencil?"

"No problem," she said, and began drying my hair briskly with a
thick towel. When she had finished, she wrapped the towel into a turban,
raised my head from the pan, and pulled the pan away. "You can line
yourself up on the bed again, and turn onto your left side."

I did as I was told, exposing my back and buttocks to her. She began
to wash me. I suppose that she worked with the practiced efficiency of
someone washing a car, but on the receiving end, her ministrations felt
sensual and tender. The water was warm. The sponge was rough, but her
hand was smooth, and she used both sponge and hand, the one to clean,
and the other to soothe, because the object of this exercise, it seemed
clear to me, was not only to bathe the patient, but to ease him. I was
grateful. I wanted to thank her, but I didn't want to reinforce the nurse-
patient relationship. I wanted it to go somewhere else.

"Thank you for explaining that theory of time," I said. "I've been
thinking about it."

"Which one was that?" she asked, sponging my shoulders and back
with professional care.

"Which one?" I asked, taken aback. "The one about time being nothing but a construct of the human mind."

"Oh. Yeah. That's a good one." The soothing hand followed the sponge,
kneading the skin and muscle. "Want another?"

"Sure. Okay."

"Try thinking of time as a tree. A tree with infinitely many branches
and infinitely many roots."

"A tree," I said. "With infinitely many branches. And infinitely many
roots. Okay."

"Now imagine it sliced." She had reached my feet. The sponge tickled, and I laughed a bit. "Tickle?" she asked, like a mischievous girl.

"Yes," I said, "as if you didn't know."

She tickled the soles of my feet with practiced skill, and she actually made me giggle. "Are you imagining it sliced?" she asked.

"Sliced?"

"Yes, sliced. You can turn over onto your back. Sliced crossways. Horizontally. Into infinitely many infinitely thin slices."

"Got it," I said, turning onto my back. I was erect. My erection was right there, making a spectacle of itself, but she said not a word nor gave it a glance and went right to work washing my face, sponging it gently, with the tenderest of attentions.

"Those slices are instants or moments in the existence of many universes. An infinite number of universes."

"The branches," I said, like a good student, while she used a small swab on my ears.

"And the roots." She winked, not in a flirtatious way, but in a way that said "think about it."

"The roots—oh, of course." She began sponging her way down across my chest. "So you're postulating an infinite number of earlier universes— the roots—all collapsing to a singularity—the trunk—"

She had reached my waist, moved right on down my belly, and was now holding my erect penis in her hand while she ran the sponge over my scrotum.

"Focus," she said.

"On what?"

"On the theory," she said, with a look that said that I was being a bad boy, violating an unspoken rule or condition of the sponge bath.

"I'm sorry," I whispered. "I'm going to—"

"It happens," she said with a shrug.

It did.

"There, there," she said, and began cleaning me with the sponge. Its roughness sent me into a quivering ecstasy that made me gasp and nearly cry out. "Hush, now," she said, as if comforting a whimpering child.

Embarrassed, grateful, I struggled to return to the theory of time as roots, trunk, and branches. "And the slices are parallel," I offered, "parallel moments in branching universes."

"You got it," she said, with a pat that was awfully close to goodbye.

"It's an attractive idea," I said quickly, to keep her there. "It offers the possibility of alternatives. On another branch of the tree of time I might not be lying in this hospital bed."

"You might be lying on a beach in Miami with Sheila and Didi."

"Or with you," I might have said, but it and all the other things I might have said about lying on a beach somewhere, about lying with her anywhere, anywhere with anyone, seemed too crude and obvious. I wanted to say something to keep her there beside the bed for a while longer, so I said, "Time sliced into infinitely many infinitely thin slices, like pepperoni, slices of pepperoni, but infinitely thin and infinitely numerous, a recipe for the ultimate pizza, with infinitely many infinitely thin slices of pepperoni, no threat to the heart, or a threat infinitely small."

That got me a smile, but only a smile, while she went about packing her gear.

"Where do you get these theories?" I asked. "Is there a big book of theories of time?"

"Maybe," she said. "But I get them from TV. I've got satellite TV. And there's the Time Channel. 'All Time, All the Time.' "

"Do they get that here?" I asked, gesticulating in the direction of the dark and silent set suspended above the foot of my bed.

"Not at present," she said, and with a blown kiss she was off.

LEFT ALONE, washed clean, lying in a hospital bed without benefit of the Time Channel, with only the beating of my heart to mark time, I had time to think. Under such conditions, particularly if one is afflicted with a life-threatening disease, as I seemed to be, one's thinking is likely to turn toward questions of mortality—actually, toward questions of vitality and mortality, life and death. Was I going to die? Well, yes. Was I going to die just then? Maybe. Was I going to die happy? Speaking as the man I seemed to be, no. Fulfilled? No. But suppose I was not going to die just then. Suppose I survived this stay. Suppose I left the hospital, allowed to think of the present episode as a warning. What would that warning be? Why, it would be the old, old warning—

" 'You must change your life, for there is no place that does not see you,' " said the voice of Sister Solace, whispering in my ear.

"Oh, shit," I said. "You scared me half to death."

"Sorry," she said, but she was smiling and hiding something behind her back, like a schoolgirl with a good report card.

"Half to death," I repeated, "and for a guy in my condition that puts me pretty close to the edge of the abyss."

"I brought you something," she said.

"What is it?"

"Something to help you begin to change your life, to begin to correct your past errors."

"Yeah?" I snarled.

Without a word, she handed me a plastic container of dental floss.

"Start with the simplest, that's the advice of the Society," she said. "And not flossing is the simplest error on your list."

"Oh. Flossing. Right."

"Daily," she admonished with a waggling finger.

"Promise," I said, crossing my heart.

She gave me a consoling pat on the cheek, whispered, "Change your life," once more for good measure—she could not be faulted when it came to giving good measure—and left me until whenever her next unscheduled materialization might occur.

Change my life. All right, I will. In what way must I change my life? I must floss more regularly; she was right about that. I must be good to my heart, too, better than I had been, apparently. I must not abuse it, must care for it and strengthen it, befriend it. Was there more? Where was that list? I wished that Sister Solace hadn't gone, so that I could review "my" list of errors and look for clues there. That wish lasted only the briefest of moments. I took another look at the top half of the master list. Following the error of murder in anger came this:

> I didn't do my homework. Habitually. I owe literally thousands of homework assignments, reaching all the way back to the third grade.

This sent a chill not merely down my spine, but rushing through my entire body. I owed something. An assignment. There was something I hadn't done. I had to write a review. A restaurant review. I really was a restaurant reviewer. Feeling the pressure of a deadline that I had ignored too long, I seized the Meal Preference Sheet and the stub of pencil and, on the back of the sheet, in a small, precise hand, wrote a review of a restaurant called Ike's, "just like that," by which phrase I mean to say that I wrote it without hesitation, as if I had already written it and was now merely duplicating it, replacing a lost copy from memory. I signed it, also without hesitation, and with the unconscious awareness that this was how I always signed my reviews, B. W. Beath.

I looked at the page incredulously, amazed by what I had done. It was then, I think, that I realized that I was not so much struggling to recover a memory as I was in the process of recovering a memory. I was living a memory. All the living I was doing was within a memory. Everything that was happening to me had happened long ago, many years ago. I am not referring to an experience of a "memory" of an earlier life, when I was an itinerant peddler selling asps to Cleopatra, but to an earlier period of *my* life, about eighteen years earlier.

"Mr. Barber, right?" asked an orderly who wheeled a gurney alongside my bed. Cerise followed him and took a position on the opposite side.

"Right," I said, as if I were sure.

"Excellent," said the orderly. "I hate it when I wheel the wrong guy down to the cath lab, you know?"

Cerise laughed.

"I'll bet the wrong guy wouldn't be too pleased about it, either," I said, shifting myself from the bed to the gurney. I wanted to hear Cerise laugh, wanted to make Cerise laugh. She did, but as she did she reached across to me, took my hand, and squeezed it, and from that squeeze I realized that there was some danger that I would not be wheeled back from the cardiac catheter lab, that I might die there. I recognized Cerise's squeeze as professional compassion, and nothing more, but I enjoyed it as much as I would have if it were something more personal, more heartfelt.

"Here we go," said the orderly, raising the railings and clicking them into place.

"Cerise," I said, handing her what I had written, "this has to go to *Boston Biweekly.* The newspaper. To the entertainment editor, Larry Boggs." Larry Boggs? How did I know that? It just came out of me. I said it "just like that."

"Okay," she said, gravely. "I'll see that it gets there."

"It's not my will or anything like that," I said, "but it is important."

"I'll take it on my break," she said, shrinking with distance.

I found it a very odd sensation to be wheeled through the hospital corridors. Of the many things that made it odd, the oddest was that I enjoyed it. I felt no embarrassment at being flat on my back and treated as if I were helpless. That state seemed entirely appropriate to my condition. I wouldn't have minded a push around the hospital daily.

"So, you're probably asking yourself, 'Is arteriography painful?' " said the orderly.

"Damn," I said. "I forgot to ask myself that."

"Hey, don't worry about it. I'm here to tell you that's it's not going to hurt a bit."

"You've been through it?"

"Huh? No. But I know all about it."

"Sort of."

"Don't confuse me here. I'm telling you you're going to be fine. Before you go into the cath lab they'll give you a sedative to help you relax."

"Okay. Good."

"In the lab, they'll give you a local anesthetic in your groin where they're going to insert the catheter—like what a dentist would give you."

"Not one of my favorite experiences."

"Then they make just a little cut so they can get the catheter into the artery."

"Oh, brother."

"The doc runs a sheath into the artery. It's a little plastic tube. That's going to allow them to insert the catheter. Hold on a minute."

He maneuvered me into an elevator.

"Once they get that sheath in, they thread the catheter in, and they run it all the way up to the coronary arteries. That's what they want to look at, right?"

"Right."

"So then they inject some dye into your blood so's the whole coronary arterial system will be visible to the X-ray cameras."

"Dye?"

"That's right. There's no pain associated with that. You are going to feel a flush of warmth kind of spreading all through you, though. Goes away after a while. Nothing to worry about. Our floor."

He maneuvered me off the elevator.

"You may feel some discomfort while all this is going on, and there is a certain risk."

"I had a feeling we'd get to this part."

"Some people do feel a little pain, some feel angina, there's some risk of injury, and a few patients die during the procedure."

"Very few, right?"

"Oh, yeah."

He wheeled me into a curtained area. He drew the curtains shut around us.

"Look," he said, gripping my shoulder with avuncular familiarity. "Find the pleasure."

"Find the pleasure?"

"You are having an adventure. All of life is an adventure, including this."

"Adventure in Arteriography."

"That's it. The secret to enjoying life is to find the pleasure in whatever is happening to you, you know what I'm saying?"

"I hear you."

He gave me a friendly punch on the shoulder and left me to savor the adventure on my own. I had hardly had time to begin the savoring before a large and very strong-looking female nurse appeared at my side.

"Matthew Barber?"

"Yes?"

"Oh, good. I hate it when I shave the wrong guy."

I laughed heartily, and the nurse beamed at me. She couldn't tell that I was laughing at the idea that there might be only one joke current throughout the entire hospital.

Without further humor, she said, "I'm going to inject you with a sedative."

"To relax me," I said.

"You been through this before?"

"No, but I heard about it."

"Mm-hm," she said, while she eased the sedative into my arm. "There. Now I'm going to shave your pubic hair at the side of your groin, where they'll be making the incision for the catheter, okay?"

"Okay."

"I'll just need to lift your gown."

She held a large gauze square in one hand and with the other raised my gown. As she did so, she swooped in with the gauze square and swept my penis and scrotum to one side; so smooth and practiced was her maneuver that she managed to preserve as much of my modesty and dignity as might have been preserved.

"Well done," I said.

She said nothing. With a disposable razor she began shaving the hair from the right side of my groin.

When she had finished, she replaced the gown and removed the gauze pad.

"You're all set," she said. "Someone will come and get you when they're ready for you. Just rest here," and she disappeared, leaving me staring at the ceiling, waiting for the sedative to do its work.

Chapter 11

As Matthew, I Remember

[Swann] had distributed his own personality between two characters, him who was the "first person" in the dream, and another whom he saw before him capped with a fez . . . enjoying, at the same time, such creative power that he was able to reproduce himself by a simple act of division, like certain lower organisms.

—Marcel Proust, *A la recherche du temps perdu (Swann's Way)*
(translated by C. K. Scott Moncrieff)

LYING THERE, idly awaiting some sign that I was relaxing, I began to recall what had happened to me, how I had come to be in the hospital. If time is just an illusion, a construct of the human mind imposed on the universe for convenience, then it isn't quite correct to say that I recalled what had happened to me. Images and sensations began to occur to me. I interpreted them as memories. I think they were memories. As they came to me, unsought, unbidden, I welcomed them. I think I may even have been smiling as they came, smiling in part at the efficacy of the sedative as an aid to recovering memory, if memories they really were.

I remembered that the night air was cold. It felt like the first really cold night of the winter. I was walking along a dark street in Charlestown, late, after too many drinks and too much excitement. I wasn't walking particularly fast, but I was breathing hard. I walked until I reached the

Charlestown Bridge, where I stopped, thinking that I would catch my breath.

Breathing hard? Yes. I was excited, and frightened. I was breathing hard because I had just been involved in a fight. A fight? Me? Not quite a fight. It wasn't anything more than a couple of swings. I had done a foolish thing, something not at all like me.

I had been in a bar, drinking, feeling lonely and sorry for myself. There were some young people at the bar, students, an eclectic cosmopolitan group of rich kids, and among them was a girl. She was attractive, sexy, flirtatious, playful, and because I was attracted to her I began talking with the others in the group, making bar talk, joking, trying to make myself interesting and amusing. I seemed to be succeeding, and she seemed to be interested, and I was elated. I was rejuvenated. I was also, as I should have guessed, and would have guessed had I not been under the sedative influence of too many margaritas, being deceived. Somehow, without exchanging a word or a glance that I could detect, these charming young people had hatched a conspiracy against me. They had plotted to humiliate me. Maybe it wasn't just something they thought of on the spot. Maybe it was a frequent amusement of theirs, making fools of men, men like me. Maybe the script was always the same, and all they had to do was find a suitable victim—a man feeling lonely and feeling his age—and dangle the bait in front of him.

"Hey, look."

"Where?"

"There at the bar. The guy drinking alone."

"Oh, yeah."

"A real Matthew Barber type."

"Let's go to work."

It worked. I took the bait. There is no fool like an old fool.

They claimed that they were going off to a party in Charlestown, and to my surprise and delight they asked me if I wanted to come along with them. I looked at the little morsel and saw only her eyes and her smile, not the hook. I said yes.

We squeezed into a couple of cabs. The girl and I got into the same one, and she sat on my lap. As daring and delighted as I felt, I also felt embarrassed, because I was sure that she had to feel my erection. She did. She made it very clear that she did. She settled herself on me, wiggled her bottom on me, in a way that made it quite clear that she felt it. I was thrilled—and I was embarrassed. How very Matthew Barber of me.

We drove, but I wasn't paying attention to where we were going. I was paying attention to my own performance, in the role of the fascinating and congenial older man. When the cab stopped, we were nowhere, but I didn't even notice that. I thought that we must be someplace where students find cheap apartments—but the truth is that I didn't think at all, just supposed. We tumbled out of the cab. I looked around, trying to get some idea of where we were, and in the time it takes to recall it they were all back in the cab, with the windows up and the doors locked, laughing, pointing at me. I was ashamed, and I was furious. I suppose I was furious with myself, but I wanted to take it out on them. I wanted to punish them for what they'd done to me. I began kicking at the cab, pounding on the windows, calling them names. They drove off, but they must have been as lost as I was, because they went only a short way and had to turn around, had to come back past me to get onto the road again. I scrambled around, looking for something to throw at them, and found a broken bit of concrete. I waited, and I threw when I thought I had the best chance of doing some damage. I hit the driver's window, and it shattered. I wanted to cheer. I think, perhaps, that I did cheer. Remembering it, lying there on the gurney, detached by sedation, I could see that I must have looked ridiculous, certainly must have looked ridiculous to the kids in the cab. They must have roared.

The cab stopped, and the driver got out. I'm sure he'd been paid to play his part in the game of humiliating me, tipped for it, but I guess he hadn't been tipped enough to cover damage to the cab, because he jumped out of the cab and came after me. I backed up, but I didn't run. Recalling it, I am revolted by the way I behaved, but right then I wanted to fight. I wasn't afraid. I was proud of myself for not being afraid, and I exulted in the fury I felt. I wanted to hurt somebody. The cabdriver would do. We were under a bridge approach, and there were construction materials around. I grabbed the first thing I found—a length of reinforcing bar, one of the rods they put in concrete to strengthen it. I began to play a ridiculous part. I took an aggressive stance, swung my weapon, and advanced on the cabdriver. I must have looked like a middle-age Neanderthal. It felt very, very good. As I recalled all of this, I understood that I had been very angry for a very long time. I was ready to make the cabdriver suffer for my anger, redress with his pain the pain that I felt.

He picked up a bar of his own. What did the kids make of all this? What did the girl make of it? I hadn't thought about that at the time, but on the gurney I did. At the time, I just wanted revenge. I wanted revenge for every offense, every indignity I had ever suffered in my life.

I attacked him. I swung at him with that bar, and I hit him. I felt the bar hit him. It must have hit his head. That's what I was aiming for. That's where I must have hit him. When I felt it—felt it, rather than saw it, I still couldn't see it, even though I could recall it—I felt—so many things at once, felt that so many things were lost in that moment. I lost any right to think of myself as a good man. I had never struck out at anyone in my life. I had thought of myself as much, much better than most people. With that one swing of the bar, I lost my illusions about myself. Some of my illusions anyway. Lost.

I dropped the bar, and I ran. I don't know what I did to that cabdriver. I don't know how much damage I did to him. I know that I hit him, and I can still feel the bar hitting him. My arms remember it, my hands remember it. I might have killed him. I might only have bruised him.

I ran. I walked. I ran. The cab didn't follow me. Was that because the driver was unable to drive—whatever that meant? I didn't want to know. I ran. I had to stop and rest again and again. I couldn't draw enough air into me. I was gasping.

With the running and the gasping for breath, the memory became very strange. It had been awful. It became strange. I began talking to myself. I was there, bent over and wheezing, and I was also there beside myself, mocking myself. The self who was standing beside me could see right through me, as they say. He knew everything that I had felt during that absurd fight, he knew how lost I felt, and he knew that I was dramatizing the moment. If he had been on another gurney beside me while I was recalling it all, he would have known what I was thinking, what I was recalling, and would have understood that I was dramatizing it as I recalled it, as if I were trying to entertain myself with the story, to make the whole episode "interesting" in the way that stories engage our interest more completely than random recollections do.

I wanted to get away from him. I wanted to get to a hospital—this hospital. When I found myself on the Charlestown Bridge, I knew that I wasn't very far from here. I tried to stand up straight, but I was light-headed, and I thought I was going to faint. It passed after a moment, and I began walking again. He kept pace with me. I walked faster.

I tried to run, tried to leave him behind. I hadn't gone far before I felt a numbness in my left armpit, in my left elbow, down my forearm, and in my little finger. I was having a heart attack. I knew it.

"I'm having a heart attack," I said.

He said something dismissive. I don't recall it exactly. It was something like "It's probably nothing." That was the way he had begun talking to me, the attitude he took toward me.

"I can't believe that I've sunk to the level of talking to myself," I said.

"I can't believe that I've sunk to the level of talking back to myself," he said.

Why had it come to this? Why had I decided to be two people? Had I decided? Or had this division just happened without my willing it? If I had willed it, why did I feel a need to talk to B. W. Beath? When I invented him, he was just a pseudonym, just a way to preserve my incognito while visiting restaurants and when writing my reviews. I'll admit that I loved the idea that my incognito had to be preserved. I felt like a spy—a kid's idea of a spy. To be honest, I think that the feeling of spying and the secret thrill of secrecy itself became the only pleasures that I got out of reviewing restaurants. After a while, writing the reviews became a chore, but the spying was always a kick.

B. W. Beath was many things that I am not. He was clever. He was suave. Worldly. I enjoyed being him. I began to dress the part, consciously costuming myself, disguising myself, before going out to visit a restaurant. I cultivated "his" mannerisms and style of speech. (It occurred to me from time to time that I was ruining his disguise; if I had wanted him to go undetected, I should have acted more like myself.) Things were under control, though. I was in control. It was a game. At some point, apparently, the game had gotten out of hand, and was so much beyond a game now that he and I were running side-by-side across the Charlestown Bridge, on the lam, running from an assault-and-battery charge. Me, Matthew Barber, mild-mannered to a fault, with blood on my hands.

"Oh, that's too much," he said. "Blood on your hands? You're exaggerating."

Perhaps I was, but I felt as guilty as if I'd killed the guy. As if we had. BW and I were running together, partners in crime. I had to stop again. I've never been much of a runner.

After a minute or two we continued, but walking, not running, and still talking. I couldn't stop talking to him, even though he responded with the kind of belittling banter that older children wield so well against younger ones.

I told him everything that was happening to me, as it happened to me, as if he couldn't feel it himself. Perhaps he couldn't. He claimed not to. I told him when I felt the numbness passing, and he told me that he had been right about its being nothing—a pinched nerve at worst. I thought that was ridiculous and told him so. I disparaged his medical knowledge and diagnostic skills. I was trying to score points in an argument with a phantom. It was ridiculous. I saw that it was ridiculous to do what I was doing, but I didn't feel that it was within my power to stop arguing with him. For everything I said, he had a reply, and to his every reply I felt compelled to reply. I could only try to escape, break away. I turned toward Causeway Street.

BW asked, "Where are we going?"

"Charlesbank Hospital," I said.

"Don't," he said, and I swear that I could feel him tugging at my sleeve, trying to restrain me, to redirect me. "You're going to embarrass yourself."

I pulled away. I began walking, slowly, toward the hospital. I didn't speak. I struggled not to speak. I didn't want to tell him that I was afraid, that I felt threatened, in mortal danger, but I had no one else to tell, and I wanted to tell someone, so I told him. He made a joke of it. I turned toward him a withering glance that I suppose he didn't even notice. He began berating me for not having gotten enough pleasure out of life. I laughed in his face—a little breathlessly, I admit—and told him that he was only demonstrating how poorly he understood me. It wasn't pleasure that was lacking in my life; it was a sense of purpose, a higher purpose, something that would make me feel like a worthy person, a man of parts. A man of parts? If I had told him that he would have pounced on it and eviscerated it. I had to get away from him.

I managed to keep silent until we came to a narrow street that led to the Charlesbank emergency entrance. I stopped and stared down the street. I didn't want to go into the hospital, but my chest was tight, and I was wheezing. The door to the emergency entrance seemed like such a plane of demarcation, a slice of time that, if I passed through it, would forever divide "before I went into the hospital" from "after I got out of the hospital," if I did get out of the hospital. I knew that I had to go, had to go through that door, and I knew that if I didn't rouse myself and make myself go to the door and through it, there might not be any "after" left in my life at all.

I began walking toward the entrance. I had never felt so tired in my life. He tried to grab my sleeve. I pulled away. A taxi turned our way, leaving the hospital, curving along the circle at the emergency entry.

"Let's get that cab," he said. "Let's go home."

I trudged on, mechanically, with my head down, as if I could feel the weight of my death on me, like a winter coat wet with snow.

I found myself at the doors, a pair of doors, flat glass doors, closed, with no handles or doorknobs, and I was confused. I couldn't figure out how I could get through them, and I thought that he might help me. I turned around to call out to him, but when I turned around I felt dizzy and I knew I was going to pass out, and as I fell backward toward the doors, I saw him get into the cab—I saw myself get into the cab—and then I fell backward toward the doors, and I expected to fall against them, but they slid open, sideways, automatically, and admitted me.

I WAS MOVING. At first I thought I was flying, in the buoyant, drifting, powerless flight of dreams, but the squeak and creak and steel firmness of the gurney corrected me.

"Where are we going?" I asked the unseen mover.

"Cath lab," said a voice.

"Oh. Of course. Right."

We went through doors. We were in a large white room. I was transferred to a table, not a table that looked as I would have expected an operating table to look, but a table more like what, I couldn't help telling myself, I would expect a table in a morgue to look like, a table on which autopsies would be performed, a slab of stainless steel, unpadded. Nor did the assembled set of doctors and assistants resemble the crew that I had seen in operating rooms in movies and on television. There were two doctors at the foot of the table, standing just beyond my own feet, and then there were several other men who seemed to be technicians more than medical personnel. That, it struck me, was entirely appropriate, since the room was well equipped with electronic devices and monitors. To my left, if I turned my head that way, I could see a large monitor, like a large and very good television set, tuned to nothing, and above me, suspended from the ceiling, or perhaps from a wall or post that I couldn't see from my angle, was another large monitor on a bracket that allowed it to be tilted and rotated so that it faced directly at the doctors at the foot of the table. Beyond that, the room was a mystery, blurring at the edges of my peripheral vision, where it fuzzed into a cloud of silver and white, of stainless steel fittings and white walls. The conversation was all in murmurs, as if everyone were awaiting a signal, the raising of a curtain, before they performed their roles, took their parts, played their parts, living in waiting time, that time that is wasted when one is waiting to do whatever is the point of one's being where one is. I, too, was in that waiting time, that limbo, though I had no idea what my part would be when the performance finally began.

The doors swung open, and in walked another, older doctor. Raising my head, I saw the two younger doctors almost imperceptibly bow theirs. An eminence was in the room, in the operating theater. The procedure could begin.

"There are no nerves in the heart," said one of the younger doctors, addressing me, acknowledging my presence in the room and my essential role in the drama for the first time, "so you need no general anesthetic, but we will give you a local at the site of the incision," and he administered an injection in the shaved area beside my groin.

As a group, they then turned away, as smoothly and as synchronously as dancers, turning inward in a contemplative adagio. With their backs to me, they bent their heads and began a conversation.

What are they talking about? I wondered. *The news? Stocks? A nurse? The one called Cerise? Me? Golf?*

After a few murmurous moments they turned back, and turned their attention to me again.

"You'll feel pressure," said one, and he bent to the shaved area.

"Pressure?" I asked.

"The incision," said another.

I felt pressure, but nothing else.

They fussed some more, and the second said, "We're inserting the catheter."

I felt nothing at all, not even the feeling that I was being invaded.

A long period of silence passed, and then the second of the younger doctors said, "You'll feel a warm flush."

"The dye," I said.

"Yes," he said. "The dye."

I began to feel the flush spreading through me, and with the warmth came a strong desire not to be where I was, but to be somewhere else . . . as Bertram W. Beath.

Chapter 12

As BW, I Take Off

He is a man on the run. . . . I'd say he was alive with a sort of "bravery." . . . He is the opposite of an exceptional character, the opposite of a hero, but what differentiates him from average people is that he never settles down in average situations.

—François Truffaut
interview included in the press notes to
Love on the Run

ON A COLD WINTER'S NIGHT, Matthew and I were walking along a dark street in Charlestown, Massachusetts, late, after too many drinks and too much excitement. We were not walking particularly fast, but Matthew was breathing hard. We had reached the Charlestown Bridge, the bridge to the North End of Boston, and there Matthew stopped. I stopped with him, and I will admit that I didn't mind stopping, because it gave me a chance to catch my breath.

Matthew said, with a dramatic display of discomfort, "I'm gasping. I can't breathe."

"I can see that," I said. "Anyone could see that. You're putting on quite a show."

"I'm pulling at the air," he went on, with that odd sense of wonder people exhibit when their own bodies betray them, "sucking it into my lungs, but it doesn't seem to penetrate me, doesn't seem to do me any good."

I said, stating the obvious, "You're out of shape."

He flapped his hand at me, as if to dismiss me, as if I were an underpaid assistant or an unpaid intern, and said, "Go away."

In the deep and reassuring voice of a friend, a true friend, who would not allow himself to be sent away, however painful it might be to stay, I said, "Never. I shall be with you always. Through thick and thin." I was surprised to find when I spoke that I, too, had trouble drawing a breath.

Matthew waved me away again and shook his head. He put his hands on his knees and tried to breathe. "I feel nauseated," he said. "If only I could catch my breath, I could—" He stood up straight, swayed a little, and then began to move again, tentatively, as if he expected to fall. I moved with him. He walked faster. I kept pace.

He tried to run, as if he meant to leave me behind. He hadn't gone far before he said, "I feel a numbness in my left armpit, in my left elbow, down my forearm, and in my little finger. This is a heart attack. I'm having a heart attack."

"It's just a pinched nerve," I said, theorizing.

"A pinched nerve?"

"More than likely. I wouldn't give it another thought."

"And in a few minutes I'd be dead."

"So? You will be someday. None of us gets out of here alive."

"Well, I'm not ready to make my exit," he said, in a voice that he was evidently struggling to make strong, defiant, and assertive, but then he lost his breath again and added, weakly, as an afterthought, "asshole."

"Such language from a sophisticated guy like you."

"I'm having a heart attack. I'm entitled."

"I doubt that you are having a heart attack, but even if you are, must it make you sink to the level of—" I stopped when I noticed that he had turned toward Causeway Street. I asked, "Where are we going?"

"Charlesbank Hospital," he said.

"Don't be ridiculous," I told him. "You're going to embarrass yourself. You're going to get everyone excited about a heart attack, when all you've got is a case of bad nachos and too many margaritas."

"Shut up."

The night was quiet. The hour was late, and Boston is not a late-night town. Matthew began walking, slowly, toward Charlesbank Hospital. He didn't speak.

"What are you doing now," I asked, "contemplating your mortality?"

"Maybe."

"Well you might, walking along these streets this late at night. How are you feeling? Remorseful? Regretful? Cheated?"

"Cheated," he conceded. "Somehow, something has eluded me. I don't know what it is, exactly, but I feel the lack of it."

"Pleasure," I suggested. "The only thing worth getting out of life. Pleasure."

"I was thinking that I've missed a sense of purpose—"

"The pursuit of pleasure is a purpose."

"A higher purpose."

"There is no higher purpose."

"I mean something transcendent—"

"Oh—the pursuit of *happiness*."

"Right now you would make me happy if you would leave me alone. Forever."

"Never. You can count on it. You can count on me. I will, as they so infuriatingly say, be there for you. Always."

We walked along in silence until we came to a narrow street that led to the Charlesbank emergency entrance. Matthew stopped and stared down the short street, wheezing. "I don't want to go in there," he said. "I'd rather not."

"That's because entering will be a turning point in your life, Matthew my friend. If you go through that door, everything that has happened to you in your life so far will have to be stamped 'before I went into the hospital,' and everything that is to come will have to be stamped 'after I got out of the hospital,' assuming that you do get out of the hospital. While you are in the hospital, you will expect yourself to come to some kind of understanding. I expect that you would. Come to some kind of understanding, that is. If you go in there, you will probably have insights. Epiphanies, for God's sake. I don't think you're up to it. Let's go home."

"Is this angina?" he asked, muttering, as if he were talking to himself, pretending to ignore me. "It's not a pain in the chest, but a pain in the back, an ache, maybe a pulled muscle."

"And it might just as easily be nothing more than the ache of an empty heart—the metaphorical heart, that is, the seat of love and hope. You have suffered several kinds of heartache, Matthew, so a broken heart seems just as likely as a heart attack."

"The back pain is gone now," he said, "the numbness, too."

"See?" I said. "It was nothing. Overexertion. Indigestion. And a pinched nerve."

Matthew wore a noncommittal look, but I suspected that he was inclined to agree. A taxi turned our way, leaving the hospital, curving along the circle at the emergency entrance. I wanted to flag it down and get out of there.

"Let's get that cab," I said.

"No," said Matthew, shaking his head. "You're wrong about this." He began walking toward the entrance. Reluctantly, I followed. Each step seemed harder than the last. I had never felt so tired in my life. Trying to take those few steps was like slogging through viscous mud that was clotting on my shoes, slowing me, exhausting me, and Matthew, beside me, seemed to be trudging through the same sludge. When we reached some steps that led to a side door of the building, I said, "Why don't we stop and rest here for a minute?"

"If I stopped here," he said, "I would not get up. I would die here, on these steps."

"You're being melodramatic."

He trudged on, mechanically, with his head down.

Then, just then, at that moment, I decided that I had no further part to play in Matthew's melodrama. I turned away and started loping toward the cab, my hand in the air, and with each stride away from Matthew, I grew lighter and stronger. When I reached the cab, I grabbed the door, swung it open, and threw myself in.

"Where to?" asked the cabbie.

I looked back at Matthew. He was at the emergency entrance, standing there, looking back at me, and the look on his face was so incredulous that it seemed like a challenge, as if by refusing to believe that I could be leaving him he was telling me that I could not leave him, that I wasn't capable of it.

"To the airport," I said, and the cab began to move.

Matthew turned toward the doors and began to collapse. As the cab pulled away, I saw him falling, slowly, toward those doors, and I saw the doors sliding automatically open to let him in.

THE CLOSER I CAME to the airport, the more I thought of warm places, and by the time the cab turned onto the airport access road, I had made up my mind to go anywhere warm, anywhere where the sun rose high in the sky at midday. I had the cabbie stop at the first terminal, got out, and rushed inside like a perp on the lam. I scanned the screen that listed departures. The first flight that met my single criterion was headed for Miami. In an hour and forty minutes I was on it.

The flight was uneventful. By the time I arrived in Miami, dawn was breaking. I had had no sleep other than a nap in the airport in Boston and another on the plane, but I felt no fatigue at all. From the airport outside Miami, I had a cab take me to South Beach. I had never been there, though I had often tried to convince Matthew that we ought to go there, dangling as bait the likelihood that the beaches would be littered with models basted with oil and sizzling on the sand. Matthew had always been too busy. In many ways, I allowed myself to say to myself, distanced as I was from him now, Matthew was a fool.

The cab ride was sunny and cheap, with a reggae sound track. I checked in at the Albatross, a small hotel at the northern end of Ocean Drive, where without the slightest pang of guilt I handed Matthew's American Express card to the desk clerk and without even the briefest hesitation signed Matthew's name on the registration card. An Alvar Aalto bowl on the corner of the desk was filled with complimentary condoms. No one remarked on my not having luggage.

My room was in the front, on the northeast corner, providing, through its jalousie windows, a breeze and a view of the beach. I shopped for a while, just long enough to provide myself with the rudiments of a tropical wardrobe, the essentials for my personal grooming, and a hundred business cards from a speedy printer.

I returned to the Albatross to shave and shower, and then, dressed in

Bertram W. Beath

Passionate Spectator

my new duds, I went out to lunch and a new life, no longer a swimmer fighting the current to get somewhere, but a drifter now, floating like a leaf on a stream, going nowhere, content now simply to be, and to see, to see what might come my way.

Chapter 13

As BW, I Learn the Lesson of Crab Cakes

Who can flatter himself that he will ever be understood? We all die un-
appreciated. It is the lot of women and of men of letters.

—Honoré de Balzac, "Ferragus," in *The Thirteen*

A LITTLE AFTER NOON, I was sitting at a table in the Puerta Cerrada
restaurant at the Denada hotel, waiting for a waiter. A waiter was passing, but he did not have the look of a waiter who intended to wait on me.
I cleared my throat to indicate that I was there, sitting at a table in the
very restaurant in which the waiter was employed, fully prepared to become a patron of the restaurant at the earliest possible moment, particularly eager to order a drink, and as likely as anyone else to leave a
handsome tip. The passing waiter showed no sign of having heard me
clear my throat, but it was hard to tell because the waiters at the Puerta
Cerrada were very discreet and tried their best to ignore anything a
customer might conceivably not have wanted them to hear. Not for their
ears the patrons' confessions, *cris du coeur*, complaints, conspiracies to
commit corporate larceny—whatever. The waiter disappeared behind the

gauzy draperies that nearly encircled the dining room, lending the room an air of summery indolence and separating it from the hotel lobby and the service area.

In time, another waiter glided by. As this one passed, I asked him, quite directly, to bring a wine list, thus: "Would you bring me a wine list, please?" The waiter did not look at me, but without breaking glide he said, "Of course," and he vanished behind the gauze.

A man at the next table chuckled. "You may never see him again," he said. "Our waiter disappeared behind those draperies quite a while ago." He chuckled again, then sighed. "We haven't seen him since."

"It was still breakfast time when we saw him last," said the woman with him, wistfully. "I asked for cream for my coffee."

The chuckler chuckled. So did the woman.

Yet another spectral waiter materialized from behind the gauze, this one carrying a plate. He brought the plate to a man dressed as a cowboy—boots, jeans, embroidered shirt, black hair slicked back, six-gun in a studded holster, bandoleers of bullets, nickel-plated cell phone (just kidding about the six-gun and the bandoleers). The plate held six hard-boiled eggs.

"He must have ordered yesterday," said the chuckler.

I considered leaving, but as soon as I began to rise from my chair, another waiter materialized beside me. "Can I get you something to drink?" he asked. "Some wine?" He flipped a wine list open as if commencing a conjuring act. Before he could make it disappear, I clasped it with both hands, scanned it, found a wine I recognized, a soft and buttery chardonnay from South Australia, and ordered a bottle of that.

A dark-haired woman in a short brown dress hurried past, apparently on her way to a table on the terrace. She halted abruptly, turned, and squealed hello to the chucklers. They greeted her warmly, and she took a seat at their table. A conversation began, but it was a sickly thing, halting and frail, likely to die before it got anywhere.

A waiter, not the one who had shown me the wine list, nor any of the waiters who had drifted through the room earlier, but a waiter all the same, brought me the very bottle I had ordered and commenced a great show of opening and icing. The chuckler glanced in my direction with envy in his eyes.

I poured myself a glass of wine. The cowboy peeled the last bit of shell from the first of his eggs, grinned, flicked his eyes around the room to be certain that he had an audience, and inserted the egg, whole, into his mouth. He chewed. He swallowed. He smiled. Bits of egg white flecked the corners of his mouth. He began peeling another egg.

"Wait a minute," the dark-haired woman said, putting the sickly conversation out of its misery. "Wait a minute." She looked into the eyes of the chuckler and said, "I'm getting the strangest feeling here. You don't recognize me, do you?"

"Well," said the chuckler, and he chuckled again.

"I don't believe it," said the dark-haired woman. She was smiling, but it was a mirthless smile.

"To tell you the truth," said the chuckler's companion, "I don't recognize you, either."

The dark-haired woman, still smiling, said to the chuckler's companion, "Yeah, but you didn't sleep with me."

She rose and extended her hand to the chuckler, who took it. Smiling, she said to him, "Have the crab cakes. They are the best crab cakes I have ever eaten in my life."

She strode off toward the terrace. The chuckler and his companion looked at each other. "I really have no idea who she is," claimed the chuckler. His companion gave him a withering smile, rose, and, gliding in the immaterial manner of the waiters, made for the gently drifting draperies and disappeared.

Or, perhaps, behind the curtains she underwent a metamorphosis, because no sooner had she passed behind the gauzy membrane than a waiter emerged from it, a particularly puzzled one, who looked around the room, found me, and, with what I would have been willing to swear was a wink—though I know well that one cannot always be certain about a wink and the conspiracy it implies—put a plate of chicken salad in front of me.

"I didn't order—" I began to protest, but the waiter was already gone.

I looked at the chicken salad. It looked good. I had intended to order the crab cakes, of course, on the dark-haired woman's strong recommendation, but fate had apparently decreed that it was chicken salad for me that day, so I ate it, and it really was quite good.

I had just finished, and was considering taking the remains of the bottle of wine out to the terrace, when the dark-haired woman came by again, on her way to the ladies' room this time, I guessed. "Pardon me," I said, rising, bringing my heels together, and making the slightest suggestion of a bow.

"Yes?" she said, surprised.

I handed her my card.

She drew her eyebrows together and looked at me, at first puzzled, then amused, as if she expected a joke.

"May I ask you a question?" I asked.

"Well, I'm just on my way to—" she said, gesticulating with my card in, it seemed reasonable to suppose, the direction of the ladies' room.

"When you return?"

"Sure. I guess." She looked at the card. "Is this a joke?" she asked.

"Certainly not," I said.

"Okay." She went off toward the ladies' room, holding my card. Her dress was quite short.

I grabbed the sleeve of the next passing waiter. Before he could object, I pulled him downward so that I had his ear. "Bring me a second wine glass immediately," I whispered. "That woman in the short brown dress is a restaurant critic with an international following."

"All right," the waiter said, and in a moment he brought a second wine glass, delivering it with an unmistakable wink.

When the woman in the short brown dress returned, I rose to the bent position the modern man assumes when he wants to show that he can be polite but is not going to become aggressively or offensively or embarrassingly so. She sat in the chair opposite mine. "Would you like some wine?" I asked.

"Well, I'm with some people—out on the terrace—"

I held the bottle, prepared to pour, and raised an eyebrow.

"Why not?" she said, and I poured her a glass.

She took a sip and asked, "What's the question? You asked if you could ask me a question."

"Are the crab cakes really that good?" I asked.

"Oh, the crab cakes," she said, shaking her head. "Crab cakes have so often disappointed me. Did you order them?"

"I was never given the opportunity to order anything. However, they served me chicken salad, so I ate that."

"Take what life brings you? That's your philosophy?"

"I have no philosophy," I assured her, "but if I did, I suppose that would serve as well as any other."

"Well, was it good? The chicken salad?"

"I have no opinions. I left them in Boston."

"Good place for them."

"I really would like to know about the crab cakes."

She sighed. "As I said, they've often disappointed me." She took a swallow of wine. "And every time they disappoint me, I promise myself never to order crab cakes ever again, anytime, anywhere, and I tell myself that I would be a fool to break that promise. And yet every time I see crab cakes on a menu I'm tempted to order them."

The cowboy got up from his table, scraping his chair as he rose, and her attention was diverted. The cowboy touched the brim of his hat to her and leered, and she smiled with the weariness of one often disappointed by crab cakes and cowboys. "I suffer from a disease," she said, returning her attention to me, "a kind of mental illness, the groundless hope that springs eternal." She glanced again at the cowboy, on his way out now. He turned suddenly and caught her looking at him. She looked down into her glass. "The problem," she continued, "is that crab cakes ought to be a good dish. They usually look good, so crispy and golden brown. I let their good looks get my hopes up. But again and again I find that most crab cakes are more cake than crab. Sometimes they're overspiced to make them 'tasty,' you know? Like someone will say, 'They got the tastiest gol-durn crab cakes over that new drive-thru place up eye-nine-oh-nine'? And some are underspiced so that the flavor of the crab will 'come through.' Yeah. One lonely crab in a carload. I know all this, know it all from bitter experience, and yet whenever I see a plate of crab cakes going by on the way to someone else, I think, 'Those sure look good. Why don't I try some? What have I got to lose?' "

Her cell phone rang. "Oops," she said, "just a minute." She flipped the phone open and said, "Hello? Oh, hi, Laura. . . . I know. Where am I? I'm here. I'm at a table inside. . . . I ran into a friend." She winked at me, a definite wink, a definite conspiracy. "I don't know. . . . We're—catching up—you know? . . . Okay." She flipped the phone closed. She drank most of the rest of her wine, held the glass toward me for refilling, and said, "Where was I?"

" 'What have I got to lose?' " I said, and poured the last of the wine.

"Okay, I'm coming to the Lesson of Crab Cakes. You see, crab cakes are full of promise, but they rarely deliver. I think the real point of crab cakes—their raison d'être, if you'll pardon my French—is to teach us that. Here it is, the Lesson of Crab Cakes: beneath the golden crust of a promise there often lies a truth that's hard to swallow. It's a lesson I guess I'll never learn."

It was a pronouncement that seemed to call for a reflective pause, so I reflected a moment before saying, "And yet you recommended the crab cakes to the chuckler."

"Who?"

"The man who didn't remember you."

"You heard all of that?" She looked around the room and added, quickly, with a shrug, "I guess everybody heard all of that." After a moment, she said, "I recommended the crab cakes because I wanted revenge."

"They're that bad?"

"No," she said, "they're actually pretty good. Not the best I've had, but good. I was hoping he'd have them, and enjoy them, because I wanted to infect him with my disease, give him a good case of the crab cakes. I wanted him to become a restless seeker, always pursuing perfection, never finding it." She smiled and winked and looked at my card, which she had placed on the tablecloth directly in front of her. "My turn to ask a question," she said. " 'Passionate Spectator,' what's that about?"

"I've—how shall I put this?—decided to step aside from life for a while. To stop playing the game. Sit out for a hand or two. Just watch."

"Mm. I get it. That's why you have the cards, right? Because spectating is what you do? Your occupation? Well. Good luck to you. You can't get out of the game, though. You know that's not possible. But watching is a worthy occupation. Seeing is bringing-into-being. It's what makes the universe happen. Bearing witness. This particular universe, anyway. Maybe. If it's true that the universe is spread all over some kind of super-space in a haze of potential until it's observed and collapses into—this."

She indicated, with a grand wave of her hand, the dining room and everything that lay beyond it, to the farthest reaches of the heavens.

"Yes?" asked a waiter attracted by her gesture.

"Another bottle of the chardonnay," said I.

"Oh, don't bother," she said. She lifted my card, held it between two fingers, tapped it, pursed her lips, and said, "Where are you staying?"

SOMETIME EARLY IN THE MORNING, after the noisy crowds that prowl Ocean Drive in search of amusement had gone looking for it somewhere else, the wind off the Atlantic began to roar in the gaps of the jalousie windows in the corner of my room at the Albatross.

"P.S.," she said, "let me ask you another question."

"Mm?"

"Do you think it's even *possible* for one person to be honest with another?"

"What do you think?" I asked right back.

"No."

She got out of bed and went to the windows and began methodically tightening them, turning the crank on each one as much as she could. The muscles across her back strained with the effort, her buttocks clenched when she stood with her legs apart to brace herself. She had an even tan, the color of honey, and there was no pale line anywhere on her to suggest a bathing suit.

"In what paradise do you sun yourself?" I asked.

She said, "I think it is impossible for any two people—and I'm not just talking about people in a relationship—any two people—to communicate with complete honesty. I think it's one of the great frustrations of being human."

She turned toward me and stood for a moment posing, displaying herself, and thinking, deciding what to do next. She decided. She set her mouth impishly, scampered to the bed, threw a leg over me, got astride me, settled herself on me, and wiggled to get me as deeply into her as she could.

"A tanning machine?" I asked. "A tanning bed? At a health club?"

"Consider the experience I'm having now," she said, apparently having decided to ignore my questions. She began rocking slowly forward and back. She hadn't fully succeeded in closing the windows, and the wind still whistled in their gaps. "If I tried to tell you about it with complete honesty, I never could. For one thing, if I started telling you what I feel, what I'm feeling now, I would be selective." She stopped rocking, raised herself and settled very slowly back onto me. She licked her lips.

"I wish I had something to feed you," I said. "Strawberries, perhaps. Or chocolates. I wish you had something to feed me. Strawberries really would be nice. I haven't eaten strawberries in a long time. Years, I think."

"I wouldn't tell you everything I'm thinking, for instance. I couldn't, even if I wanted to. There isn't time. If I got started, I'd have to explain all the references—who's who and what happened when, starting with my first sexual experience." She laughed, and the laughter rippled through her and through me. "But I'm not going to do that, because I am acutely aware of the wisdom of leaving some things unsaid—though I don't always let that wisdom guide me. I would probably leave out anything that I think is nobody's business but my own." She rose again, settled again, rose again, settled again. Pale sunlight began to slant across the bed, and the wind seemed to slacken.

"Strawberries with cream," I said.

"I would also leave out anything that wouldn't show me off to good advantage, anything that wouldn't portray me in the light in which I would like to be seen—and anything that I thought you wouldn't like to hear." She wiggled as she had before to get me more deeply into her.

"Cream and brown sugar. Dark brown sugar."

"And another thing: I'm feeling some things that can't be expressed in words, not adequately. There just isn't any way that I can make an equivalent in words to the physical sensations and emotions that I'm feeling." She let herself fall toward me and arrested her fall with her hands on either side of my shoulders. "I couldn't make any other adequate equivalent, either. All art fails me here." She extended her arms to raise her torso and shook her hair, then leaned forward to brush one nipple across my lips, then the other. "The only way that you could understand my feelings fully and completely and honestly would be to feel what I feel." She extended her arms to push herself up and away again, and she began raising and lowering her hips, regularly and slowly. "Maybe someday we'll have the technology that would allow all the activity of my brain to be transmitted to your brain, so that you could experience what I'm feeling, but still the experience wouldn't be the same, because your brain isn't identical to mine, so it would have things going on in it that weren't going on in mine, so my experience would be colored by your feelings, your memories, your desires." She drew a sharp breath, stopped moving for a moment, exhaled slowly, and resumed the rhythm. "It wouldn't be identical to my experience anymore. It would be your version of my experience." She lowered herself slowly until she was lying on me, whispering in my ear. "So, even though I had tried in all good faith to communicate my experience"—another sharp breath—"to you"—another—"fully and honestly—oh—you would be incapable of—ah—of—receiving it—unh—in the same pure form—oo—wow—in which it was sent." She let herself go limp and sighed into my ear. After a while, she whispered, "That's it, you see? It can't be done. Real honest communication is impossible."

"We'll have strawberries and cream for breakfast," I said.

"If you like," she said. "I don't usually eat breakfast. But we will definitely have crab cakes for lunch. I heard about a place on Collins Avenue that I want to try." She stretched and turned onto her side, facing me. "My name is Sheila, by the way," she said, and closed her eyes, and in a while, with the breeze sighing in the jalousies, Sheila fell asleep. Shortly after that, so did I.

Chapter 14

As BW, I Meet a Rebel Angel

Here the general average of intelligence, of knowledge, of competence, of integrity, of self-respect, of honor is so low that any man who knows his trade, does not fear ghosts, has read fifty good books, and practices the common decencies stands out as brilliantly as a wart on a bald head.

—H. L. Mencken, "On Being an American"

THE NEXT AFTERNOON found me lying on a chaise longue (which was costing me ten dollars for the day) on the beach (which was costing me nothing, if we don't count the price of my room at the very reasonably priced Albatross hotel, which was $189 a day), scanning the sunbathers with my miniature binoculars (which had cost me $129.95). I concealed my scanning by draping a towel (provided free by the Albatross) over my head and the binoculars. Anyone who noticed me, would, I hoped, assume that I was meditating in some new fashion. Actually, I was looking for Corellians.

Earlier, in the morning, while Sheila and I were breakfasting on strawberries and cream on the terrace in front of the Albatross, I had read an article in the *South Beach Buzz* about these Corellians. They are followers of Massimo Corelli (no relation to composer Arcangelo or novelist Marie), who believe that life on earth was created as a laboratory experiment by beings from a planet "in our galaxy but not in our solar system." According to the *Buzz,* the Miami chapter (fifty strong) was hosting a group of their Canadian cousins, and all of the assembled Corellians would be meditating daily on the beach. Sheila went off to meet her friends and resume the quest for the perfect crab cake, but I did not go with her, because I was curious about these Corellians. I wanted to infiltrate their number and observe them to see if I could find out why they believe what the *Buzz* said they believe.

The people closest to me, right beside me, almost too close for comfort, were passing the time smoking and glaring at one another, which might count as meditating. *Are they Corellians?* I wondered. I decided on the direct course of investigation; I would ask them.

"Excuse me," I said. "May I ask you a question?" I presented my card.

They examined it closely, first turning it this way and that, apparently to confirm beyond doubt their original impression that it was a card, and then reading the name and job description in an accent that led me to ask, "Are you German?"

"Yes, we are German," said the young son, who may have been repeating a memorized lesson. "We are a family on vacation. We are here to 'soak up the sun.' "

The daughter, who was soaking up the sun in an attractive, even provocative, manner, flashed her eyes at me, smiled, and displayed her tongue stud.

"Explain this, please," said the father, showing me my own card.

"Ich bin ein leidenschaftlich Zuschauer," I said, "if I remember my high-school German correctly."

"Ein Spion?" asked the boy eagerly.

"No, no, not a spy, just an idle watcher."

The father of the group glanced uneasily at his wife and daughter, then fixed me with the stare of one who would like to have me clapped in irons.

"Well?" he said, in a tone that impugned my motives.

"Well," I said, defiantly, "may I just ask you one question?"

"You have already asked us a question," said the boy. "You asked, 'Are you German?' "

"Ah! You're right," said I. "Sharp lad."

"What is the question?" asked the father, clearly eager to have me ask it and then get on with the forced march to the dungeon and the rack.

"Are you Corellians?"

"No!" boomed the father. "We have already told you that we are Germans."

"Let me put that another way," I said. "Do you think that life on earth was created by aliens as a laboratory experiment?"

The father's eyes popped. "Sir," he said, with ominous calm, "I ask you to take your passionate spectacles elsewhere and leave us alone."

"Yes. Certainly. Of course," I said, and retired to my chaise.

In a moment, the boy's shadow fell across my eyes. I looked up to find him holding my card.

"May I ask you, sir," the boy said, turning the card toward me so that I could read it, exactly as his father had, but without the threatening note, "does one have to go to university for this?"

"Well, I did," I said, "but it isn't necessary. You can just go to SpeeDee Print on Collins Avenue and get some cards printed."

"I think that I would like—" the boy began, but a mighty roar of unmuffled engines overwhelmed and distracted him. Two young men on personal watercraft had come flying up out of nowhere on their way to some other nowhere and were now buzzing in circles, making waves and noise, apparently uncertain about where the way to nowhere lay. "My sister and I would like to pilot powerful personal watercraft," the boy shouted, "like those fortunate bastards out there," he added, tilting his head in the direction of the water, "but," with a curl of the lip, "Father considers them a frivolous waste of money and gasoline, so we are condemned to sit here and bake in the sun like plums becoming prunes."

"I dislike prunes," I remarked.

"I dislike prunes very much," said the boy.

Our attention was diverted by an enormous woman who arrived just then and spread on the sand a towel too small to hold her. She was wearing a black one-piece bathing suit but immediately rolled it from the top down, reducing the top to a black hoop around her hips and revealing great spheroid masses of herself. She then tried to loll. In the attempt, she twisted, turned, grimaced, and grunted.

The boy and I observed her in silence for some time.

Failing to find a position that would fit all of her onto the towel, she at last gave up lolling and began to read instead. She had brought with her in a large canvas bag a thick paperback book, well worn, called *The Vampire's Vacation*.

"You have the card," I said to the lad. "Why don't you ask her?"

"If she's German?"

"No. If she's a Corellian."

"Oh, yes. The alien experimentations."

He walked over to her towel and said, "Excuse me, madam. May I present my card?"

She looked up at him, shading her eyes with her hand, wrestled herself onto one elbow, extended a plump arm, and took the card. She read it. Her lips moved as she did. "Is this a magazine?" she asked. "*Passionate Spectator?*"

"No, it is the designation of one who stands just a bit to the side of life and watches it," said the boy, doing quite a creditable job as an apprentice or squire.

"Interesting," she claimed.

"And so I would like to ask you a question."

"Yes, well, go ahead."

"Are you a Corellian?"

She squinted at him and said, with a little laugh, "No, I'm Catholic. Why do you ask?"

"I was wondering whether you believed that humans were put here as part of a laboratory experiment."

"I guess you could put it that way," she said, with a fuller laugh. "I hadn't thought of it like that, but I suppose that is what we believe. Eden, and all that."

The boy didn't know where to go from there. He turned and looked to Mentor for guidance. I waved him back to my side.

"A dead end, a dry well, a frozen waste," I said. "Some avenues of inquiry will get you nowhere. However, here's something interesting." I handed him the binoculars. "I spotted, some distance down the beach, a man, in his late sixties, by my estimation, retired, I suppose—Florida is famous for its retirees—strolling along, looking at the women, and,

I think, selling something. You'll find him easily; he's wearing a knit shirt, green shorts, white socks, a red fanny pack, and black sneakers."

"Oh, yes," said the boy. "I see him."

"Not the one with the blue fanny pack."

"What?"

"Just a joke."

"Oh. Yes. A joke."

"I thought that he might be a Corellian—not because he was meditating, though you will notice that he does give each of the women a good long look, which I am willing to count as a form of meditation—but because he seems to be proselytizing."

"Yes?"

"Yes. While I watched him, he approached several women, and some of them allowed him to stay and chat for a while. May I have the binocs?"

"Of course," said the boy, and returned them to me.

No sooner had I brought the curious retiree into focus again than a very tall and very beautiful blonde walked across my field of vision, blocking my view of the retired man and diverting my attention from him. She was the sort of statuesque beauty who can divert the attention of a heterosexual male of a certain age, equipped with binoculars, caroming through life perusing passing attractions. I followed her with the binoculars, ignoring the retiree.

The blonde attraction was wearing a tan cotton shift and tan espadrilles. She spread a large towel on the sand, smoothed it, and looked it over. She may have been meditating on the smoothness of it. She smoothed it a little more. She may have been meditating on smoothness as a concept, or as an unattainable ideal in the field of towel-spreading. The retired man had noticed her, too. He stood stock-still and watched her untie her espadrilles, take them off, and set them neatly side-by-side on the sand beside the towel. Then she stood and with a twist and a flip and a second twist put her long hair into a sinuous knot atop her head. Then she raised her arms and removed the cotton shift, and a sigh escaped from me, drifted off across the sand, embraced her, tickled the fine fair hair on the nape of her golden neck, and dissipated in the dry heat.

The retired man walked up to her and said something to her. She looked at him quizzically, as if she couldn't believe that she had heard him correctly. She raised her hand to the back of her neck as if my sigh still tickled her there, and she shook her head. The retired man spoke again, and she laughed and shook her head again. Then she turned her back on him, squeezed lotion from a tube with the brand name "Golden Fruits" into her hand, and began rubbing it onto her breasts.

"I wonder what he said to her," I said, to myself, but aloud.

"Perhaps he is also looking for some of these Corellians," muttered the boy.

The retired man resumed his progress along the beach, meandering from woman to woman, missing none, and after a while he reached the enormous woman directly in front of me and the boy.

"Excuse me," he said to her. "Would you like to buy a Cuban cigar?"

She looked up at him, shading her eyes with her hand. With a roll of her head in his direction, she said, "A cigar?" Her dudgeon was rising. "Certainly not! Do I look like the sort of person who would poison her body with tobacco?"

"My apologies," said the man, with all the meekness of a little person with something to sell. He turned and, because I was sitting right there and unavoidable, looked at me. I looked at him. He looked at the boy.

"My father will probably buy one," said the boy. "The man there in the green bathing costume. He likes a good cigar." The retiree started in the direction of the Germans, but toward the boy's sister, not his father.

"*Mein Begleiter,*" I said to the boy, "will you watch my belongings for a few minutes while I go and find out if that statuesque blonde is a Corellian?"

"Shouldn't I come with you in case you encounter any difficulties?"

"Next time," I promised, and in a few strides I was beside her. "Excuse me," I said. "May I ask you a question?"

"Please," she began, and she was about to ask me to go away, I think, to allow her to lie in the sun and think of nothing and no one for a while, but I handed her my card. She took it—with some reluctance—and read it. With a little sigh and a look, as if she were telling herself that she ought to know better than to encourage me, she said, "What's the question?"

C.\

"Do you subscribe to the notion that life on earth was created by aliens as a laboratory experiment?"

She burst out laughing. "That is definitely not the question I was expecting," she said. She looked at my card again. "Is this a joke, or a pickup line, or a serious question?" she asked.

"Door number three," I said.

"Well," she said, "to be honest, I am no longer sure."

That was definitely not the answer I had been expecting.

"Let's try this question," I said, settling to the sand beside her. "If we and our fellow creatures are the result of a laboratory experiment, how do you think the experimenters would rate the results?"

"Ah," she said. "That's a question I can answer."

"And the answer is?"

"The answer is that the results aren't in yet."

"Ah. So you take the position that we're continuing to evolve."

"Yes, of course we are."

"Getting better all the time."

"That depends on who is defining 'better,'" she said. "You have to bear in mind the fact that evolution has nothing to do with progress. Evolution is just the—let me see how to put this—it's the cumulative change in a species of organism, over a very long period of time, resulting from the relative success that some individuals achieve in reproducing themselves in comparison with others of their own kind."

"Mm-hm," I said, squinting into the dazzling light reflected from the Golden Fruits lotion on her smooth skin.

"Bear in mind, always, that the competition for reproductive success is among organisms of the same type. It's not about a species carving out a niche for itself, competing with other species. It's about individuals competing with other individuals for reproductive success within a species. When we regard the process, bringing our exalted understanding to bear on it, we see that it's a competition to become the model for future generations, because subsequent generations of a species come to resemble the individuals who are most successful in the mating game, and that recognition leads many among us toward the teleological error."

"I knew that," I said, with a wink of the eye and the satisfied grin of an educated man.

"Good. I'm glad. But I'm not so sure that you have really internalized it, because your remark about getting better all the time seemed to me to have a little suggestion of the idea of progress in it."

"I was just trying to be amusing."

"Oh, of course."

"I was hoping that by being amusing I might gain some small advantage in the competition for reproductive success."

"Okay—I see—very funny—but I want to make sure that we agree that progress is not a part of the evolutionary idea," she said, waggling her finger in the admonitory manner of a schoolmarm. "We say that it's about competition, but that's an interpretation of the facts, not a description of them, and it betrays our tendency to see consciousness everywhere."

"The solipsism of the sentient," I said.

"If you like. Just remember that, in nature, evolution is just change brought about by chance. It's adaptation, not improvement. Individual organisms that are very successful at mating pass their genetic characteristics on to the next generation to a degree that less-successful individuals do not. And that's it. That's all of it. Progress is not a part of it, but adaptation is, over a very long run. Agreed?"

"Agreed. Do you want me to rub some of this lotion onto your back?"

"Oh, yes, please do."

I HAVE VERY STRONG THIGHS," she said, later, after dinner, in bed in my room at the Albatross, and she proved it by flexing her thigh muscles, tightening her legs around my ears.

"Mmph," said I.

"Returning to the subject of the human experiment, let's just consider intelligence for a moment."

"Mmph."

"Think of the well-known bell-shaped 'normal' curve."

"Mmph."

"If the people at the right end of the curve are the people with the full complement of human intelligence, then those at the top of the peak in the middle, the single biggest group, are endowed with only half the intelligence of those. They're halfwits."

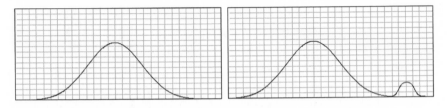

FIGURE 3: Bell curve (left) and bell curve shifted, with a bump (right).

I burst out laughing and raised my head to look over her belly and into her smiling eyes.

"Do you think that an unkind statement?" she asked.

"No, no," I said. "I recognize that it's a statement of fact—at least that it's statistically likely."

"Yes, and it scares the shit out of me when I'm driving a car, let me tell you, the thought that half of the people on the road are halfwits."

"Or worse."

"Exactly. The ones down there at the far left end of the curve, those are the nitwits and dimwits, and you see that there are fully as many of them as there are of the smart ones, the fullwits."

"But what I want to know—"

"—is what I predict for the future. Will tomorrow's halfwits move up toward the fullwit end of the curve or move down toward the nitwit end?"

"That's it."

"Well—what I really think is happening, and will continue to happen, perhaps at an accelerating rate, is that the bulk of the curve is shifting to the left, toward the nitwit end, but that a smaller curve is developing at the smart end, a bump on the curve there, another little bell of its own, and over time the area between them will grow less and less populous, so that we will have a massive mountain of people with less than half a brain and a little hill of people with more than half a brain—very much like the shift in distribution of wealth that is happening here economically in society."

"Mm-hm," I said, bending to my work again, but for a moment listening to her with only half an ear or only half a brain, because a memory had returned to me, unsought, unsummoned, but not unwelcome, the memory of the first meal I ever ate in a restaurant on my own. To be more precise, it was the memory of the dessert I had with that meal. It was butterscotch pudding, and it was so rich and surprising, so unlike the sort of pudding that my mother made from a powder in a box, that after my first taste of it I looked around the room to see if people were watching me eat it, because my pleasure was so great that it seemed like something I ought not to display in public.

"But this is an artificial evolutionary change," she continued, "because the reproductive success of everybody on the lower half of the curve, from the halfwits on down, is being manipulated—enhanced—by their smarter cousins, the ones in that little hill on the right side of the curve, who are favored by the experimenters."

Her mention of the experimenters made me raise my head again to see whether her expression indicated that she was serious about what she was saying. She wore a little smile, but I allowed myself to think that the smile was my doing.

"So you do believe—" I began.

"Oh, no," she said, very quickly. "I do not believe. That is the attitude of those Corellians who are prepared to fall on their knees before our alien Makers and beg them to grant us grace, or at least a little kindness. I don't belong to that group. I am one of those, the few, who mistrust the motives of our Makers. The Believers call us the Cynics; we call ourselves the Rebel Angels."

"You think there's a conspiracy," I said, "between the alien experimenters and a favored group of human beings?"

"Oh, yes," she said. I returned to licking her, and she said it again, "Oh, yes."

She sighed and stretched and tightened her thighs around my head and added, "The dumb ones are being bred to be consumers. This has been going on for a long time, of course, but early efforts were quite crude and also misguided."

"Mmmm," I assented into the depths of her. That pudding that I ate, that first night on my own as a little man of the world, was so smooth, so thick, and yet so yielding, that eating it, the act of licking it from the spoon, was a sensual pleasure in itself, not a pleasure apart from the flavor, but a pleasure that augmented the pleasure of the flavor and in turn was itself augmented by the flavor in a crescendo of ascending sensuality. Eating butterscotch pudding that rich and smooth and creamy was an experience I had never had before. I had never eaten any other food that gave such pleasures to my lips and tongue. Certainly my mother had never served anything like it. It would have embarrassed the entire family.

"In the old days, our Makers didn't quite understand how to make use of the halfwits. They thought that those dullards were most valuable as workers, and so they had their agents—the humans who are in cahoots with them, the ones we call the Collaborators—teach them to think of themselves as workers, but only a very, very dull person wants a life of all work and no play, so the workers began to feel dissatisfied and exploited, which led to Marx and all the rest of it, but now the Makers are much more savvy and much subtler. Slower, please. If you don't mind. Slower."

"Mm. Mm-hm," I said. After my first small, tentative spoonful of that butterscotch pudding, I understood that the ordinary way of eating, putting the spoon in one's mouth and swallowing the contents, as one might eat chicken soup, was not the right way for this. This called for something like playing with one's food, rolling the pudding on the tongue, around the mouth.

"Our Makers finally understood that the great mass of people would never enjoy working but loved buying things, and so, working through the Collaborators, they taught them to play a new role. They taught them to be Consumers. What's a Consumer? Someone who buys from his master the very shackles that keep him in wage-slavery. The Consumers have to think that they're content if they're to continue to play their part, so what their masters the Collaborators sell—and teach the Consumers to buy—is the appearance of a good life. It's a shallow life, furnished and decorated with kitsch, but it's heaven for halfwits."

I gave her a flurry of quick, light tongue-taps, soft as the flutter of a hummingbird's wings.

"Oh! That is heaven," she said. "You've really got me going. This is turning into a rant. Consumers and their masters: Collaborators. By now the Collaborators have got the Consumers convinced that trading their labor for beer and hamburgers and television and very large toy trucks makes them happy. All day, every day, through every conceivable medium, they are taught to buy what the Collaborators are selling. They are taught all they really need to know: what to buy, what to eat, what to wear, how to drug themselves into the daze that is sold as happiness."

I slid my tongue into her, probed her, poked her.

"And if the Consumers are convinced that this role makes them happy, perhaps it actually does make them happy, but from the point of view of the Collaborators their happiness is immaterial, even their vestigial role as workers is immaterial, because ultimately the only reason for sending the Consumers to work is to put enough money in their pockets to buy what they produce, and the only point of the whole money-go-round is to send the profits to the Collaborators."

I surprised her with the hummingbird's flutter.

"Oh, you are really quite a genius at that," she said. "The only reason for the existence of the Consumers is to enrich the Collaborators, who look upon the mass of halfwit Consumers with a contempt that approaches loathing. They improve the breed—for their purposes—by teaching that the best Consumers are the ones who have the most junk, that a four-wheel-drive lawn mower and sneakers that glow in the dark are attractive in a mate. Listen to those Collaborators sometime when they're talking about 'meeting the needs of the Consumers.' You can practically see them smirk. Sometimes I expect them to wink."

I bit her. It was ever so gentle a bite, a love bite, but still it was a bite.

"Yow!" she said, appreciatively. "Meeting the needs of the Consumers, indeed! They are quite happy to 'meet the needs of the Consumers,' just as they would be happy to meet the needs of swine if they were farmers. Swine need fodder to feed on and mud to wallow in, and the farmer breeds his swine with care and meets the needs of his swine gladly, because the farmer knows what the swine does not: that one fine day the farmer will eat the swine for dinner."

She sighed and stretched and spread her thighs and sighed again.

"And that is all I have to say about that," she said, "for now."

Chapter 15

As BW, I Attend the Unveiling of the Limo Fountain

How can we escape the conclusion that no art can do without a soupçon of deliberate effect, a dash of kitsch?

—Hermann Broch, "Notes on the Problem of Kitsch"

THE NEXT EVENING, I was sitting at the bar at El Zoológico, a Cuban restaurant on Ocean Drive, drinking a mojito. The woman on the bar stool next to mine was drinking a mojito, too. She took a sip, through a straw, and as she sipped she slipped, slowly, off her bar stool. She grabbed my shoulder to stop herself, brought her eyes close to mine, and smiled vaguely. She couldn't quite place me, though we had been sitting side-by-side for the length of time that it had taken me to drink most of my mojito, and I had given her my card, which lay on the bar in front of her, as soaked as her coaster.

She squinted at me and mumbled, mostly to herself, "Oh, yeah. You're the spectator. Passionate Spectator. Sounds like an old radio show."

"You're right. It does," I said, restoring her to her perch.

She picked up my card, peered at it, and said in the resonant voice of a radio announcer in the middle of the last century, "And now—Moe Hito, the King of Quality Furniture, brings you this week's episode of 'Bertram W. Beath, Passionate Spectator.' "

"Very amusing," I said.

"Oops," she said. "Sorry. No offense."

"This is a beautiful bar," I remarked by way of changing the subject.

"You should see the ceiling," she said, as if it were forbidden or hidden. It was right above us, though, where it ought to have been, so I looked up. So did she.

"Whoo!" she said, clutching at me to steady herself. "Makes you feel upside down."

It *was* a remarkable ceiling. It resembled, in an abstract way, a river bottom. Looking at it did make one feel upside down, as if one were swimming in that river and peering down at the bottom, but with gravity operating in reverse. The effect must have been particularly pronounced for the slipper, who had had more mojitos than I.

Mojitos were so popular at the Zoo that one of the two bartenders was entirely engaged in mojito pre-prep. He would put half a lime, a sprig of cilantro—which replaced the conventional mint in the Zoo's signature version of the drink—and some sugar syrup—which the menu asserted was real cane syrup, from sugar cane—into a sturdy glass. As he prepared these glasses, he stacked them, one inside another, in a tower.

Thanks to the work of the prepper, all the main bartender had to do to complete a mojito was grab the topmost glass of a tower, mash the lime and cilantro with a pestle, add lots of ice, fill the glass with rum, and squirt a little soda into the mixture. *¡Mira! ¡Un mojito!*

While the slipper and I were admiring the coordinated dexterity of the bartending team, a guy wearing a black cap and a desperate look rushed up to the bar and asked the prepper, "Have you got a TV?"

"No TV," said the prepper. "No TV."

"Jeez!" said a second guy, also capped and desperate. "We're missing the game!"

"Aren't there any bars around here with the game on?" asked capped-and-desperate guy number one.

The slipper turned toward him and grabbed his shirt. "Are they still playing that fucking game?" she asked. "My ex-husband was always watching that game. I thought it would be over by now. What's the score?" Capped-and-desperate guy one unclamped the slipper's hand and with a parting sneer went off in a huff with his pal. I ordered a second mojito.

The slipper leaned toward me and whispered, in the manner of an old chum sharing a confidence, "Celebrity sighting!" She nodded in the direction of the doorway, where a fiftyish couple was entering. They were dressed in simulated yachting outfits, navy blue with gold piping. On their blazer pockets were decorations that resembled heraldic emblems.

I raised an eyebrow questioningly, and the slipper identified them for me: "The Duke and Duchess of Kitsch," she said. She did not laugh at that, did not even smile.

The duke did smile. He smiled continually, and he nodded in the direction of the slipper and me, acknowledging us with affable condescension. "Fifteen minutes!" he called to us, his exclamation point an even broader smile. Why he called out in that manner I had no idea. I smiled back and raised my glass to indicate that I was friendly or, at the least, that I meant the duke no harm. Turning to the duchess then, the duke said, "That strange creature we passed on the way over here—she was a man, wasn't she?"

"A freak," said the duchess.

"What kind of freak, exactly?" asked the slipper, pivoting suddenly.

"A man-woman," said the duchess, "a girl-guy or laddie-lady, a person of a sex too complex to define, short, slight, moon-faced, with a double chin, pale skin smooth as silk, wearing a minidress and patent leather boots, thigh-high, with platform soles, who strutted and displayed herself and attempted to attract the passersby," and the duchess strutted and displayed herself, as if she were wearing thigh-high boots with platform soles and attempting to attract the slipper and me.

"No shit," said the slipper. "Sounds like my old friend Denise, née Dennis. Must have come for the unveiling." With a shake of the head and a satisfied sigh, she added, "Friends. You can't beat 'em." She availed herself of my steady shoulder to climb down from her stool and then, with the aid of the wall, she made her way to the doorway and slipped through it into the night.

"Fifteen minutes, my dear," the duchess called after her.

"*Dos mojitos, por favor,*" said the duke, smiling.

After no more than half a mojito's time, the slipper returned and, making good use of my sturdy frame, regained her stool.

"It's scary out there," she said with a shudder. "Ocean Drive is full of people looking at the attractions, like the place is one continuous street fair. They walk along, and they look around, and when the attractions start to thin out, they stand around in confusion, wondering what to do next, and they look at one another, and shrug, and turn around and walk back the other way, and when they get back to where they started they're convinced that there are no more attractions left to see, so they get into their cars and they drive home and they watch that damned game."

The duchess let a moment pass, then pushed her empty glass toward the bartender and said, "*Un otro, por favor,* for I so desperately need a connection with the sublime."

"We really ought to be going," said the duke.

"Hello?" called the duchess to the bartender. "I must be going. Put that in a plastic cup, will you?"

The duke and the slipper drained their glasses, and the slipper climbed down. I had no intention of going with them wherever they were going, but the slipper tugged at my arm and said, "Here we go. Time to go. Let's go." So I went.

When we were outside, walking along Ocean Drive, I said to the duke, "Just curious, your grace, but where are we going?"

"Where are we going?" said the duke. "Ho-ho-ho."

"Ha-ha-ha," said I, "but seriously, where are we going?"

"Why," he said, "you are serious. I assumed you were a friend of Ivy's."

"Ivy?"

"Here!" said the slipper. "Present, pickled, and plastered."

"Oh," I said. "We just met this evening. Minutes ago, actually."

"Ah-ha," said the duke. "Well, we are proceeding to the unveiling of the Limo Fountain."

"The unveiling of the Limo Fountain," I said.

"A gala," said the duchess.

"And we have arrived," said the duke.

We had reached the Shangri-La-La, a high-rise pile just outside the

Deco district. In the plaza at the entrance to the hotel, klieg lights scanned the sky for enemy aircraft, crisscrossing above a massive something draped in white fabric. Arranged along one side of the drapery was a crew of models and musclemen, ready to remove the wrap when the time came.

Quite a crowd had assembled, possibly thousands.

"There seem to be models in great abundance," I remarked.

"Provided for the occasion," said the duke.

"In Miami, half a dozen models are brought out for the opening of a delicatessen," the duchess explained, "a full dozen for the opening of a health club, two dozen for a restaurant, and so on."

The slipper stopped at the draped sculpture and looked up at it. Dizziness struck again, and she held my arm tight.

"Maybe we ought to leave it like that," she said. "Under wraps."

"Come, now, my dear," said the duchess, as if she hadn't heard. "It is time to meet your public."

The duke and duchess arranged themselves on either side of the slipper and each took an arm. They marched her around the edge of the crowd and up to the entrance of the Shangri-La-La. They conversed briefly with some people with clipboards and headsets, and then the duke and duchess, with the slipper clamped firmly between them, took a long step up onto a platform, where they stood before microphones, bright lights, and television cameras.

"Good evening, everyone," said the duke, in a voice so assured that it silenced the crowd at once. "I am the Duke of Kitsch, and this is my duchess."

"Howdy, y'all," said the duchess.

"If you listen to 'Drivin' with the Duke and Duchess' on Smooth Radio 109, you already know us, of course."

"But whether you do or not, it must be a treat to meet us."

"I would think so."

"So would I."

"Me, too," said the slipper.

"She speaks!" said the duchess.

"Ladies and gentlemen," said the duke, propelling the slipper toward the microphone, "it is my very great pleasure to welcome you to the unveiling of the Limousine Fountain—"

"Limo Fountain," said the duchess.

"Of course," said the duke. "The Limo Fountain. It gives me great pleasure to welcome you to the unveiling of the Limo Fountain and to introduce you to the woman of the hour, our dear friend Ivy, the artist known as I-V-Y."

"Hey," said the slipper, "that's me."

This occasioned laughter and applause. I joined in both.

The slipper blinked at her audience and said, "I'm amazed so many of you showed up." She began fumbling in her pockets and eventually came up with a slim personal digital assistant. "Stainless steel," she said, displaying it to the crowd and tapping its handsome case. She contemplated it. "I've never worked in stainless steel." She contemplated it some more. "It doesn't rust, right?" She paused. "Right?" she said again, louder.

"Right!" called a few voices from the crowd.

"Well, wrong, actually," she said.

Those in the crowd who had not joined the chorus tittered with superior glee at the hasty and ignorant among them.

"It's an alloy, see, and it does react with the oxygen in the air—which is what we call rusting in the case of regular old steel—but the oxidized layer can't react further. It just lies there on the surface and prevents any further oxidation. Cool, huh?"

She displayed the PDA again, using the back of it like a mirror to play reflected light across the crowd.

"What's that, you say?" she called out, cupping her ear as if to hear an objection from the crowd. " 'How come we don't see that oxidized layer the way we see rust?' I thought you'd ask that. I'll tell you why." She leaned in to the mike. "You see the oxidized layer on common steel, and on bronze, which is what the Limo Fountain is made of, but you don't see the oxidized layer on stainless steel because the oxidized layer on stainless steel"—she brought her mouth against the mike so that her words exploded—"is thinner than the wavelength of visible light."

She waited a moment for that to sink in.

"Makes you realize how strange the world really is, doesn't it? I mean, if there is something right there in front of us, and we can't see it, what else are we missing?"

Another moment.

"Tiny alien invaders so small that we can't see them?"

Nervous laughter.

"Billions of them, living in the pores of your skin? Waiting for the right moment?"

More nervous laughter, mingled with puzzled murmurs.

"And that brings me to art," she asserted, "because art shows us what we can't see. What we don't see or won't see. Makes us see. Enables us to see. Gives eyesight to the blind! Hoo!"

"Hooray for art!" cried the duchess.

"Now there are the blind," said the slipper, "and there are the blind. That is, the blind and the blinder. And the even-blinder-than-that." She paused, consulting the screen of the PDA. "But that isn't what I was going to say," she said. "At least, not according to this."

She turned the screen of the device toward the audience and allowed them to see her look of puzzled surprise. More applause, more laughter.

"According to this, I was going to say, 'Those who have no experience of wisdom and goodness, and are always engaged in feasting and similar pleasures, are brought down, it would seem, to a lower level, and there wander about all their lives.' "

"You got that right," said the duke.

" 'They have never looked up toward the truth, nor risen higher, nor tasted of any pure and lasting pleasure.' "

"You said it," said the duchess.

" 'In the manner of cattle, they bend down with their gaze fixed always on the ground and on their feeding-places, grazing and fattening and copulating—' "

"Amen, sister," shouted someone in the crowd.

" '—and in their insatiable greed for these pleasures they kick and butt one another with horns and hoofs of iron—' "

"In that damned game!" said the duchess, recognizing the theme as the slipper's hobbyhorse.

" '—and kill one another if their desires are not satisfied.' "

" 'Hoo!' " said the duke, quoting the slipper.

The slipper let a moment pass, then added, "Plato. *The Republic.* Pretty cool, huh? Prescient, right? . . . Right?"

"Right!" called a few voices from the crowd, probably not the voices of those who had embarrassed themselves earlier.

"It's all about that damned game, as the duchess said. That game that's always on. Every time I turn the TV on, they're playing that fucking game. They're going at it with balls and sticks and bats—and it never ends. Never ends. Yeah. Well, my work is about that. What else?" She consulted her assistant. "Oh, yeah. I was going to say something about kitsch, because that's the other thing my work is about, and that's the other thing about that game. It's kitsch, that game, because it's pointless, or rather because its only point is distraction."

The duke and duchess exchanged looks.

"See," said the slipper, "the essence of kitsch is motive. It's the willingness to go for effect rather than truth. To move an audience rather than saying something. To appeal to the heart and not the head."

"You're losing them," warned the duke.

"Oh, yeah. Hey, sorry I'm getting so technical here."

"Why don't you just let the work speak for itself?" said the duchess.

"I think I'll just let the work speak for itself," said the slipper. "Let the veil be rent asunder!"

"Ahh, in just a moment," said the duke, rushing to interpose himself between the slipper and the microphones. "We'll be rending the veil asunder in just a moment, but first I want to make sure everyone knows that immediately following the unveiling, reproductions of the Limo Fountain will go on sale in the boutique to my right." He indicated a tent.

"Yes," said the duchess, at his side, rising on her toes the better to be seen and heard, "you can have a full-scale model—"

"Well, not full-scale—"

"No, of course not! I meant to say 'fully functional.' Full-scale would be—well, it would be wonderful, wouldn't it, but we don't have anything on that scale—except the original, of course."

"But the reproduction is—"

"Fully functional. That is, it sprays water and everything."

"It would make a fine addition to a suburban front yard, I would think."

"Oh, indeed."

"And we have a cute little version small enough to keep on your bedside table. Not fully functional. No spraying water."

"It would make a great paperweight, wouldn't it?"

"Indeed it would."

"Well, my dear, shall we unveil this fountain?"

"Oh, let us!" She leaned closer to the microphone and called out, "Strapping lads, haul away!"

The oiled beefy boys hauled with choreographed effort and choral grunts, and the drapery began to slide along the hidden contours of the work beneath it, until it reached a critical point and slid with a sailcloth sigh to the plaza pavement. The fountain stood revealed.

It was a stretch limousine rampant, rearing as a steed does in an equestrian statue, its massive haunches flexed, hind tires compressed under the weight, its long back bent, its foretires pawing the air, its hood and front bumper drawn back liplike, its grille teeth bared. Mist sprayed from its radiator cap like steam from the nostrils of a straining steed. A kink in the exhaust made it resemble a stallion's pizzle, and water arced in a fine stream from it. The limo was peopled with fat figures, made of stacks of balls, like bronze snowmen, leaning from windows and rising like prairie dogs from a multitude of openings in the roof: the driver leaning from his window, swatting the limo's flank with his driver's cap, urging it on; a drunken frat boy spewing bronze vomit down the side below one window; a bronze pop diva standing up through a sunroof, waving to her fans, one strap of her tiny dress fallen, revealing her right breast; a baseball player, a hockey player, and a hip-hop gangsta brandishing the tools of their trades: a bat, a stick, an automatic; a prom king tearing the wrapper from his queen; a developer, a potentate, a candidate, and a judge, stuffing bundles of bronze bucks into one another's mouths; and below them, in the shadow of the limousine, a herd of indistinguishable little figures, of indeterminate sex, scrabbling for the bills and coins that were falling from the passengers' hands and pockets and dribbling from the exhaust, where a bronze likeness of the slipper herself squatted, smoothing with her bare bronze hands rough metal to shape the back bumper.

THE NEXT MORNING, very late the next morning, when the slipper and I had awakened in her thickly curtained bedroom, she walked to the door that led to the balcony, slid it aside, and stepped out into the sunlight.

I lay in the bed, looking at the ceiling, listening to the play of water from the fully functional reproduction of the fountain we had set up in the tub, late in the evening, while the slipper's friends were still congratulating her and toasting her in her own champagne. She returned to the room, walked to the bedside, and picked up a smaller reproduction from the bedside table.

"I sometimes wonder if today's satire is not inevitably tomorrow's kitsch. I mean, I work in a satirical mode, and I like to think my work has a bite to it, like a really good radish, but no sooner do I make a statement than it becomes a lawn ornament or a gewgaw. This culture has a boundless capacity for sucking anything—everything—into the realm of kitsch."

She put the reproduction back on the bedside table, carefully, and stared at her hands, surprised by them, as if she had never really noticed them before. "These are quite magnificent hands," she said. She held them in front of her, examining them, admiring them, marveling at their strength, flexing them. "They know my thoughts and feelings better than I do myself. So it seems. At times, anyway." She knelt on the bed and pressed her hands on me and began to mold me, to make of me what she wanted, and I began to feel the privileged wonder of a medium taken well in hand.

Chapter 16

As BW, I Am Present at the Goosing of the Hamlet Project

I was the shadow of the gray goose slain
By the radome nose of a prop-jet plane . . .

—Ramblin' Jack Shade, "Pale Fire Blues"

I CHECKED OUT of my room at the Albatross, took a few of the complimentary mints from one of the Alvar Aalto bowls on the counter and a few of the complimentary condoms from the other, and waited for the taxi I had summoned to take me to the airport. I waited. I waited. I began walking back and forth in front of the Albatross.

At ten o'clock the taxi arrived. "To the airport," I said in the commanding tone I use with taxi drivers.

At 10:45 I stood at the Hummingbird Airlines counter.

"You're booked on a flight to Long Island's MacArthur Airport via Pittsburgh," the clerk announced, in a tone that suggested I might have forgotten.

"Interesting," I said, as if I had.

"But the flight to Pittsburgh has been canceled because the Pittsburgh airport is fogged in."

"Aha."

"You can wait here for another flight."

"Mm."

"Or you could catch the shuttle bus to the Fort Lauderdale airport and catch the twelve-forty flight to Washington, where you can make another connection to Islip."

"Point me to it," I said.

She pointed, and I made my way with graceful haste through the terminal in the direction in which I had been pointed.

I boarded a blue-and-gold van, taking a seat directly behind the driver. A woman slid in beside me, opened a computer case, and from it removed a presentation folder embossed with a logo and the slogan "Hamlets are Home Towns."

She began rehearsing, reading passages from a text silently, then closing her eyes and mouthing the words, or perhaps a paraphrase of the words, as if she were making a presentation, a pitch.

The driver arrived, and the van lurched off at a promising speed, startling the pitcher out of her practice pitch. Her folder slid from her lap to the floor. I bent to retrieve it. As I presented it to her, she said, "Thanks," and added with a nod in the direction of the driver, "I thought this was ground transportation."

I chuckled to indicate that I had a sense of humor, then added with a nod in the direction of her presentation folder, "You've been rehearsing."

"Yes, but I think I shall stop for now. Motion sickness."

"Do you mind my asking what you're rehearsing for?"

"No."

She let enough time pass to convince me that she was my kind of woman.

"What are you rehearsing for?" I asked.

"I have to make a presentation—"

"A pitch. I thought so."

"Yes, you're right. A pitch. I have to pitch an idea, a whole way of life, really."

"Hamlets are home towns."

"Right again, but it's not nice to read a girl's documents."

"I'm ashamed of myself, but please do tell me more."

"We call it the Hamlet Project," she said, "and it is at heart an attempt to replace ugly, wasteful suburban sprawl with small communities, and at the same time reverse a trend in American housing toward racial, ethnic, social, and economic balkanization via the gated-community concept."

"You don't pitch it that way, do you?"

"No. Of course not. I pitch it all rose-tinted and honeyed, but I'm tired, and yours looked like a sympathetic ear."

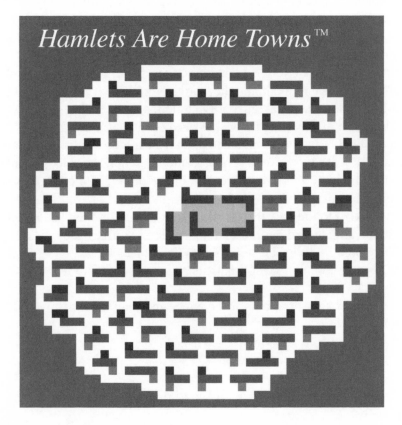

Hamlets Are Home Towns™

FIGURE 4: A hamlet, plan view (courtesy of the the Hamlet Project®).

"Well, it is a sympathetic ear, and I have another of them, and a pair of sympathetic eyes as well." I gave her my card.

"What are *you* pitching?" she asked.

"Oh, nothing. Nothing at all. I have nothing to offer. Nothing beyond a pair of sympathetic ears and a pair of sympathetic eyes."

IN QUITE A BIT MORE TIME than it takes to tell, we reached Fort Lauderdale, arriving just a couple of minutes after the 12:40 flight to Washington had taken to the air.

"Well, what now?" we asked each other, standing at the check-in desk where we had received the bad news. I was, I will be the first to admit, hoping that the pitcher would suggest our taking a room at an airport motel where we could fill the idle hours until the next day's 12:40 flight began to board.

"There's a one-oh-four to Washington," suggested the desk clerk, who seemed to have no news but bad.

"We'll take it," said the pitcher.

I liked that "we."

The clerk, whose white plastic name tag identified him as Jerry, Reservations Specialist, began tapping at his terminal's keys, and in another moment he was able to hand us tickets for Washington, which was not Long Island but was a step in the right direction.

When we were in the air, the pitcher continued her explanation of the hamlet concept, assuring me again that I would not be hearing her pitch, but the facts behind the pitch.

"The idea we're—putting forward—is a hamlet, a little village, as a better place to live, a better way to live, than a swath of suburban sprawl with the equivalent population."

She had hesitated just a moment before saying "putting forward," and I thought that in that instant of hesitation she had considered using "selling" instead of "putting forward."

"I think a bit of the pitch is finding its way in, here and there," I said.

"Well, it's unavoidable, I guess. I do practice saying these things."

"I don't mind. Go on."

"Take a section of a suburban subdivision where a thousand people are living now. At four people per family unit, that's two hundred fifty little houses. Each of them has its precious quarter acre, so that's sixty-two and a half acres of land, about a tenth of a square mile."

She reached into her bag and produced a map showing a tenth-of-a-mile square superimposed on a suburban subdivision. She did not rummage. She was well organized. Even though she produced the map without any rummaging at all, she did not seem to be dealing with me in a practiced manner. She was, I think, natural, though not spontaneous. How could she possibly be spontaneous after so much rehearsal?

"In the hamlet," she said, "the basic footprint of a townhouse is just twelve hundred square feet. We've got an ideal population of two thousand. That's five hundred units, occupying six hundred thousand square feet of land. Double that, to allow for walkways and public squares and playgrounds and such, and you've got a total of one million two hundred thousand square feet, or a little less than twenty-eight acres. That leaves thirty-four and a half acres open."

I noted the unmistakable note of triumph in her last remark. "Thirty-four and a half acres," I said, in a voice full of wonder, as one who marvels

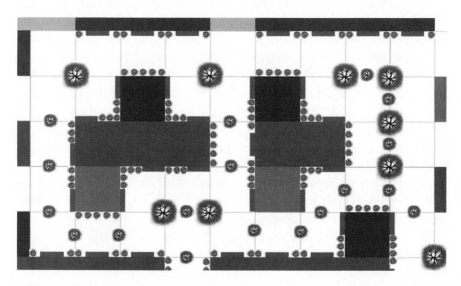

FIGURE 5: A neighborhood within the hamlet, bordering on the downtown business area (visible at top).

that there can be such vastnesses. "How many hectares would that be?"

"About eleven point three," she said. "Don't mock me."

"I'm not. Honest. What do you do with that open land?"

"Well, we can do many things, depending on what suits the area, but typically, we would have a mix of things, maybe some small-scale agriculture, truck farming, specialty farming—boutique farming, if you want to call it that—and we would allow some acreage to return to the wild, which can be the worst of the land, since the ducks and frogs and slugs don't care, and some might be parkland, maybe some simple ball fields, quite possibly a water park."

I raised my eyebrows.

"People love 'em," she said, "and it helps persuade them to give up the backyard with the aboveground pool."

I laughed, because I thought she expected me to, and our flight attendant tossed us a couple of baglets of sugar-coated nuts. I ordered a Scotch. The pitcher said, "What the hell," and ordered vodka. "So tell me something about you," she said.

"There is nothing to tell about me. I wander. I watch. I listen. And right now I am thoroughly enjoying listening to you. Go on."

"Well, remember that we've got an ideal population of two thousand—twice the population of the swath of suburb the hamlet replaces. That's partly for the economics of the venture. Essentially, the hamlet can be built for the equivalent of the cost of buying the houses and land, which makes the total cost twice that. So if we sell twice as many units, we can break even."

"And that's all you're after?"

"Oh, yes," she said, as if I had accused her of having her slim hand in the till. "But there's another reason for the two thousand figure. Two thousand is a population large enough to support a few small businesses within the hamlet itself. That means you can have a luncheonette, a convenience store, even a small grocery, right in the heart of town, an easy walk from wherever you live. A circle with an area of twenty-eight acres has a radius of about six hundred twenty feet, just a few steps longer than two football fields, so even from the perimeter a walk to the center of town for a quart of milk is no big deal. We include twenty-five commercial buildings. These are on the same scale as the residential buildings,

but they are all in the central area so that they're—well—centrally lo-
cated. Basically, that means twenty-five storefronts and fifty small office
suites. There are lots of things that this means for the hamlet. For one
thing, you'd be surprised to know how many people run small businesses
from suburban houses. A hairdresser, a CPA, even a dentist, may be running a business in a finished basement. They can still do that from a
townhouse, of course, since they're roomy, but many choose to locate in
the hamlet's downtown. They feel more professional. They can schmooze
with other business people, have lunch, that kind of thing. They become
part of a group, a community. So almost immediately you have lots of
small businesses downtown, and you have employment opportunities right
in the hamlet. We generally figure that about nine hundred people in the
hamlet will be in the employment pool and that a hundred fifty can be
fully employed in local businesses, with another fifty providing services
and another fifty locally employed part-time. That's the equivalent of a
hundred seventy-five employed locally full-time. Just about twenty percent of the employables."

"Wow," I said, nonjudgmentally.

"It's a lot to absorb."

"Oh, it is, but I'm absorbing it. It's fascinating."

We landed in Washington, deplaned, and scurried to the ticket counter,
where we learned that Islip was now fogged in, but we could get onto a
4:45 plane to Baltimore, where there was, for the time being, a break in
the fog.

"Baltimore?" said the pitcher. "Isn't that right next door?"

"Yes," admitted the reservations specialist, "but it gets you closer to
Islip."

"How long is the flight?" I asked.

"About fifteen minutes," said the res spec.

The pitcher and I burst out laughing at that, but we got ourselves
ticketed.

WHEN WE WERE SEATED side-by-side in a five-stool airport bar at-
tended by a retiree supplementing her Social Security payments, the
pitcher sipped her second vodka and said, "We have one-, two-, and
three-story units, with twelve hundred, twenty-four hundred, and thirty-six

hundred square feet of living space, respectively. Each has another twelve hundred square feet of garage and storage belowground. They're grouped in clusters of five, with the two-story units predominating, so that overall we've got twenty percent of the little ones, twenty percent of the big ones, and sixty percent of the middle-sized ones."

"Which Goldilocks would have found 'just right,'" I said.

"Yes, exactly. The big ones are really huge, the little ones are actually quite roomy for a couple, and the middle-sized ones would be fine for the three bears and Goldilocks, too. We define the outer shell in broad terms, and we offer a number of architectural plans and complete building packages, but people are free to build something else, so long as it fits within the footprint and the basic shape of the shell. Oops. We've got to get onto that plane."

From the gate, we walked down a flight of movable stairs onto the tarmac, where our plane awaited us. It was a DeHavilland Dash 8 turboprop, a "high-wing" design, in which the wings, and the engines mounted in them, were fixed above the fuselage, at the front of which was a tiny cockpit, within which we could see our pilot and copilot squeezed chummily together, and below that a black hemispherical "radome nose" within which lay the plane's radar equipment. In the passenger cabin were thirty-seven seats, and when all of us who hoped, someday, to arrive at the MacArthur Airport in Islip, New York, were seated, we filled twenty-three of them.

"Do people do that?" I asked.

"Do what?"

"Build something else, rather than taking a package."

"Twenty-eight percent do. Of those, most are builder-designed, and not really much different from what we offer ourselves, but a venturesome seven percent hire architects and go after something more unusual. In practice, with most of the people choosing a package, and most of those choosing a brick facade, you get a certain continuity of design, a sense of stability, but not uniformity of design, since you find surprises sprinkled here and there."

We took off, not with the sprint and leap of a jet, but with the workmanlike rise of the propeller plane, like a weekend hiker mounting a hill. We banked slowly to the right, and at one point in our banking, the plane seemed to pause, then go on banking and climbing. The pitcher looked at me. "We hit something," she said, eyes wide.

"What?" I said, not actually asking what we had hit, but merely registering astonishment.

"I don't know," she said, mistaking my astonishment for inquiry, "but we hit something." A moment later, she said, "We're going in a circle."

"Really?" I said. "I don't feel it."

She nodded her head and said, "We are," and the sole flight attendant hastened down the aisle to the cabin, disappeared within, then reappeared almost at once and said, "Ladies and gentlemen, we're returning to Washington. We've hit a goose."

WHEN THE DEHAVILLAND Dash 8 turboprop was on the ground again we deplaned and walked toward the airport, taking a route that brought us around the nose of the plane. There we could see that what had once been convex was now concave.

"I'll bet that goose is a goner," quipped the pitcher.

ALL TWENTY-THREE OF US travelers slumped, or attempted to slump as best we could, in the rigid seating provided in the airport lounge, fiberglass molded to fit the bottom of no one I have ever met, while we waited for another Dash 8 to be brought around to make the attempt. While we waited, the pitcher continued, and we slumpers listened, angling our slumping in her direction as she progressed, in the manner of pilgrims bored by the delays along the road to Canterbury.

"The hamlet is solar powered," she said, wearily, "but it's part of the power grid. The units all have sloping roofs and are aligned to favor their catching the sun—that's part of the design shell that we require—and the roofing material itself is photovoltaic: it generates electricity. We have five hundred thousand square feet of roof in the hamlet, and that area can generate five thousand kilowatts."

A woman of sixty-something, overweight, with lacquered hair hennaed to a golden color like the wrapper on a chocolate mint, took a little plastic snap-top case of dental floss from her purse and began to floss her teeth, among us all.

At that point, the pitcher stretched, yawned, and fell asleep.

After a moment or two, a slumper asked, in a whisper respectful of the pitcher's slumber, "How many people are there living in this hamlet?" I laid it all out for him, and for the other slumpers, who listened in the manner of people with nothing better to do.

"So," said one when I had finished and he had finished tapping at a PDA, "in the sunny south, the hamlet makes enough electricity for its own needs and then some."

"It could actually sell power to the utility grid," said another, a rival perhaps, tapping at her own PDA.

"In the north," said the first, "they have an excess in the summer, but they have to buy from the utility in the winter."

"They're almost self-sufficient in the long run, but not quite," said the rival, with a sigh of disappointment.

The flosser, having completed her work, dropped the spent floss onto the mousefur carpet, snapped shut the snap-top case of dental floss, and observed, "They could go over into self-sufficiency by building an array, a solar farm, on the open land. Add a hundred thousand square feet, and they can sell energy."

"That sounds enormous," objected a slumper.

"It's just—" said the first of the tappers, tapping at his PDA.

"—two point three acres," said the second of the tappers.

"No more than the area that about nine of the houses used to occupy," said the first tapper, "a single suburban block."

"I have to say that I'm not crazy about the idea of a solar farm," said the flosser. "Aesthetically, I mean. There doesn't seem to be any way to make it look nice."

"But from the hamlet's point of view you're making electricity," said the first tapper.

"And you've got more local employment, a few extra jobs," said the second.

"Hey, I'm getting sick of sitting around here," said a slumper who had until then been silent. "Who wants to share a cab to Baltimore?"

He got three takers, and as the four of them made for the sliding doors that led to ground transportation, the flosser asked, "Anybody want to bet they beat us there?" but those of us who remained had hardly seen the last of the backs of them when a reservations specialist came to us

and announced that "they" were bringing out another plane to replace
the one that—she hesitated, apparently not having been equipped with
an airline-sanctioned term for what had happened to the first Dash 8.

"—got goosed," said the flosser, growing considerably thereby in my
estimation.

WE FLEW to Baltimore without incident, the pitcher dozing in the seat
beside me, her head resting on a pillow that I had placed on my shoulder.
She slept with the trace of a smile on her face, and I wondered whether
she was dreaming of a successful presentation to skeptical suburbanites,
or whether she was, perhaps, dreaming of living in the hamlet, sleeping
in her own bed there, in her own unit, and I began to give some consid-
eration to living there myself. I had just stepped out the door of my unit
and begun ambling the zigzag walkways on my way to the center of
town, where I hoped to find a congenial *tertulia* in a cozy pub, when we
touched down, and the pitcher stirred.

"Where are we?" she asked, baffled.

"Baltimore," I said.

"What time is it?"

"It's about eight-thirty."

IN THE TERMINAL, we found the group that had traveled by taxi waiting for us, gloating. There had been some unexplained, and perhaps in-
explicable, disappearances since we had gathered in the airport lounge in
Washington, and we were now a group of nineteen, all of us still bound
for Islip, and still determined. About half a dozen of us went foraging for
food, leaving the others slumping vacantly in the rigid seats, gathered in
a small area, for companionship, and for exclusivity, to keep out those
who were not of our tribe. As I set off in what seemed to be a promising
direction, I could hear those left behind beginning to recount for one another the tales that bound them together, stories about the inconve-
niences and indignities they had endured on the journey, and, of course,
the already legendary goose.

It was the wrong time for finding food. The airport was in its slack
mode, with few flights in or out, and the franchise chains were closed or
closing, statistical analysis having determined that this was the time to

swab the surfaces with powerful detergents, not the time to feed the few who were so foolish or unlucky as to be stuck there en route to Islip. I found one source of food, and only one, in my chosen direction: the last nine of a day's stock of soft pretzels hanging limp and lukewarm in an outlet where a lone swabbie pushed litter around the tiles with a mop. I persuaded the swabbie to sell the pretzels to me, though he was not officially a pretzel vendor, and I carried the pretzels and all the packets of mustard that he and I could find back to the tribe, where I added them to the gatherings of the other hunters: bags of chips, bars of candy, bottles of watery juice drinks, and plastic cuplets of jelly, jam, and marmalade. A feast.

While we were eating, the pitcher said, to me, but with an audience that might have been gathered in a ring of firelight, "Now we get to the automobile. What we've done is provide another level of the town exclusively for vehicular traffic. The entire area below ground level, with the exception of the support system and the areas necessary for distribution of services and the sewage system, is where all the traffic flows, not only the vehicles that belong to the residents, but the delivery vans and garbage trucks, all of it. When the conditions aren't suitable for building below ground—if excavating would be too expensive or if the water table is too high, as on Long Island—we build above, raising the whole hamlet one story above the surrounding area, making it a little town on a hill."

IN TIME, and a very long time it was, we were called, and when called we went, with the uncertain weariness of people who have been too long in airports, to another DeHavilland Dash 8 turboprop, wherein we chose the seats we wanted. So, a short while later, I was sitting in a window seat somewhere south of Manhattan, with the pitcher sleeping on my shoulder, bound at last for Islip, New York, and the MacArthur airport.

Behind me, a woman was saying, "But the kid kept on complaining that his ears hurt, and his mother gave him gum to chew but it didn't do any good, and he kept whining and complaining, and finally he started, like, shrieking, and I'm sitting right next to him, so I put my hand on his arm and shushed him and he's like 'Who the hell is this?' but he's ready to do anything to stop his ears from hurting, so I said, 'Hold your nose

and blow, as if you were blowing your nose,' and I held my nose to show
him how to do it, and he grabs his nose and blows so hard that you could
see his face get all red, and he blew his eardrums out."

Eighteen passengers and the flight attendant—everyone in the cabin
but the sleeping pitcher—burst out laughing, welcoming the consolation
of laughter from whatever source it came.

THE NEXT MORNING, in a room at the motel nearest the airport, I regarded the pitcher standing at the mirror putting the final touches on her
makeup and decided that I had to ask the question that I had to ask.

"I have a question for you," I said.

"Mm."

"Where do they barbecue?"

She turned, slowly, to look at me, with her lipstick held in one hand, a
thumb's breadth from her lower lip, and panic in her eyes.

Chapter 17

As BW, I Discover Humanity in the Phantoms

To walk out your front door as if you've just arrived from a foreign country; to discover the world in which you already live; to begin the day as if you've just gotten off the boat from Singapore and have never seen your own doormat or the people on the landing . . . —it is this that reveals the humanity before you, unknown till now.

—Pierre Hamp, "La Littérature, image de la société,"
quoted by Walter Benjamin in *The Arcades Project*

I SAILED THE SEA on a ferry, briefly, and arrived on East Phantom, the largest of the islands in the Phantom Archipelago that stretches from Montauk to Block Island. I registered at an elaborately luxurious and outrageously expensive bed-and-breakfast on Main Street. Among the amenities of the place was a day pass for the East Phantom Physical Culture Club, "The Friendliest Little Gym in the Phantoms." I walked the length of Main Street, found the club, and entered. Behind the desk was a young man chewing on a carrot and scowling. His name tag said that his name was Virgil. I handed my pass to Virgil, who scowled and handed me a towel. Virgil was built like a bulldog, and when he scowled he looked like a bulldog. I started toward the men's locker room.

As I turned, a barrel-chested man in his late fifties, a member, to judge from the card that he wore around his neck on a lanyard, approached the desk and said to Virgil, "Come here a minute. I've got to talk to you. Come here."

I stole a glance and saw that the barrel-chested man was gesticulating in the direction of the locker room. Assured that I would be able to hear what the man had to say, I abandoned the idea of returning to the desk to browse through the credit-card applications.

The youngster, with the look of one who anticipates having to listen to a long and disappointing joke, groaned, but followed the man into the locker room anyway.

"Listen," said the barrel-chested man when the door had swung shut behind them, "I want to tell you something, but I don't want you to get upset about it, you know what I'm saying?"

"Yeah, I guess so."

"This place is a class act, am I right?"

The youngster shrugged.

"I mean it's supposed to be a class act, right?" He poked his finger in the young man's chest.

"Right," said the young man.

"But when the ab machine breaks and it isn't replaced or there isn't maybe another ab machine that you got in reserve in case one breaks, but instead the ab machine just disappears, that is not a class act, you know what I'm saying?"

"I know what you're saying."

"Well?"

"Well what?"

"What are you going to do about it?"

"Me? What am I going to do about it?"

"That's what I'm asking you. What are you going to do about it?"

"Nothing."

"Nothing?"

"I don't hold the purse strings here, you know what I'm saying?"

MOMENTS LATER, I was climbing an endless set of stairs, and trying to concentrate on a sharp exchange in the letters section of the *New York Review of 'Pataphysics,* but I was being distracted by the television monitor in front of me, where a clumsy young crab fisherman was squinting

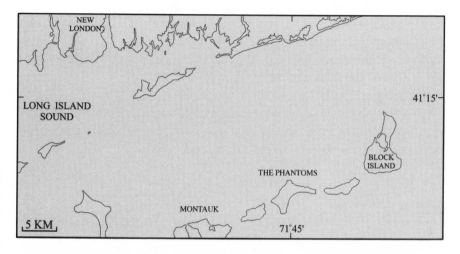

FIGURE 6: The islands in the Phantom Archipelago stretch from Montauk, on the tip of Long Island, eastward to Block Island.

and grimacing and trying his damnedest to catch some crabs. The sound was off, but subtitles ran within a black band beneath the picture.

I asked the man to my right, "What are we watching?"

"Don't ask me," he said.

"Okay," I said. I turned toward the woman to my left, to ask her what we were watching, but the man on my right continued.

"I'm the wrong guy to ask. Totally the wrong guy. Definitely the wrong guy to ask."

"Uh-huh."

"I mean, what the hell do I care what we're watching? It's all marketing! That's all it is. You want to know what I say?"

" 'It's all marketing'?"

"Exactly! That's what I say." He pointed at the screen, where the hapless crab fisherman had brought up a mess o' flotsam and jetsam, and said, "I'll tell you what that is. That is the end of culture, that's what that is. This culture sells products, and it sells stupidity, and it sells violence. It's all marketing." His belt of stairs slowed and stopped. "Remember what I said," he advised me.

" 'It's all marketing,' " I said, raising a clenched fist.

He raised a clenched fist in return, and I wondered whether by chance
I had joined a clandestine cell.

The woman to my left pulled her reading glasses down on her nose
and followed the man with her eyes as he walked away.

"It takes all kinds," she said.

Since my band of stairs was close enough to hers to allow me to read
over her shoulder, I did. She was looking through the classified ads in the
back pages of a women's magazine. One ad asked:

What Do Women Want Most?

The rest of the ads seemed to offer answers. Women want careers:

Get Paid for Reading Books
Become a Medical Transcriptionist
Assemble Simple Crafts at Home
Become a Beauty Queen

They want knowledge:
Earn Your High-School Diploma
Access Anyone's Inner Thoughts
Look into the Future!
Star-Plans from Certified Malibu Psychics

They want love:
Meet Eligible British Gentlemen
Love Advice from the Witches of Salem
Make Your Love Come to You
Tap the Love Power of Your Guardian Angel

And they want orgasms:
Increase Your Orgasms!
Enjoy Boundless Orgasmic Release
Guaranteed Orgasms with Orgasmatron
Reach Orgasm with Electro-Tongue™!

The woman took her cellular phone out of her fanny pack, flipped it open, and dialed.

"Hello?" she said into the phone. "I need some advice. . . . Okay, a star-plan. . . . Okay, I'm trying to decide whether to take the cash or the payments . . . in the Lotto. . . . No, I didn't win . . . not yet. . . . I haven't even bought a ticket yet. . . . I never bought a ticket in my life. . . . Yeah. . . . But I'm going to. I could use the money. . . . Right. . . . You can get so much a year, or you can have it all at once, but not as much. . . . No, no, no, you don't understand. . . . See, you have to tell them when you buy the ticket. . . . Yeah. . . . Yeah, I was taken aback. I didn't realize you had to do that. This is a first for me. . . . Of course it's a big decision. . . . That's why I need some advice. . . . What do you mean, short or long? . . . Huh? . . . I can get a long-term psychic star-plan or a short-term psychic star-plan? . . . Well, I don't know. It depends on whether I take the cash or the payments, right? I mean, I would need the long-term if I take it all at once, but I could go year-to-year with short-terms if I take the payments. . . . I don't know what to do. I'll call you back." She flipped the phone shut. "Not in this lifetime," she muttered.

On the screen, the crab fisherman had finally gotten the knack. He was hauling in crabs like mad and dreaming up a scheme to market the little critters.

"Would you mind changing that?" asked the woman. "I've seen it."

I can be obliging when it amuses me to be. I dismounted my endless staircase and walked to the set, which hung from the ceiling on a pivoted platform like those used to suspend television sets in front of patients in hospitals. I had to rise on my toes to press the channel button. I moved through a few channels without finding anything that drew any sort of comment from the woman until I came to a channel where a smiling fellow was sitting in an upholstered chair, saying, "—and when we come back, we'll have Dr. Ravenel here to tell us how to talk to our kids about drugs. Don't go away." His every word was transcribed as he spoke and appeared in the subtitles below the picture.

"That," said the woman. "I better look at that." She leaned in my direction. "I'm worried about my daughter," she confided, and then, to indicate just who was worrying her, she jerked her head in the direction of a young goddess on a torturous device at the far end of the room. The girl was on pedals, her feet strapped to the pedals, and she was standing upright, holding rubber handles, and climbing as one might scramble over rocks at the steep end of a mountain trail, above the tree line. Her scrambling was a regulated clamber, though, regularized and ritualized by the limits imposed by the engineering of the machine. When she sensed that she was being observed and turned in the direction of her mother and me, I saw that her face was disfigured by a sneer. She was climbing at a furious pace, but suddenly she stopped, unstrapped herself, and dashed across the gym floor to a scale. She must have been an ounce or two over her target, because after weighing herself she dashed back to the climbing machine, strapped herself in again, and began ascending at an even fiercer pace.

LATER THAT EVENING, I was sitting on a bar stool in a restaurant called Village Hardware. It was called Village Hardware because it was in a building that had once housed a hardware store by that name. The stool I had chosen was at the right end of the bar, around a corner, the only stool beyond the service bar, the stretch of bar-top turf that was reserved for the waitresses. Perched on this stool, I could lean against the exposed brick wall and chat with the waitresses while they waited for their orders, and I didn't have to watch my back. In my capacity as a restaurant reviewer in the Boston area, I once received from one of my readers, a retired CIA agent, a long, friendly letter full of advice on how to choose seating that would offer advantages in an unexpected firefight, and I have tried to follow the advice ever since. That correspondent would have approved of this bar stool, since it provided long views of the only two entrances to the room, no opportunity for approach from behind, and a nearby window for a quick escape.

There was one table to my left, a table squeezed in where there should not have been one, squeezed in to squeeze a few extra dollars out of the space. Four people could dine there, but not in comfort. I suppose that this table had originally been intended for cocktails only. There was a two-seat banquette against the wall and two chairs were opposite the banquette, inches from my feet. Two couples were shown to the table.

The hostess—let's call her Rita—pulled the table out from the banquette, and a man and woman slid into position on it. Then Rita repositioned the table, and the other man and the other woman seated themselves on chairs so that the two men, who were nearer to me, were facing each other, and the two women were also facing each other. The man on the banquette took his napkin from the table at once, as a gentleman should, flipped it open, and spread it on his lap in a fluid and nonchalant gesture that was almost quick enough to prevent me from seeing that the hand of the woman beside him was under it.

The man on the chair put an unlit cigar into his mouth and said, speaking around the cigar, rolling it in his mouth as he spoke, "Nobody can believe what a deal I got on this house—not even you can believe it, right, Sandra?"

The woman on the banquette shrugged her bare shoulders and twisted her mouth into a crooked grin and leaned toward the center of the table and said to the man on the chair, speaking in the measured tones of someone who has said what she is saying several times before and wants everyone to know that she has, "No, Derek, I cannot believe the deal you got on the house." The napkin in the lap of the man on the banquette rolled and rippled like a bay on a windy day, and the man with the rippling napkin in his lap burst out laughing.

Derek smiled around the cigar and rolled it in his mouth again, and said to the man on the banquette, "You don't believe it, either, do you?"

"It's amazing," said the man on the banquette.

"Bet your ass it's amazing," said Derek, and he struck a match.

"You're not going to light that, are you?" asked Sandra.

"What?" said Derek, looking around the room with the contumacious air of a guy who had struck a good bargain for a month's rental on a house in the Phantoms that wasn't really very far from his boss's house and not much farther from the beach. "Somebody's going to object?"

"I'm going to object," said Sandra. "I don't think you can smoke a cigar in here."

"All right. Okay," said Derek, and he dropped the match into his water glass and put the cigar into his shirt pocket. "You know," he said, "I'm thinking people are nuts to rent a place like that. I mean, what if we just like trash it?" He laughed, picked up his water glass, saw the match in it, and waved it in the direction of a bus boy. "What do you think a house like that goes for?" he asked. "A couple of million?"

The napkin rippled, and the man on the banquette said, "I don't know."

"Three million?" asked Derek. "The houses down the street probably go for three million."

"Yeah, but Derek, those houses are like huge and they're right on the water," said Sandra.

"This is practically on the water," said Derek.

"Down the street," said Sandra.

"I didn't say it was on the water," said Derek. He nodded at the man on the banquette and asked, "Did I say it was on the water?"

The napkin surged and roiled.

"No," said the man with the roiling napkin in his lap. He smiled at his menu.

"It's practically on the water," said Derek. He took the cigar from his pocket. "I'm going to go out and smoke this," he said. "Anybody want to come with me?" No one in Derek's party said a word, so he stood and took the forearm of the woman on the chair beside him. "Come on, Terry," he said. "Come with me." She rose and followed him with the resigned air of a woman who was dependent on him for her ride home, and the napkin heaved as if a whale were breaching.

"Another?" asked the bartender.

"No thanks," I said, though another would have been nice.

I asked for the check, paid it, and left. In the parking lot, Derek was leaning against a vehicle the size of a small bus, holding the cigar toward Terry and saying, "Come on, just try it once."

I walked back to the bed-and-breakfast in the quiet spring evening and retired for the night, alone.

Chapter 18

As BW, I Observe the Diners at the Crab Buffet

A simple walk through a thousand nesting boobies may not be a religious experience, but it has a deep spiritual quality.

—Harold J. Morowitz, "The Galápagos,"
in *Mayonnaise and the Origin of Life*

VERY EARLY the next morning, I was on the beach. I was the only person on the beach as far as I could see in the direction of Block Island, where the sun was rising, or toward Montauk, where mist lay over the water and the shore. The tide was low, as low as ever, since it was the spring tide, the full-moon tide. The beach was wide, the water way out, leaving horseshoe crabs of many ages and stages of development stranded on the beach.

An encyclopedia will tell you that the horseshoe crab is a large, primitive marine arthropod related to the spider. Its heavy dark brown exoskeleton, or carapace, is domed and shaped like a horseshoe. Its body is divided into a broad, flattened, semicircular front part (the prosoma), a tapering middle part (the opisthoma), and a pointed, spiky tail-like part (the telson). In other words, they look ridiculous. They look like the battle helmets of Neanderthal legions, something cobbled together on short notice out of mismatched bits from the bottom of the fauna-parts bin.

Their respiratory organs are made of thin leaves that are fitted like the pages of a book onto one pair of flaplike appendages on the opisthoma. Rhythmic movement of the appendages circulates water over the surfaces of these "book gills" and drives blood into and out of the gill leaves.

The antiquity of the horseshoe crab is humbling to a member of a younger species, such as ours. They are sometimes called "living fossils" because they resemble fossil trilobites and eurypterids of the Paleozoic era. Horseshoe crabs first appeared in the Upper Silurian period, and a number of fossil species have been described. The American species, *Limulus polyphemus,* is common along the Atlantic coast from Nova Scotia to Florida. It lives in shallow water, preferring soft or sandy bottoms, and reaches a maximum length of nearly two feet (sixty-one centimeters). They have survived for so long. As a species they have seen so much. They have been witness, if only from the sidelines, to the entire history of humankind. They've seen it all—and yet—they have a fatal flaw.

Horseshoe crabs have five pairs of walking legs attached to the prosoma. These legs enable the crabs to swim awkwardly or burrow through sand or mud, but they are short and weak, too short and too weak to allow a crab to right itself if it is turned onto its back. The telson might do the job, might flip an inverted crab, but it's poorly placed, exerting its leverage longitudinally rather than laterally, and the muscle that moves it is too weak to make it effective. In the spring, when many, many horseshoe crabs are stranded on the sand, upside down and helpless as Gregor Samsa, herring gulls come winging in and eat them alive.

That was what was happening around me on the beach while I walked.

Of the many crabs that had been left on the beach by the outgoing tide, some were making their lumbering way back to the water, but many others were not because they could not. One unhappy accident or another had flipped these upside down, and they could not right themselves.

The overturned ones lay there helplessly waving their legs. Herring gulls swooped down on them and pecked at them, whirling upward with morsels in their beaks. I watched. Who could resist? There they were, presented in their own shells, defenseless, like a seafood salad bowl.

Silent though they were, they seemed in their frantic gesticulation to be signing to the gulls, saying, "Eat me!" Waving their five pairs of useless walking legs, they seemed to be beckoning, urging the gulls toward them. "Come, come, come and eat me. Please. Help me fulfill my destiny in the grand design."

The gulls were noisy at the crab buffet.

A WOMAN CAME RUNNING my way. She was running hard and well. She was strong and lithe. She was wearing blue shorts and a blue athletic bra, both crafted of some cunning fabric that clung to her as closely as her own sweat, which gave a silken sheen to her skin in the early morning, early spring sunlight.

"Good morning," she said as she drew near. She seemed not to be out of breath at all.

"Good morning," I replied.

"A glorious morning, isn't it?" she said, brimming with life and health. "A glorious morning to be alive."

"Yes," I said. I raised my index finger to indicate that I would like a moment of her time and added, "May I ask you a question?"

She paused, jogging in place, and tilted her head to one side, non-committally.

"What's the question?" she asked.

I swept my arm outward across the scene of slaughter on the sand and asked, "What do you make of this?"

She looked where I had indicated that she should look and saw what she had not noticed before. For a moment she was transfixed. She stopped running in place. Across her face, like a succession of darkening clouds, swept horror, revulsion, and anger. Then she clenched her jaw and fell to the fight. She plunged into the thick of the struggle and struck out on the side of the crabs. Screaming, she flailed her arms at the gulls. She ran among the crabs, batting gulls away from the overturned ones, righting the hapless creatures as quickly as she could, nudging them over with her running shoe, or bending to grab them and set them on what legs they had left.

"Help me!" she shouted.

It was not a time when producing a card and explaining my detachment would have been effective, I thought, so I joined her. As she fought, she grew more bloodthirsty. No longer content merely to scatter the gulls, she wanted to punish them. She struck them with her hands and fists, and she kicked at them. I imitated her, but I wasn't her match in fervor or technique. It was a pleasure to watch her body at work.

"You're good at this!" I shouted.

"Tae kwon do," she shouted back. "I never expected to use it!"

We stood and surveyed the field. There were no overturned crabs now. Gulls screamed at us from above, just out of reach. They were not pleased. They swept down at us, pecked at our heads. They were bold. They were foolish. The runner struck with invisible swiftness at one, and it fell to the sand as if it had never had the gift of flight. She pounced on it and with savage glee twisted its neck. She turned with sudden shyness toward me to see if I had witnessed the act. She saw that I had. She shrugged like a girl caught with her hand in her panties, and she threw the gull to the sand. She began walking toward the water. I walked with her.

We took our shoes off, waded in, and washed our hands in the foam.

"Well, that was ridiculous, wasn't it?" she asked.

"It was—"

"Ridiculous—but satisfying—very satisfying." She looked back at the carnage on the field of battle and sighed. Then, suddenly, she shook her fist at the sky and screamed, "Do you call this fair?"

I allowed a decent interval to pass, then asked, "Do you call it fair?"

"No," she sighed. She shook her head. "No, I don't."

"Do you think it is part of a grand design?"

"A grand design?"

"A master plan."

"Oh. Do I think there is a god, in other words?"

A cluster of busy gulls not far from us began screeching and cawing, fighting over some bit of a crab that one of them had found on the sand. Together we watched the gulls struggling for a moment.

"No," she said, "I don't—but if there were, he would have to be a real son of a bitch, wouldn't he? I mean, just look at this!" With a sweep of her hand, she indicated the massacre of the crabs. "If there is a god, how does he excuse himself for this?"

She looked at me questioningly. I shrugged.

"Maybe this is the designer's idea of a joke? Horseshoe crabs are the butt of a divine joke? Do the heavens ring with laughter now, right now, this minute?"

She looked upward and seemed actually to be straining to hear the laughter.

"Maybe we are all laughable in the eyes of God," she said. "Maybe there's a built-in flaw in all the creatures here, every one of us on this beach at this early hour, every one of us on this planet now and always, something about each of us that makes us as laughably flawed as these crabs, lying on their backs, waving their pathetic little legs in the air."

She took a breath.

"Maybe he's not nasty, though," she conceded. "Just stupid. If there is a designer, maybe he bungled the horseshoe-crab project. 'Uh-oh, what have I done now? The thing is incapable of righting itself. It's defenseless on its back. Ahh, so what? Nobody's going to notice.' Is that it?"

She put her hands on her hips and observed the scene on the beach for another moment.

"You know," she said, "divine stupidity is not such a bad explanation. Why else did the creator not create a world in which the living beings were sustained in some way other than eating one another? Was the creator too stupid to see that it might be possible, that he could have given the animals the same powers as the plants and allowed them to make their dinner from sunshine and dirt?"

She threw water on her face, wiped it off, and shook her head.

"No," she said. "I don't see a design in this. It's too savage and too stupid to have been designed. Nature is beautiful at times, and ugly at times, but always absurd. I try not to be annoyed by the nastiness of it. I try to tell myself that it is absurdly human of me even to see nastiness in it, but I can't always manage it. I sometimes wish we hadn't evolved to the point of understanding, you know? Life would be easier. Easier to take. The crabs and gulls are better off, in that way. I suppose the crabs don't care, really. They can't care. They don't know how. And for that matter, I suppose the gulls are nothing more than hungry."

We watched the gulls gleaning for a while longer.

"So much death requires an antidote," she said, and she took my hand

and led me to the rolling dunes on the other side of the beach, where, in a hollow that caught the warmth of the weak sun, she stripped off her jogging gear and lay on her back in the sand, arms and legs wide, easy pickings.

LATER, WHILE WE LAY ON OUR BACKS, watching childlike clouds drift overhead as if they had nothing to do, she said, "It happens every spring, but every spring it takes me by surprise. I suppose something in me makes me forget from spring to spring. I suppose it's a part of spring that I would rather deny. The tendency to interpret the crabs and gulls as human is irresistible, of course. 'All you can eat at the crab buffet!' And the gulls come crowding in. Everybody loves a bargain. Everybody's a glutton at heart. I would be if no one were watching, if I knew that no one would ever be watching, no witnesses. They're like fat people at a steam table, elbowing one another aside. And they're so fucking noisy about it. They boast when they've got a crab, but then they're surprised when others come rushing over for a taste, and then they're all screaming noise again, trying to defend their crabs. 'My crab! My dinner!' The ones without crabs wail over their misfortune, cursing the fates or the creator. 'Why must the world be so unfair?' The crabs are quiet. No screaming from them. They keep their thoughts to themselves. The crabs have been here much, much longer than the gulls. They probably expect to survive, in the long run. They probably see a design. 'The gulls may seem to be winning today,' they think, 'but the designer gave us the strength of the patient and simple, and we are sure that we will endure.' Sure. If you were born here, on the Phantoms, as I was, it's very hard not to see the gulls as the city people and the crabs as the locals. We have the strength of the patient and simple. Will we endure?"

She stretched and sighed.

"Give me another shot of life, stranger," she commanded.

Chapter 19

As BW, I Pick Up a Few Things in East Phantom

There are people who would be disliked, even boycotted, if they lived an ordinary community life in town or city. But if they keep traveling, always saying goodbye, they are treasured and loved. Their short periods in one place are like an actor's moment on the stage—they can keep to their star hero role that long at least.

—Dawn Powell, diary entry

I WAS SITTING OUTDOORS at a charming little café called Annette's, in charming little old East Phantom. For the sake of my heart I was eating the vegetarian special, a platter of root vegetables, field greens, and cunningly molded tofu.

An elderly couple was sitting at the table to my right. The elderly woman was eating a salad, and the elderly man was eating a bowl of soup. Two girls were to my left. Both were eating sandwiches and french-fried potato cubes. An enormous stainless-steel van was parked at the curb. There was a sign on the side of the van:

HARRIMAN & SONS
DUCT CLEANING COMPANY

In the van, two guys were eating hero sandwiches. I had, spurred by envy, convinced myself that they were veal parmigiana heros, with extra cheese and sliced hot pickled peppers.

The elderly woman said to the elderly man, "Do you mind if I taste your soup?"

"No," he said. "I don't mind. Why should I mind?" He sighed and pushed the bowl toward her.

"What's that for?" she asked.

"What's what for?"

"The sigh."

"I can't sigh? Go on—taste the soup."

Girl one nodded at the van and said, "My mom got those guys in."

"Who?" asked girl two.

"The guys with the truck."

"What do they do?"

"They suck your ducts."

Girl two asked, "What does that mean, 'They suck your ducts'?"

"They put like a big vacuum cleaner onto the ducts—where the hot air goes—you know, to heat the house. Then they suck out all the dust and shit that's in there."

"Oh," said girl two. She sucked on her iced tea, made it slurp, and giggled.

The woman tasted the soup. "Oh, that's delicious!" she said. "That's just wonderful!" She took another spoonful, then pushed the bowl back toward the man. "Wonderful!"

A BMW convertible was parked in front of the duct suckers' van. A fortyish woman got into it on the passenger's side, opened a small white box, removed a chocolate truffle in brown fluted paper, put the truffle into her mouth, and tossed the fluted paper on the ground.

"Such delicious soup," said the woman. She was silent for a moment, and then she said, "I'm surprised you didn't want some pepper in it."

The man sighed again. "It was fine," he said.

"A little pepper—" said the woman.

"Look," he said. "I'm done already."

Girl one said, "It helps with allergies. That's why my mom wanted to get them in."

"I thought she did get them in," said girl two.

"Nah. She was going to. They came for an estimate, but my father didn't want it. He was like, 'It's my house. I'll take care of it.' "

"You said she got them in."

"No."

"You did. You were like, 'My mom got those guys in.' "

"Really?"

"Well? Yeah? Really."

"I didn't mean that. I meant she wanted to get them in."

The elderly man paid the check. He stood and offered his arm to the elderly woman, who took it, and he supported her as she rose from her chair. They began walking, slowly, away.

The girls watched them go. I watched the girls watching them. I wondered what the girls thought of them, of their halting steps, the way they searched the ground in front of them for the smallest obstacle that might trip them up, the way they clung to each other.

Girl one said, "My mom never really had a house."

Girl two said, "What?"

"That's the way she felt, anyway."

"Yeah?"

"It was like she was always living in somebody else's house? Her parents' house, and then living with roommates, and then my dad's house? Because the house was like everything my dad represents, all that fake rich stuff."

Girl two said, "Yeah."

A fortyish man jumped into the driver's seat of the BMW. "What's that?" he asked the paper-tossing woman in the other seat. "Candy? Jesus, what is it with the candy? You spend a week at Canyon Ranch, you finally lose some weight, and then you're back on the candy diet?"

"Oh, shut up," said the paper-tosser. She put another truffle into her mouth and tossed its fluted paper on the ground.

The fluted paper landed in front of the elderly woman. "Did you really have to do that?" she asked the tosser.

"Huh?" said the tosser.

"Would it kill you to get out of the car and walk to the trash can?" asked the elderly woman.

"Fuck you, lady," said the tosser. "If it bothers you so much, you pick it up!"

The driver leaned across the tosser, grabbed the box, shook the truffles onto the ground, threw the box after them, shouted, "Pick 'em all up!" and accelerated away from the curb.

Girl two asked, "So what did she do?"

"Who?" asked girl one.

"Your mom."

"Oh."

"Did she make your dad get the duct suckers?"

"No." The elderly man bent stiffly and began picking up the truffles. The girl watched him for a moment, then bent her head and poked at a potato cube. "She hung herself," she said after another moment.

"What?" said girl two, and then, again, almost shrieking, "What?"

"Hung herself," said girl one. "In the garden. From the pergola."

The duct suckers got out of their van to give the elderly man a hand. I thought about helping him myself, but three would have been a crowd, would have attracted more attention than the elderly man or his elderly darling would have welcomed, I decided.

GIRL TWO sat there for a moment, her eyes wild. Behind those eyes I could see her mind racing, searching for a way out, a way to get away. From the desperate look on her face I decided that under the numbing weight of such crushing news she could think of nothing better than "Hey, I gotta go," or something equally lame, and she seemed about to say that or something like it. So, because I am a man who rises to the occasion and is often inspired to action when others are paralyzed by indecision or fear, the fear of doing one of the many wrong things that present themselves as the only alternatives in difficult moments, I rose, walked to the girls' table, and presented my card.

"Excuse me," I said to the daughter of the suicide, "but I couldn't help overhearing, or, to be more truthful about it, I listened with increasing fascination as you unfolded the details of your mother's—unhappiness—her despair."

"You were eavesdropping," she said, looking deeply into my eyes, looking for some evidence there that I might be the one who would listen to her with the sympathy she sought, craved, needed.

Girl two was regarding me with her mouth agape and her eyes wide, full of the astonishment we feel on those rare occasions when our prayers are answered.

"I was," I admitted. "You could almost say that I am a professional eavesdropper—'almost' because I am not paid for the eavesdropping I do."

"It's a hobby?"

"More like a mission."

Girl two said, in a cautionary tone, "We should go."

"You go," said girl one. "I don't have anything to do. I'm just going to stay here for a while and see what I overhear."

"That's the spirit," I said.

Girl two looked at me with eyes that said, approximately, "I'm not sure whether I should thank you for relieving me of the burden of listening to what I expect would be a painful and embarrassing outpouring of grief and shame and guilt from my dear friend girl one, or whether I should castigate you severely for eavesdropping in the first place, interrupting in the second, and usurping my rightful place as sympathetic listener in the third, or whether I should just call the cops in the likelihood that your intentions are evil, but a part of me, a growing part, just wants to get away, go home, have a swim, wash the whole experience away, ignore it, forget it, whatever."

"I'll go then," she said aloud. She rose, came around the table and hugged her friend, then started toward me, and for a moment I thought she was going to hug me, too. She didn't. She extended her hand and, as she had been taught, said, "It was nice meeting you."

I took her little hand. "It's a nice afternoon," I said. "You should go for a swim."

She looked at me then with fear in her eyes, the fear that I had the uncanny ability to read her mind. She clutched her bag to her breast and backed from the table, then turned and walked briskly away.

TOGETHER, the daughter of the suicide and I watched girl two as she walked away. At the curb, she stopped and turned toward us. She brought

her hand beside her cheek and extended her little finger downward toward her mouth and her thumb upward toward her ear and mouthed
"Call me."

The daughter rippled her fingers in a wave and looked down at the
table. Girl two turned again, crossed the street, and in a moment was out
of sight among the cars in the parking lot.

"You miss her," I said.

"I do. I really do." She sat in silence.

"I'm listening," I said.

She seemed about to say something, then shook her head, just
slightly, bit her lower lip, looked down at the table in front of her, and began running her thumbnail along the pattern of the tablecloth.

"I have nowhere to go and nothing to do," I said. "Don't feel rushed."

"You're unemployed?"

"I'm on sabbatical."

"You don't seem like the religious type."

"What?"

"Sabbatical. Do you know what it means?"

"Time off for good behavior?"

"Rest. As in a day of rest. As in the Sabbath?"

"Really? Of course. It's right there, staring at me, isn't it?"

"The seventh day, the day when God rested. From that day of rest
comes the Old Testament command to let the land lie fallow every seventh year."

"You are surprising me. Go on."

"It's in Leviticus: 'Six years thou shalt sow thy field, and six years thou
shalt prune thy vineyard, and gather in the fruit thereof; but in the seventh
year shall be a sabbath of rest unto the land, a sabbath for the Lord: thou
shalt neither sow thy field, nor prune thy vineyard. That which groweth of
its own accord of thy harvest thou shalt not reap, neither gather the grapes
of thy vine undressed: for it is a year of rest unto the land.' "

"You don't seem like the religious type, either.' "

"My mother."

"Oh."

"And that's where the sabbatical comes from. The college professors'
sabbatical. A year of rest. The seventh year."

"When one is like the lilies of the field," I said, to demonstrate that I could quote the Bible if necessary—for a seduction, for example. "No sowing. No reaping."

"Yes." Again, she looked deep into my eyes. A long moment passed. "Do you think it's true that the eyes are the windows to the soul?" she asked.

"No," I said, truthfully.

"You're probably right. I've been looking into your eyes, trying to discover something about you, and I can't see anything there. It's as if there is nothing inside you. No one inside you."

"You're quite right," I said. "I am not one of those people who hears an inner voice, who thinks that there resides within him a different self, someone much better, or someone much worse. I am all there is to me— all shell, no white or yolk."

This was too much table-talk tennis, and she frowned at it.

"Look," I said, taking her hands in mine and taking encouragement from my not being refused, "I'd like to do something for you."

"For me, or to me?"

"Both," I said honestly.

"What would you like to do for me?"

"I would like to make you understand how easy it is to get away."

"Get away?"

"To disappear, to make like a breeze and blow, to pass through life leaving no more impression than a breath, the tickle of a breeze."

"You mean to get away from"—she rolled her eyes—"all this?"

"Yes, but without having to hang yourself from the pergola."

"Go on."

I had to find some way to say it, to tell her what I was, what I had become, sell it to her, pitch it to her, before I lost her, before she turned her attention to something else, or simply rejected me and my gray-haired advice.

"You walk—" I began.

"—away," she said, with a frown, already disappointed by the advice she expected to hear.

"No, no," I said quickly. "Not away. Not toward. Through."

"Through—what?"

"Life. The world. It all."

"Doing—what?"

"Well—" I said, sighing at the failure of communication I was beginning to feel forming like a fog of cotton wool between us.

"Digging it," she said.

"You are surprising me again," I said.

"You want me to go on the road?"

"Not necessarily. One can travel a great deal in Concord—or East Phantom, for that matter. I'm suggesting that you step aside from"—I swept my arm to indicate the restaurant and everything beyond it—"all this."

"Step aside."

"Remain in it, but cease to be of it."

"Pass through it like a breeze, invisible."

"Like the passing of a noble gas."

She giggled.

"I hadn't meant that to be funny," I said.

"But it was," she said.

"Forming no bonds, leaving no trace, so that those you leave behind begin to wonder whether you were ever really there at all."

"Words of wisdom," she said. It was an assessment. There was no irony in it.

"Thank you," I said. There was no irony in it.

"Would this have saved my mother?"

"I don't know. But I think it might save you."

"Is it the pursuit of pleasure?"

"Not pursuit. More a case of taking pleasure where you find it. I seem to prefer to keep moving, but it isn't necessary."

"And do you like it—everything you see?"

"Like it, dislike it, love it, hate it—I don't feel any of that anymore. I left my heart in Boston. I experience it. I watch it, I taste it—"

"—and you eavesdrop on it—"

"Yes."

"You slurp it."

"Slurp it?"

"The world is your oyster. It's here so that you can see it—taste it, touch it—and your experiencing it is the reason for its being here. That's the solipsism of the idler, the drifter, the slacker, the dharma bum."

"You really are an amazing girl."

"How long have you been doing this?"

"Not very long, really, but long enough to have learned how salutary it can be for someone who would rather not be in the world."

"What have you seen—touched—tasted—?"

"Ah, well. Where shall I begin? I've seen a cowboy eat eggs whole—"

"Raw?"

"Hard-boiled."

"With the shells?"

"No. Shelled. But otherwise whole. Not in bites."

"Hm," she said, disappointed.

"I've seen the way the sun gleams from the lotion called Golden Fruits—"

"I use that."

"—I was a witness to the unveiling of the Limo Fountain; I've seen the radome nose of a turboprop plane indented by a goose—"

"And what have you learned?"

"That hasn't been my object."

"Still, it happens."

"Yes. Despite one's best efforts."

"So?"

"I've learned how difficult it is to make oneself understood, and how difficult to understand. I've learned that crab cakes are rarely as good as they look, that most people are fools, that the mojito is a bracing drink, that satire seems to slide with time toward kitsch, that people in adversity will huddle together, that fairness is not a concept nature knows, that one can get one's ducts sucked—"

That earned me a smile.

"What I've really learned is how to go on living," I said, and I meant it.

"Yeah," she said with a frown and downcast eyes.

"You can, too," I said. "Will you try?"

"I'm not sure I know how," she sighed.

"Just begin to wander. Let yourself be carried along by the crowd. Amble the streets. Wander willy-nilly. Learn to do nothing. Develop a passion for observation. Just promise me that you'll try."

"I will. I promise. I will try."

"Be patient," I said. "It takes a while. Try it for fifty years."

"Fifty years?"

"Yes. In fifty years, I think you can learn to live as I do—and that you will have learned to enjoy it."

"Fifty years," she said, laughing and shaking her head.

"After fifty years, if it hasn't worked, I'm certain that there will still be pergolas aplenty."

"Okay," she said. "Okay."

I reached across the table and touched her cheek.

"So," she said, "now that you've saved my life—what next?"

"Well—I—"

"Are you going to try to get me to go to bed with you?"

"I'd hate myself in the morning if I didn't."

IN THE MORNING, on the ferry, we stood side by side at the rail, looking into the wind, toward Montauk, with the sun warming our backs.

"Do you mind my asking where you're going? I know I shouldn't, but—"

"I don't mind at all. I'm going back to Boston."

"I hadn't expected that."

"Neither had I, but I left someone there—"

"Don't you always?"

"Yes, but this is different. I left someone with a misimpression, a misapprehension, a delusion—"

"Don't you always?"

"Yes—"

"—but this is different."

"Yes."

"Who is this poor deluded creature?"

"A heartbroken man named . . . Matthew Barber."

Chapter 20

As Matthew, I'm a Little Mixed Up, but I'm Feeling Fine

Noise provides a Darwinian network with the raw materials for creativity. . . . The process we call thought results from the Darwinian sculpting of network noise in the absence of external training. . . . The essence of associative thinking is to mix things up and then separate the good from the bad.

—Frank T. Vertosick Jr., *The Genius Within*

MR. BARBER?"

"Yes?"

"I thought we'd lost you there for a minute."

"I drifted off, I think. The sedative—"

"You're feeling relaxed, then?"

"Yes, quite relaxed. Very relaxed."

"No discomfort?"

"No. None."

"Except for the fact that this steel table you have us on feels as cold as a slab in a morgue."

"What was that?"

"Nothing. I was just thinking aloud—the sedative—"

"We're just finishing up here. It won't be much longer."

"You're back," I said, subvocally, surreptitiously.

"Yes, I'm back. I began to feel—how shall I put this?"

"Guilty."

"I wouldn't go quite so far as that."

"But you came back."

"Yes, I did. I had the feeling that there was unfinished business between us, and, to be quite honest about it, Matthew, I had the feeling that
you needed my help. So, at great personal sacrifice, I've returned to
sunny Boston. What have you been up to in my absence?"

"Well, as you see, I am an inmate of this institution—where they take
my chest pains quite seriously, by the way."

"The solipsism of the medical profession. In their eyes, we are all
more or less diseased. We need them so, don't you know."

"Perhaps we are all diseased, one way or another."

"All right!" said one of the doctors, with what sounded disturbingly
like a sense of relief at having plumbed the depths of my heart without
killing me. "That's that!" He smiled at me triumphantly.

"That's that?" I asked, hopefully.

"Actually, not quite," he admitted. "We'll be leaving the sheath in until we've decided whether you're going to need an angioplasty, but we'll
have you taken back to the ward for now. Get you off this 'cold slab.' "

RETURNING TO THE WARD, wheeled back on the gurney, I sensed a
tension in the room and began to understand that there had been doubts
among my wardmates about the likelihood of my return.

"They're glad to see me back, relieved for me." For a moment, I wondered if there might not be applause.

"Except for the ones who bet against you," sneered BW. "They're out
a few bucks."

"They wouldn't wager on the life of a wardmate. We're all in the
same boat here. There's a kind of brotherhood, a bond—"

"What the hell is this now?"

"What?"

"The little old woman who's been sucking lemons. What's she after?"

"Oh. Sister Solace. I should have been expecting her."

As soon as I was back in my bed, she moved as close to me as she could get, grasping my hand with the fervor of one who really had feared that I might not return. She had probably only been concerned that I might die before she managed to console me sufficiently to get full credit for the effort, but nonetheless I was pleased to think that she cared, if only in her own odd, self-centered way. If she cared, perhaps someone else cared, too, and not merely those who had bet on my survival.

"Welcome back," she said. "You've been in my prayers."

"There's a chilling thought," said BW.

"Thank you," I said, with a childlike smile.

"Let's continue, shall we?" She consulted a list, "my" list. She glanced up suddenly, as if something very important had nearly escaped her. "Have you flossed?" she asked.

"I—flossed—sure—I'm not going to let a day go by."

"Wonderful! Now let's get to work on that timidity problem."

"Timidity problem?"

She read from the list: " 'I have been far too timid.' "

"You wrote this?" asked BW.

"Not really—I'll explain," I said. "Go along with the gag."

"What gag? You *have* been far too timid."

"Take it one day at a time," the good Sister urged me. "Tell yourself that you are going to be a bolder person today than you were yesterday."

"Say, I might learn to like this woman," said BW.

"If you have been timid and timorous in the past, apt to flinch at the sound of a backfire, to cringe at the sight of a cockroach, to curl up in a fetal position when it's time to pay your taxes—"

"Apparently she's known you all your life."

"—then today is the day you stand up to someone, or at least to something."

"Tell him, little woman."

"Picture yourself doing so. Visualize yourself doing so. If necessary imagine yourself doing so." She paused. "Are you doing it?"

"I'm trying," I said, "but I don't think I'm very good at this sort of thing."

"Imagine yourself buying a newspaper or a package of breath mints at a newsstand."

"Okay, got it."

"You check the change you're given—"

"She's got you," said BW. "You do that. If you've got fifteen cents coming back, you check to see that it's all there."

"—and to your surprise, you find that the change you have been given is insufficient to make up the full amount that you tendered, after the cost of the goods you have purchased had been taken from it."

"That happens," I said with a shrug.

"Now I want you to see yourself saying, hear yourself saying, feel yourself saying, 'Just a minute there, pal, you owe me another nickel.' "

"She's tough," said BW.

She looked at me, tilted her head, and raised an eyebrow. Apparently she wanted me to actually say it.

"Just a minute there, pal," I said with as much annealed iron in my voice as I could manage in a hospital bed, "you owe me another nickel."

"You want I bust your fuckin' head?" growled BW. "Ged ouda heah."

I laughed. Sister Solace took it for self-satisfaction.

"See?" she said. "You can do it. Now I'll bet you're eager to get out of here and give it a try. Well, I'm sure it won't be long." She gave me a consoling pat and moved on to her next charge.

I FELT GOOD. I thought that the angiogram had gone well, and I felt better now that it had been done, not merely because it was over, but because I was allowing myself to think that it had cured whatever malady my heart might have had. I was beginning to think that I would like some company, some visitors. I was thinking, just trying the idea on for size, that I might call my ex-wife, Liz, or my ex-girlfriend, Belinda, or my ex-girlfriend's daughter, Leila, or my old friend, not ex-friend, Effie, and when I thought of calling Effie, my heart leapt up, and felt not at all like a sick or wounded heart but like a heart in love, a strong heart, an engine. I was quite surprised by the feeling when first I felt it, but as little as a couple of heartbeats later I wasn't surprised at all. Effie. Of course. I was in love with Effie.

"Mr. Barber?"

"Yes?"

It was the eldest of the doctors who had stood at the foot of the slab in the cath lab, the eminence, now standing at the foot of my bed.

"I'd like to talk to you about your heart and discuss the options open to you."

There was in his tone something that said that the options would be few.

"Did I have a heart attack?"

"Yes. A mild one. There has been some tissue damage. Some death of tissue in the heart. You don't want to have another."

"No," I said.

Without my noticing it, Cerise had moved beside my bed.

"This is nice," said BW. "This is very nice."

She took my hand, in the kindest and most compassionate way, and her kindness and compassion sent fear coursing through me like an icy version of the flush-inducing dye. I paled. I shivered. I looked at the beautiful Cerise. She returned my look with the sort of look she might have worn had the eminence just drawn the bedsheet over my lifeless face. I like to think that it was a look of regret for what might have been, for all that might have passed between us if I had survived.

"Shit," said BW. "I don't like the direction this is taking."

"You have a significant blockage in two of the arteries that bring blood to the heart," said the eminence.

"That doesn't sound good," I said.

"I should have stayed where I was," said BW.

Cerise tightened her grip on my hand and raised it, bringing her other hand around it, too, so that she was now holding my hand at about the level of her waist.

"In my opinion," the eminence continued, "we should perform an angioplasty to reduce the size of those blockages and enlarge the arteries, then follow that up with medication that will reduce the level of blood cholesterol, reducing the likelihood of this occurring again."

I allowed myself to squeeze Cerise's hand a bit, and she was so kind as to press my hand against her belly.

"When will we do this?" I asked.

"As soon as I can schedule you for the lab again," he said. "Tomorrow afternoon?"

"Okay," I said, cool as steel, a battle-scarred veteran of life's slings and arrows.

"CERISE," I said, when the eminence had left us, "may I use the phone?" Thinking of Liz and Belinda and Leila and Effie had taken my thoughts out of the ward, out of the hospital, out into the city, where all the minutiae of my out-of-hospital life whirled around me like litter thrown up by a dust devil on a turbulent day. I saw it all, all at once, and it dizzied me, daunted me, intimidated me, but I wasn't going to be intimidated anymore, wasn't even going to be the sort of person who could be intimidated anymore. In the workaday world, I was, I saw from the stationery and business cards in the swirling trash, not merely an employee of a toy company, but one of its vice presidents. What a ridiculous occupation for a grown man. Two ridiculous occupations: toy-company executive and restaurant reviewer. That would have to change. Mentally reading the information on my own business card, held at arm's length in my mind's eye, I called my office. I said that I was under the weather and wouldn't be in for a few days. I offered no further information, didn't mention the hospital or my heart, and I hung up without giving a number where I could be reached. Such behavior would cause talk. It might eventually come to be regarded as having been the first little mistake that led to the end of my career in the toy business. So be it. I was embarking on another career. I was going to make myself worthy of Effie, woo her, and win her.

I dialed her number. I didn't have to think about it or try to recall it. I just punched the numbers. Apparently I called her often enough to know the number well.

"Hello?"

Her voice brought everything back. If what we mean by the past is nothing more than what we remember, then my brain held all I knew of Effie, and the sound of her voice set off an electrical storm in there, with every memory crackling back and forth and amplifying every other. Graduate school. Her enthusiasm for teaching. Her bewildering choice of law school. Her pro bono work for the downtrodden and neglected. Her resilient idealism. Her sweet smile. Her perfect little breasts. Her annoying husband.

"Effie, it's Matthew."

"Matthew! Hi. How are you?"

"Not so well, to tell the truth."

where I hoped to find a quiet spot so that I could prepare myself for meeting Effie in the morning. I hoped to bring all I wanted to say to her to the eloquent simplicity of I-know-me-too.

"You're as good as in there," said BW.

"You—you disgust me—go away."

"I've been away."

"Be away again."

"I will, I hope, but I'm here quite specifically to help you with something."

"I can't think of anything that I could possibly want your help with."

"That cabdriver—"

"Cabdriver," I said, instantly disconsolate. I had allowed myself to forget that cabdriver.

"About that cabdriver—"

"I've done a horrible thing. I'm guilty of a terrible act."

"Matthew—"

"I could be caught. Tried. Convicted. Executed."

"Calm down."

"I can be found. I can be tracked down. I used my credit card at the bar. Left it there. I picked up the check. What a fool."

"Have you checked the newspapers? Have you seen any report of the incident? Any headlines screaming MURDER IN CHARLESTOWN?"

"No—but maybe the body hasn't been discovered yet. Maybe he isn't dead. He might be in this hospital now. Maybe it hasn't been reported."

"Hmm. That's an interesting possibility. Now why do you suppose it might not have been reported?"

"Maybe the kids paid him off. Paid him to keep quiet."

"But why would they? They wouldn't be trying to protect you."

"Well—maybe the cabbie thought the kids and I really were together. Maybe he threatened them with the cops and they paid him to be quiet. They'd be worried about losing their allowances."

"Look—"

"Wait a minute. This is a bit of luck. I didn't use my own name with the kids. I told them to call me BW. None of them knows who I am."

"Permit me to point out that the name B. W. Beath is published throughout Boston and the surrounding metropolitan area above each of

"What's wrong?" she asked, with real concern. Perhaps she l[c]
as I loved her. Or perhaps it was only a deep and enduring friends[
if so it was strong and genuine, and could be turned to love. I cou[
her, if I could make myself worthy of her.

"A pushover," said BW. "She's as good as yours."

I tried to ignore him.

"I've had a heart attack. I'm in Charlesbank."

"Oh, no. Can I see you?"

"Yes. I'm sure—" Had there been visitors in the ward? I hadn't
ticed. But surely a man scheduled for angioplasty would not be den[
the solace of a visit from the woman he loved.

"I'm on my way."

My heart raced. I saw it on the monitor. I was going into a panic.
wasn't ready to see her. I wasn't presentable. I hadn't thought about wha[
I was going to say.

"Tomorrow, if that's okay," I said. "I want to see you, need to see you,
more than I can say, but tomorrow morning. Okay?"

"Okay." She was disappointed. I could hear her disappointment. How
wonderful it was to hear her disappointment. "Does Liz know? Do you
want me to—"

"No. Not yet. No one knows but you. I'll take care of all that, but after I've seen you. I really need to see you, want to see you."

"Okay. I'll be there as early as they'll let me in."

"Thanks." I took a breath. "I love you." I said it as I meant it, as a
lover, not as a friend.

She paused for the length of my new basic unit of time, a heartbeat,
and then said, "I know. Me too."

She hung up. There was no need for her to say goodbye. "I know" and
"Me too" were entirely sufficient, four little words, said softly and deliberately, as if she had been expecting me to declare myself for a very long
time and had thought about her reply for an equally long time. They had
about them the simplicity that comes after long deliberation. "I know"
encapsulated all our history. "Me too" offered us a future.

ELATED, I got myself out of bed and, walking with my right leg straight
to avoid disturbing the sheath in my groin, made my way to the sunroom,

my highly regarded and avidly devoured evaluations of the city's restaurants and watering holes."

"Maybe the driver couldn't go to the police. He might be an illegal immigrant. That's a real possibility. I can get away with this."

"Well, well, well. You've turned a corner there, Matthew, my lad."

"I've been here in the hospital for a while, out of sight. When I get out, I could take a leave of absence. For my health. Go away somewhere. That makes perfect sense."

" 'Hide out till it blows over,' as they used to say in old movies. No one will ever know."

"I will know."

"You didn't quite make it around that corner, after all."

"In my heart, I will know."

"Cue the violins."

"I'll always be stained by it. My soul is blemished."

"I could have predicted we'd get to the blemished-soul idea eventually."

"This cannot be undone. Heretofore I have lived—"

" 'Heretofore'? Well, lah-di-dah."

"—I have lived all my life, with only momentary lapses, trying to do the right thing—"

"Are you kidding?"

"—and worrying that I might do something wrong."

"That I'll grant you."

"Even, at times, worrying that what I thought was the right thing might be the wrong thing."

"That I will also grant you."

"Now, at a stroke, I have done a thing that is unambiguously wrong, and it has made me marvel at how little I have done that has been right."

"Wait a minute—you're rehearsing, aren't you?"

"In being so assiduous about not doing wrong, I have done almost nothing right."

"It's a pitch. You're practicing a pitch. You're hoping to sell yourself to Effie."

"I think there was a time, when you and I were young, when I meant to do right, not merely to avoid doing wrong."

"You want her to take you on as a project, add you to her good works."

"I'm not a bad man. I could have done more that was good, but at least I haven't done so very many things that were bad."

"Let's see—murdering a cabdriver—"

"Just one."

"One that counts for quite a lot, though."

"I can expiate that one. There is still time. I can do enough that is right to outweigh that one wrong."

"Sure. Why not. How much could it take?"

"Can I do this alone? No. I need help. I need you, Effie. In so many ways that I have not allowed myself to admit to myself, you are my better self, my 'better half,' as people used to say."

"Just a gol-darn minute there, pal—"

"You are what has been missing from my life. Together, we can do something that is good and right."

"I'm beginning to feel superfluous."

"What a team we could be. You will bring the zeal and the deep understanding of the right thing to do. You will bring the conviction that will keep us from flagging. I will bring my business skills."

"I've got to hand it to you—you really know how to sweet-talk the gals."

"Maybe that doesn't sound like much, 'my business skills.' It is what I have to offer, though. I know how to get things done. I've learned how to get things done. I've learned how to get people to do a job. You don't know that, Effie."

"She'll be melting into your arms."

"I can't say that to her, can I?"

"Not unless you're trying to send her out of the room in tears, vowing never to speak to you again."

"It's true, though. I could help her. Again and again, when she has laid out one of her projects for me, in the few minutes we have to talk at a party or a dinner, I've told myself that she would need organizational savvy to succeed, and that she didn't have it, and that without it she was going to fail."

"Oh, well, 'organizational savvy.' Why didn't you say so? That's much sexier than 'business skills.'"

"All right. I won't say any of that, but I'll join her. I'll work alongside her. Together we will do good things. Great things. Together we will be whole."

"That sounds wonderful. Just wonderful." He sighed theatrically and said, "If only you didn't have to tell her about killing that cabdriver."

"Oh. That."

"She isn't going to like that. I suspect that she disapproves of killing cabdrivers on principle."

"She is a woman of principles."

"She is that—and probably pretty solidly antimurder. You know how those do-gooders are."

"But I have to tell her. If I don't—it will stand between us."

"Okay. I've had enough of this."

"It will always be there, preventing us from being truly together."

"Matthew—"

"Like an uninvited guest—"

"Before you go any further on the uninvited guest theme, give me just a moment to fulfill my mission."

"Mission?"

"My reason for coming back to you, Matthew, my boy."

"Just to annoy me—that was my assumption."

"I came to tell you that you never even hit him."

"What?"

"You swung. You missed."

"Missed? But I felt it—felt the bar hit him—"

"I was there. I saw it. I saw the whole thing."

"I can still feel it—feel the memory of it."

"I know what I saw."

"I saw blood."

"You think you did. I witnessed no blow, saw no blood."

"I know I did."

"I hate to be critical, but you want to believe that you saw blood."

"That is a disgusting accusation."

"You want to make yourself more interesting for Effie. A greater challenge. A more difficult undertaking."

"Ridiculous."

"Yes, it is."

"I don't believe you."

"You will."

"What do you mean by that?"

"In time, you will believe what I'm telling you."

"You want me to believe that I didn't hit him?"

"As I said, it was a swing and a miss."

"If that's the case, then—"

"There is no need to say anything about it, to anyone, ever."

"It might as well not have happened."

"It might as well not have happened."

Chapter 21

As Matthew, I Reject a Self-Improvement Plan

Jack was a healthy young lad, but he did not like to work, and would sit at his ease all day long, and not think of the many ways in which he might make himself useful. . . . He had not a bad heart, but was so heedless that he scarcely noticed what was going on around him.

—"Jack and the Beanstalk," from the Young Folks Series, 1888

I WENT BACK TO THE WARD and slept for a while, but in the night the nurse who woke me every night to draw blood from my arm woke me again. As usually happened, I awakened while she was already in the act of drawing blood from my arm, and as always she treated me gently, cooed to me, and comforted me. When she had finished, when she withdrew the needle from my arm, I said, "Thank you."

She ran her hand along my arm, caressing me, as always.

"Thank you for—comforting me," I said.

"You're quite welcome," she whispered.

"I need a little comforting now and then."

"I know," she said. "Me too."

Those four words. *I know. Me too.* Effie's words. How dare this night nurse use them? She smiled, but I saw now that it was an automatic smile. The tenderness that had seemed to be in her appeared too easily, as if she were mocking me.

When she was gone, I whispered to BW, "Did you hear that?"

"I heard it."

"She's got her nerve. 'I know. Me too.' As if just anyone could use those words, those four particular words in that particular order. They should be Effie's forever."

"A moment ago, your heart was bursting with gratitude for her comforting touch, and now you would deny her four little words?"

"They're Effie's words. Effie's and mine."

"Go back to sleep."

"I can't. I need to get up and walk around a bit."

I PACED THE SUNROOM for a while, then stood at the window, in the middle of the night, looking out at the street, watching, with idle interest, the slowly passing cars, few and far between, wondering where those people were going at this lonely hour, and wondering what kind of reception I might get from Effie in the morning when I told her about my plans to remake myself. BW seemed to have stayed in the ward to sleep. I felt that I was alone. I could think without fear of ridicule. I could let my thoughts go where they would. I could worry as much as I wished. I could even wring my hands a bit if I wanted to do so. I did. Would Effie see that I was sincere? Would she applaud my intentions? Would she decide on the spot to leave her husband, Richard, and be with me? Or would her sweet little face contort with pity? Would she struggle to suppress a laugh? If I were to die in the afternoon, on the cold slab in the cath lab, would she miss me? Would she regret the time we never spent together? I began to doubt my chances, and all the hope that I'd invested in Effie's affection for me. I began to doubt that anyone would miss me very much, and I began to doubt that Effie thought of me, felt about me, any differently from anyone else. If she felt anything, I feared that it might be something painfully close to pity. Would she even wait while I underwent my ordeal downstairs? She would. Of course she would. She had said, "I know. Me too." Those were the words of a woman who would wait—except when they were usurped for baser uses by people who barely understood them. She would wait here, in the sunroom. *What a shame,* she would think when they brought the news of the catastrophe in the cath lab. *What a shame that he never became the man I once thought he might have been. What a shame.*

"It would be nice if she would let up on the not-the-man-he-might-have-been business and spend a dreamy while imagining the sex you might have had."

"I thought you were asleep."

"I was. I'm not."

"Feel free to go back to sleep at any time."

"I had a bit of an insight, or perhaps it was an inspiration, during my brief doze."

"And now I'm going to hear all about it."

"The thought occurred to me that while you are renovating the old Matthew you might work toward something along the lines of your old friend Peter Leroy. There is a man!"

"Peter? He's a feckless dreamer."

"A dreamer, yes, but he has the luck of Jack about him. The luck and the pluck of Jack. Jack's luck, Jack's pluck."

"Jack?"

"The lucky, plucky lad of beanstalk fame. Seller of cow. Planter of beans. Climber of stalk. Stealer of goose. Slayer of giant."

"Feckless, too, wasn't he?"

"Only early on. He did steal the goose and bags of money and regain the family castle, remember, and the tale teaches us, I think, that pluck begets feck, in the long run."

A nurse came up to me softly and asked, "Mr. Barber?"

"Matthew," I said.

"Can I get you anything? Do you want some juice? Coffee?"

"No," I said. "No, thank you."

"A sympathetic ear?"

"No. No, thank you. That's very kind, but I'm okay."

"I thought you were talking to someone—"

"I—I guess I was talking to myself—"

"Are you sure you wouldn't like to sit and talk for a while?"

I would have loved to tell her everything, everything that I had done, everything that I was thinking, hoping, but she would never have understood, not really, not fully, and I couldn't have made her understand, couldn't have exposed myself sufficiently fully for her to understand me, not in the time available to me.

"I guess not," I said. "I'll go back to bed. In a minute."

She smiled and turned to go.

"Tell me something," I said, on impulse. "Which direction are we facing?"

"Ah—let's see—it's—south."

"You're sure?"

"I think so. Yes. I'm sure."

"Thanks. I just—wanted to get my bearings. It's foolish, I guess, but I wanted to know where I was. It's something I like to—something I need to know. I need to know which way is which."

"I know," she said. "Me too."

She really did seem to know exactly what I meant. There was in her voice a tone of real understanding, as if she had experienced precisely the need I had been trying to describe to her.

"They must teach that tone in nursing school," said BW. "Fascinating."

"It was real this time."

"And the words?"

"Words?"

"She said, 'I-know-me-too.' "

"Oh. She did? I didn't notice."

I sat for a while just looking out at the night, because I didn't want the nurse to see me try to figure out which way my bed was facing. When enough time had passed, I walked back to the ward, keeping careful track of the turns I took, and back to my bed. It faced east. I tried to convince myself that it was an omen, that by facing east when morning came I would be ready for something new, ready to become someone new.

"Someone more like your friend Peter."

"A feckless bumpkin? No, thank you."

"It was 'feckless dreamer' last time."

"Feckless just the same."

"But plucky. You've got to give him that."

"I'll give him that if you insist."

"And essentially happy, happy at heart, unlike my present interlocutor."

"Ignorance is bliss, if I remember correctly."

Chapter 22

As Matthew, I Am Forced to Alter My Assumptions

pity this busy monster,manunkind,
not.

—e. e. cummings

WHEN I WOKE the next morning, the morning of the big day, the day of my transfiguration, Effie day, I knew where I was. I knew that I was facing east, and I knew that I was in the Charlesbank Hospital. I experienced no moment of disorientation during which I wondered where I was, wondered why I wasn't in my own bed. I was pleased that there was no disorientation. I like to know where I am, especially when I don't quite know who I am.

While I was flossing my teeth, the thought occurred to me that I might confess to Effie. Not merely tell her about the cabdriver, but make it a confession. Admit all. Throw myself on her mercy. And yet, in that contemplative Zen-like state that comes over one while flossing, I asked myself whether it was really possible that nothing had happened—nothing criminal, that is.

"More than possible," said BW. "As I told you, that's the way it was."

"It's true that I haven't seen any notice in the paper."

"Nor will you."

"Can it be possible that what I feel so guilty about never happened?"

"You've had dreams that you thought were real—"

"Yes, that's true."

"You've embarrassed yourself sometimes by speaking of things that never happened, that you've dreamt."

"You're right. It's like Cerise's theory of time."

"Cerise's theory of time. I must have been absent when that was discussed. Will it be on the exam?"

"It's not really her theory. She collects them—theories of time. One of them says that what we call the past is nothing more than memory, and memory is just a state of organization of the neural networks in the brain."

"One can almost dance to it."

"Could it be that the fight with the cabdriver happened only in my memory? Never in fact?"

"My version is quite a bit simpler."

"Why shouldn't memory be just as clever as imagination, just as inventive? If imagination can envision things that might be but never yet have been, why shouldn't memory be as adept at recalling things that never were?"

"I can see no reason."

"The fight, such as it was, might only have occurred in those moments that are still missing from my memory, the time between my watching you get into the taxi as I fell through the automatic doors and the time when a nurse put a nitroglycerine patch on me."

"As a tussle in the tangled tentacles of the neural network that is you?"

"Yes. That. That, and nothing more."

"And so, when dear little Effie of the heart-shaped face arrives, it would probably be best to say nothing at all about it, since it is certain to sound to her like the crazed raving of a man who's slipped off his rocker and onto the floor."

"Matthew?"

There she was. Effie. Standing at the foot of my bed, leaning toward me, tentatively, as if she were not quite sure that the man she saw was me.

"Yes," I said. "It's me. I must look a little odd—"

"You do look a little pale," she said, coming at once to my side, leaning over me, and kissing me with all the affection of a friend of very many years, without a word about having thought that I was not alone because I had seemed to be talking to someone.

"Effie. Sit. Please. Sit here. Bring the chair close. Pull the curtain, will you? Just pull it around on that slider. That's it. I want to talk to you. I want to say something to you. I want to say many, many things to you."

"I brought you a book—and a little CARE package of spices and hot sauces—for the hospital food—"

"Thank you, but first I want to talk to you, okay?"

"Okay."

"Effie—"

"Matthew?"

"Don't interrupt me."

"I didn't mean to. I didn't think you had started."

"It's just that I have to say all of this straight through without interruption or I'll never say it all. I'll lose the—pluck."

"Pluck?"

"Courage."

"Oh. Right. Like 'plucky lad.'"

"Exactly. Ready?"

"Ready."

"Here goes." I took a breath. I smiled at her. "Effie," I said, "I love you."

"I know—"

I raised my hand.

"Oops. Sorry."

"I have loved you for years, for so long that I'm not certain when I started loving you. I'm tempted to say from the start, from the moment we met—"

"Too pat," whispered BW.

"I'd say that except that it sounds so pat that it makes the claim of love seem as unlikely as the claim of love at first sight, so I'll say that I think it may have been the morning when I came to your place to go to work with you and you had a cold or something or possibly just didn't feel that you could go to work that day and I made you toast and tea and you sat up in bed with your little breasts exposed as if our intimacy was an assumed thing. If not earlier, it was then."

"From the look on her face, I'd say that she doesn't remember that particular morning."

"You may not remember that. You may not have thought anything about it at the time, but it made me feel as close to you as a—"

"Not 'husband'! She has a husband."

"—a lover—as close as if we were lovers—and had been lovers for some time. I wished that we had been. I still do. And this love that I feel for you has deepened over the years, grown and deepened."

She squeezed my hand and smiled.

"That's good," said BW. "That girlish smile. She likes this."

"Over the years, as my love has grown, so has my admiration. I've watched what you've done, all the good things you've done, admiring you from a distance."

That brought a frown to her face, and a shake of the head, but also another squeeze. I pressed on.

"And I've admired you so much—the way you've always gone to bat for the downtrodden and needy. You've made me proud. I ought to be ashamed to say that, because there's something possessive about it, as if I had had some influence on you that made you do the wonderful things that you've done. I've felt pride because—because of what I said about feeling that we were lovers. You weren't just 'Effie.' You were 'my Effie.' "

"That's better. The girlish smile is back."

"Lying in a hospital bed gives a person time to think. Perhaps too much time to think. If you're afflicted with a life-threatening disease, as I seem to be, your thinking is likely to turn toward questions of mortality— actually, toward questions of vitality and mortality, life and death. Am I going to die? Well, yes. Am I going to die now? Maybe. Am I going to die happy? In my case, no. Fulfilled? No."

"You're rolling. This is good stuff. I didn't think you had it in you."

"But suppose I'm not going to die now. Suppose I survive this. Suppose I leave here, alive, and I am allowed to think of this episode as 'just a warning.' What will that warning have been? I've come to understand that it will be the old, old warning: you must change your life. I've heard the warning, and I will change my life. And I'm not just talking about taking better care of my heart. There must be more. There must be a purpose to my living if I'm allowed to live. And the 'I' who is allowed to live must be worthy of the gift of life. So I must change my self as well. And I will. But in what way? To what end? I know the answer to that, too. I will make myself worthy of you, Effie." I put my finger to my lips quickly because I could see that she meant to speak. "Effie, I want to ask something of you," I said, squeezing her hand. "Let me be with you, in some way, any way. I would love to be your lover, but I'd settle for being—anything. Your friend. Your disciple. Just take me in. Let me be with you. Be my reason for living. Be my reason for being a better man."

I was finished, and I felt that I had finished badly. I had intended to show her that I could be useful to her. I'd wanted to say something about our becoming a team.

"Oh, Matthew, I don't know how to tell you this," she said, with a squeeze of the hand that I recognized as a squeeze that was meant to confer solace.

"Oh, that's not good," muttered BW. "Those words are rarely a preamble to 'I just can't live without you.' "

"I've just barely begun to admit this to myself," she said, looking down at the floor. "I hardly have the words for it, although I find sometimes that I'm talking to myself about it. All those things that you said about me, the things I've tried to do, they—I—I've failed—completely failed."

"No," I said. "Failed? You haven't failed. You've done wonderful things. You—"

"It's my turn to ask you not to interrupt," she said.

"Sorry."

"I tried. I'll give myself that. I tried to help. I tried to save everybody. I tried to save people from—themselves. I failed"—she put her finger to her lips as I had done, and I stopped myself from objecting—"but I don't think that anyone could have succeeded. People are not really—susceptible of improvement."

"There's more to this girl than I thought," said BW with something like pride in his voice.

"I have followed an arc of disappointment and disillusionment that I could never have predicted. I began as a compassionate girl—before you even knew me—when I was a girl—a child. I was the one who wanted to adopt the stray dogs and orphans. And I did—to the degree that a girl can. Then one day I began to ask why there should be stray dogs and orphans. How could people, collectively, allow so many to suffer in the midst of plenty? Something should be done. Somebody ought to do something. And that began a lifetime of trying to make people see that something should be done and trying to push them into doing something." She drew a breath and shook her head. "What a waste it has been—a waste of time and effort. It has cost me my marriage—and the affection and companionship of my children—and it has all added up to nothing—to less than nothing, because people have gone on making a mess of things far faster than I could clean up after them."

"Did you catch that about her marriage?"

"I did, but shut up. I'm listening."

"Worst of all, I guess, it has cost me all my illusions about what I once thought was the essential goodness of people, of human beings as a species. We're not good. We're really quite awful. 'This busy monster, manunkind.' Remember the poem?"

I nodded.

"Manunkind." She repeated it with a sigh and a frown. "As a species, we seem to be a case of arrested development. Actually, I'll say to you what I say to myself. I think 'they' are a case of arrested development. I think I'm better than they are. I'm sorry that I'm one of them. I'm ashamed to be human. I despise my species."

"This is one of those moments when one would like to hear 'present company excepted,' don't you think?"

"Shh."

"We are still fighting over whose fallacies are true, whose fantasies are real, whose superstitions are proof against death, whose system of oppressing the weak and stealing from the poor is the one right way to run the world. We claim—and many of us really believe, more's the pity—that we have God or justice or right or destiny on our side. We kill—rape, torture, mutilate, and maim—in the name of all that we hold good and holy."

"Don't you and I have an appointment in the cath lab, Matthew?"

"We get it wrong, always, in every possible sense of wrong. And we consume everything in sight, laying waste to all the world. Eat it, use it, kill it, slash it, burn it, pave it, mark it as ours, ours! We seem to be on a blind mission to mark every inch of the planet with our scat. We bully the other creatures as mercilessly as we bully the weak among our own. We will not share. We will not play fair. We are not the best species to hold dominion over this planet. The other animals are much easier on our earthly paradise and much kinder to one another. They don't band together to vanquish and subject the other tribes. It's a shame that we are even here."

"She's beginning to sound like a lapsed Corellian."

"Why did we have to evolve into a beast with enough intelligence to ruin everything but not enough to restrain ourselves from doing it? We are unworthy of ourselves, and we live in a manner that is unworthy of the gift of life. Getting and spending and laying waste—I can't bear to watch it any longer." She put her hand to her brow and shook her head. "I'll tell you what was the last straw. I volunteered as counsel for a nonprofit group, the Hamlet Project. I think I told you about them, didn't I?"

"I—I guess you did—yes—"

"Well, I went to one of these meetings they hold to try to convince people to endorse the little Shangri-la they're going to build for them, and I sat there getting more and more disgusted. The rancor, the suspicion, the pettiness, the underlying hatred and envy, the underlying greediness and stupidity of these people. After a while, sitting there in that hot room, they began to smell, and I began to feel sick. I said to myself, 'Why am I trying to improve these people? Why am I trying to improve people, period? It will take a million years before they are what I wish they would be.' That's when I decided that I didn't want anything more to do with them. I'm leaving. I refuse to bear witness to all the awful things that human beings do. In another age, I would be retiring to a charterhouse. I'm going to Maine. Richard is letting me have the cabin there. I will not watch this horrible farce any longer. I'm going to step aside from life for a while, human life, all the affairs of manunkind. I'll tend my garden. I'll try to live so that I do as little harm as possible. I won't take a paper, I won't watch television, I won't listen to the radio. If people are going to make a mess of everything, they are going to have to do it without me. I won't play my part anymore. I just won't. I will not be a spectator in this circus of horrors."

"Matthew?"

It was Cerise.

"Yes?" I said.

"They're ready for you in the cath lab."

"Oh. Effie—"

She squeezed my hand again. I thought I saw, in the blinking of her eyes, the suggestion that she might cry.

"Will you wait for me?" I asked. "Wait till I get back from the angioplasty?"

"Of course I'll wait. I'll be right here—or wherever I'm allowed to wait."

"The sunroom is probably best," said Cerise.

An orderly wheeled a gurney beside my bed, and I shifted myself onto it. During the transfer operation, not a maneuver that displayed me to best advantage, the thought occurred to me that it would be polite to introduce Cerise and Effie, but I never got the chance because Sister Solace appeared, in her sudden, silent way, and said, "There is a chance that he won't come back."

"What?" ejaculated Effie, demonstrating by the force and suddenness of her utterance that even one so thoroughly disillusioned by the behavior of her fellow creatures could still be shocked.

"We're required to tell you that," said Cerise, apologetically.

"The insurance company makes us say it," added the good sister.

"Your chances are very, very good," said Cerise. "Only a tiny percentage of patients who undergo the angioplasty procedure experience any complications at all."

"And only a very small percentage of those actually die," said Sister Solace, "but the fact that some do might make you want to see if you can't get in one quick little bit of reform work before you go down there. Why don't you call your mother?"

"My mother is dead."

"Dead? But—you—you put on your list—something about—that you ought to call your mother more often."

"That's not my list. It's a list that goes around the ward. I stole it." To the orderly I said, as I might to a cabdriver, "Let's go. I've got an appointment."

"Stole it!" squealed Sister Solace. "Stole it! You didn't even list stealing as one of your shortcomings!"

"It wasn't my list," I repeated as I rolled through the door.

Chapter 23

As Matthew, I Check Out

THEN I NEARLY DIED. That is, Matthew Barber nearly died. It was a matter of belonging to that élite group of patients who experience complications from the procedure and nearly die from them. BW, however, was convinced—and remains convinced—that it was Effie's decision to retire to a cloistered cabin in Maine that nearly killed me, him, us. All the way to the cath lab, he never let up.

"A cabin in Maine," he said. "That sounds cozy."

"She's right, though, about the evils of mankind, humankind, manunkind."

"Oh, of course, but—Maine!"

"It's beautiful."

"It's cold."

"It's peaceful."

"It's cold."

"There is a nobility to what she's doing, I think."

"Let me just remind you that it is cold in Maine."

"This renunciation—or as she put it, a refusal to bear witness—"

"If you want to do something equally noble—"

"I do. I do."

"Then let me go. Let me go somewhere else, somewhere warm, where the women are willing."

"You mean forever? I don't think I can do that. I'd have to do it myself—"

"You could."

"I'm going to Maine—if she'll let me."

"A place renowned throughout the world for the severity of its winters."

"In time, I may persuade her to return to her good works."

"Cold in Maine is like coffee in Brazil: they've got a lot of it."

On the cold steel slab, while I was being angioplastied, he left me alone. Each of us pursued his own thoughts, I suppose. Mine were of the future I had allowed myself to imagine with Effie, a future of good works and, as reward for self-sacrifice, nights of cuddly love and mornings sunny with self-satisfaction. When I was on my way back to the ward, on the gurney, being wheeled by the orderly, I made the mistake of admitting to BW that I regretted the loss of that imagined future.

"I still have a vision of the two of us side by side, serving up steaming bowls of soup to the hungry," I said wistfully. "And yet, if she wants to be reclusive for a while, I'll gladly be reclusive with her."

"Speaking of Maine," he said, "they have an embarrassment of cold up there, a superfluity of it. They are rich in cold, those hardy citizens of Maine."

"Splendid isolation. Snowbound. Alone at last."

"If they chose to, they could export it, so abundant is the supply of cold in Maine."

"I can see the two of us curled up in front of a fire, snuggling, far from all the woes of the world."

"But, no, they won't share their cold, they keep their cold for themselves, those thrifty citizens of Maine, laying down a good supply in the winter months when it falleth from the sky like a gift, so that they'll have it in the summer to put a good chill on the waters of the old swimmin' hole."

"Effie, a crackling fire, a fluffy comforter—"

"Just do me one favor."

"That depends on what the one favor is," I said cagily.

"On nights when your crackling fire and your righteous Effie won't keep *me* warm, when I am chilled beneath your comforter, let me go, for at least a while, where I will."

"And where will you go?"

"I will search for perfect crab cakes. I will strive, and I will seek, and with luck I may find, but find or not, I will not yield."

A coldness gripped me. It was an inner cold, ice at the heart, frigid as death. It deepened, thickened, and spread.

"Something is wrong," I said.

"Nothing's wrong now," said the orderly. "You're all finished. You'll be home tomorrow."

"No," I protested. "Something is happening to me." I was beginning to sweat, and I could feel panic spreading through me as if I'd been injected with it.

We continued into the ward. I was awaited. Effie was not there, not that I could see, but Cerise was, and Sister Solace, and a male nurse whom I recognized, and my fellow inmates. All turned toward the entrance at the sound of the creaking and rumbling gurney.

"Something is wrong," I announced as I came rolling in.

"Matthew?" Effie was there, beside me, holding my hand.

"Effie. I wanted to go to Maine—"

Suddenly I was surrounded.

"What are you feeling?" asked the eminence in the deep voice with which eminences are endowed.

"I'm going numb," I said, "and cold, and I'm full of anxiety—I can't keep still."

"Get him back down to the lab," said the em. "Call down and have it cleared for him. I'll be right there myself."

We hurtled along the corridors. It was a wild, wild gurney ride, great fun in memory, a nightmare in the moment. The obvious urgency of the rushing orderly stunned the onlookers into silence as we came by, the metal rattling and ringing with his hustle, a man with a mission, on a matter of life and death. I was, for a moment, as I came rattling by, the center of attention—

"A cynosure, but a momentary cynosure," said BW. "I suppose all cynosures are cynosures for a moment merely—"

The people I passed observed me openly, with evident concern.

"Oh, yes, with all the passing passion of spectators at any of the miniature dramas chance provides to spice a day. You are a break in the routine. Your passing on a ringing gurney may not be enough to be remembered, but it is enough to slice the morning in two for some of your spectators, into 'before the guy came by on the gurney' and 'after the guy came by on the gurney,' with the guy on the gurney—the guys on the gurney, if you like—moving through the hospital like a sweeping second hand, marking time."

"You're enjoying this, aren't you?" I said.

"In my way," he admitted. "It's all part of the show."

"I knew that a part of me was enjoying it—but I hadn't realized which part. I don't think I've ever—shared your feelings before."

"Oh, please."

"No—I mean—we have our conversations—but I've never been aware of feeling what you feel—or thinking what you think—before. You're real, aren't you?"

"As real as any of the other phenomena within your mind, Matthew. As real as a memory. As real as a wish."

"I envy you."

"For what?"

"I envy you—and I'm fully aware that you are part of me, but I envy you all the same—for having found the secret to enjoying life."

"Ah. Yes. You envy me my skill as a passionate spectator."

"I do. Yes. For you, I recognize now, there really is some part of every experience that is a pleasure."

"Well, at least a diverting curiosity."

"I envy that attitude. I want some of it."

"Come wandering with me. We'll go on the bummel."

"No. No. I'm not ready for that. I never will be ready for that, I think. I don't want to be you, don't even want to imagine being you for a greater part of every day than I already spend imagining being you, but I wish that I could achieve some smooth synthesis of the two of us."

"A sort of Matthew Beath? Or B. W. Barber?"

"Or—"

"Mr. Barber?" said the voice of the eminence when I was again flat on my back on the steel slab.

"Yes?" I said, impatient with him for interrupting.

"We're going to use a different type of device this time."

"Fine," I said, eager to have them get at it so that I could go back to my mental work.

"In the procedure you had earlier, a balloon is inflated within the artery to compress the plaque against the arterial walls. However, the balloon can be left inflated for only a limited period of time, because the balloon itself blocks the flow of blood. This time we will be using a balloon that is actually shaped like an elongated doughnut, so that when it is inflated there is a hole in the center through which blood can flow. This allows us to leave the balloon inflated for a longer period of time."

"Sounds good," I said, and laughed when I realized how idiotic I sounded saying so.

"Make yourself as comfortable as you can," he said, in a tone that was almost, but not quite, apologetic, "because you'll be lying here for a while."

"Go to it," I said.

"And try to get it right this time. My attorney is waiting for me in the sunroom."

"What?"

"My fiancée is waiting for me in the sunroom," I muttered.

He clenched his jaw, gave me a tap on the shoulder, and nodded in the manner of one determined not to make a fiancée a widow before she has been a wife.

"Where were we?"

"You were saying that you wished you could achieve a synthesis of the two of us: Matthew Beath or B. W. Barber."

"Or something that you suggested to me—whenever it was—when we were awake in the middle of the night and I was worrying about how to make myself acceptable to Effie."

"I believe that I suggested a Matthew Barber renovated in the style of your old friend Peter."

"Yes."

"You, however, dismissed him as a feckless dreamer."

"I still think he's a dreamer, and I still think he's feckless, but I liked what you said about his having pluck. I've never had much pluck. I'd like to have some pluck."

The catheter snaked its way into my heart.

"Am I to gather that you are thinking—" he began.

"I'm thinking of a three-part amalgamation, just thinking about it, and right now, focusing my thoughts, I am making a deliberate attempt to imagine what life might be like . . . as Peter Leroy."

Chapter 24

I Am Called for a Voir Dire

If you see a good promotion idea, steal it. Morality does not enter this particular picture. You are competing with everyone else who is selling something. You probably thought that you were just competing with the other taxidermists in the neighborhood, right? Wrong, wrong, wrong. Who says people have to spend their money on taxidermy? Not only do they not have to spend their money on taxidermy, but there are manicurists and pedicurists out there who are trying to get them to spend the taxidermy budget on their hands and feet.

—Darryl O'Farrell, *Creative Self-Promotion for Taxidermists*

DARRYL O'FARRELL IS A GENIUS. Everything he says is inspiring. After reading the passage that I have placed as headnote to this chapter, I began to look around me for promotional ideas to steal, and I seemed to find a good idea everywhere I looked. I even ran into a good idea—literally. Perhaps Darryl O'Farrell's words had spurred me into a particularly receptive and creative frame of mind, or perhaps the morning was an extraordinary one, singularly rich in examples of promotional ideas as some mornings are singularly rich in the odor of curbside garbage, but I seemed to see techniques worth stealing all around me. For example, while I was on the crosstown bus, heading for the subway, I noticed that there were placards on the bus, advertising cards that fit into frames attached to the curved area where the sides of the bus met the roof. I had noticed these before of course, but only in the inattentive way that one notices on the sidewalks of New York the black blobs that once were chewing gum, noticing them, but not taking the time to stop and examine them, to measure them in order to calculate the mean, median, and mode of their size and volume, not counting the number of blobs on a block in order to extrapolate from that the number in the entire city, so as to calculate the mass of pressed gum citywide, never taking the time to sketch the shapes of a large number of randomly selected blobs to determine whether in the aggregate, on average, their shapes tend toward the circular, nor the time to observe a typical set of blobs to develop actuarial tables for the longevity of blobs in areas with various levels of pedestrian traffic, and certainly never taking the time to write a grant proposal for the study of sidewalk gum blobs, however revealing such a study might be. On this day, the bus placards, formerly no more interesting to me than sidewalk gum blobs, glowed as if lit by lightning. My fellow riders seemed to be reading them avidly. Why had I never noticed how popular a pastime the reading of bus placards was? Wouldn't they be an excellent way to promote my services? Of course they would! Next to

INJURED? OFFENDED? *Sue the Bastards!*
CALL NOW: 555-SUIT

a rider might see

AGING? DYING? *Write your Memoirs!*
CALL NOW: 555-MEMO

A great idea. Great. And right there for the stealing.

"But the trouble with that idea, brilliant though it may be," said Matthew, "is that it would cost money."

"Yeah," I said, crestfallen. "That's the trouble with so very many of my ideas—and Darryl O'Farrell's, to be truthful about it."

As I left the bus, it was with a sinking feeling, caused in part by the realization that it really does take money to make money, and in part by the fact that it was a "kneeling bus," one of those that genuflect to bring the steps closer to the curb before the disembarking passengers descend

FIGURE 7: Lampposters in Manhattan, on East 90th Street.

them. Head down, discouraged again, I elbowed my way through the knot of people waiting to board the bus, clustering as they like to do right at the spot where the disembarking passengers have to pass if they are to get to the subway entrance. I made a quick right to dodge a particularly large example of the urban overfed, when—*bonk*—I was struck by a good idea. Looking up, I saw taped to a lamp pole several homemade advertisements for independent contractors in the service sector of the economy. Here was a method of self-promotion that I could put into effect for next to nothing. This was worth stealing.

INVIGORATED AND EMBOLDENED by my own stroke of promotional brilliance, I entered the Jury Assembly Room determined to approach Sullivan Sullivan about writing his memoirs. If necessary, I was prepared to employ flattery. I would praise his style. People like to have their style praised. They like to think that they have a style. They particularly like to think that they have "a certain style."

"Chief Clerk Sullivan," I planned to say, "I was fascinated by your booklet on the reliability of witnesses. Not only was it chock-full of thought-provoking ideas, but it had a certain style, too, I thought."

I was surprised to see a trio of potential jurors clustered around the desk at the front of the room, where Sullivan Sullivan was wont to preside. I understood at once what was going on. These people were attempting to curry favor. They reminded me of three classmates of mine in my 'pataphysics seminar in college, a trio of sciolists who were always attempting to curry favor with Professor Gemurmel. Knowsall, Blowhard, and Windbag—I'll never forget them. Knowsall had an irritating way of prefacing any comment with a self-deprecating shrug and an apology for being about to say something that put him in the company of heavyweight thinkers. "I'm afraid this is going to sound a lot like some of the things Spinoza says about the essential unity of all that is, but," he would begin, and then he would make a commonplace observation that his preface had elevated to a level the rest of us couldn't attain even if we actually had something to say. Blowhard's tactic was to drag in an analogy from some arcane science, the folksier the better. "I don't know if you've ever seen the fishmongers of Cadaqués lay the fish they call *merluz* on the grass to dry," he would begin, and then beguile old Gemurmel with a tale out of his summer vacation while the clock ticked toward the end of the hour. Windbag knew only one thing well: the complete works of Samuel Johnson. At the start of a discussion, he clambered up onto Johnson's shoulders, quoted him, sometimes aptly, and considered his oar sufficiently wet for the week. These three fawning jurors put me in mind of them. They put me in mind of them so completely that as I observed them they seemed to metamorphose into Knowsall, Blowhard, and Windbag completely, making allowances for the passage of time. What were they after, I wondered? Maybe they were hoping that Sully would discharge them early or that he would assign them to the trial of their fondest dreams. We all have our dreams. There must be those who dream of sitting in the jury for a ghastly murder, just as there must be those who dream of eating eggplant. Here were three people who were after something, just as they had been back in our 'pataphysics seminar.

"Don't feel so superior," said Matthew. "You are a person after something, too. You want him as a client."

I chuckled at that. "You're right," I admitted, "but I am not going to descend to that fawning business. I'll take a position in the group around Chief Clerk Sullivan, but I will not condescend to join it. I will remain aloof—"

"Merely an observer," said BW, "curious, simply someone who wants to find out what's going on."

"I'm afraid this is going to sound a bit like some of the things that Mario Vargas Llosa said about Flaubert," said the one who resembled Knowsall, while clasping Sully's booklet on the reliability of witnesses to his breast, "but if I understand you correctly, you're suggesting that a witness's testimony is derived from life but never taken directly from life, that the testimony—if you'll forgive the seemingly frivolous comparison—is more like a country sausage, a conglomerate of many experiences, as a sausage is a conglomerate of many bits of pig and many bits of many other things, some of which experiences would seem to an impartial observer to be unrelated to the incident that the witness is testifying about, some even having occurred well before the incident and having been dredged from deep subconscious memory by some attractor element in the incident or in the witness's perception of the incident, and some perhaps not even experiences that the witness has had at firsthand, but possibly remembered bits of books or movies or television news clips or even just rumors that he's heard in bars, and then all of these ingredients get combined higgledy-piggledly in the mixing bowl of the brain, are mixed and mashed and mingled, and are eventually stuffed into the casing of language, and served up to the jury as a digestible, even savory, version of the truth. Is that right?"

"That's a very interesting way of putting it," said Sully, clearly flattered by the adulation of this acolyte.

"Well, it lacks the clarity and rigor of your presentation, of course," said Knowsall, "but—"

"I don't know if you've ever stood in one of those tiny village church-
yards in Ireland on a dewy morning and watched a spider at work on its
web," said the one who resembled Blowhard, "with the dewdrops glis-
tening in the morning light so that you can see the effects on the web of
the shifting tensions imposed by the breeze or the lightest landing of a
mayfly, allowing you to see in the quivering dewdrops the way the data
from the edges are telegraphed to the spider, but if you have, I think you
must be asking yourself, as I am, 'Aren't we really dealing with a network here?' I know that, as I read *On the Reliability of Witnesses,* I was
struck by the insight—implied, I think, by the statement that imagination
is distributed throughout the brain—that the witness's memory estab-
lishes a network of associations among experiences—not merely an ag-
glutination on the order of a sausage, something that is essentially stable,
but rather a vibrant, flexible, and essentially unpredictable information-
processing system that—"

"I'm sure we all recall Samuel Johnson's memorable definition of a
network," said the one who resembled Windbag.

"I know that," I said to myself.

"Better keep it to yourself," cautioned Matthew. "You'll probably get
it wrong."

"Go on and put your oar in," urged BW. "What have you got to lose?"
And he pushed me into the circle.

" 'Any thing reticulated or decussated, at equal distances, with interstices between the intersections,' " I blurted.

"Um, yes. Exactly," said Windbag, looking not at me but at the floor
between us, where the gauntlet would have lain if I had actually thrown
one. "It is, I submit, those interstices that are the little troublemakers," he
went on, chuckling, just as he used to do in Gemurmel's seminar, whenever he supposed he had made a witty remark, "because they invite the
witness to fill them—with almost anything that does not destroy the apparent integrity of the network."

"Isn't that stating the obvious?" I said. "Surely you recall that Chief
Clerk Sullivan mentioned that the stimulus for a witness's inventions may
be a vacancy toward which people seem to turn, a vacancy that implies
a missing someone?"

"Yes, of course, but I—"

"Forgive me for sounding so much like William James," said Knowsall, "but might it not be the case, Chief Clerk Sullivan, that a good deal of the distortion in a witness's testimony arises during the process of consciously trying to recall something forgotten, that effort we make to try to reclaim a certain something that we feel to have been in our mind, even to the extent that we seem to feel that it ought to be in a certain place in the mind, a place to which we keep attempting to turn, but where we find only a vacancy—"

"A vacancy, yes. Exactly that," said Windbag. "That's what I was getting at with the network concept—the spiderweb analogy—"

"If the mind is a network," I said, anticipating him, "then the essence of thought is not information alone but noise as well."

"That's what I was going to say—"

"That's what Chief Clerk Sullivan himself said," I said, flipping the pages of the booklet to find the place. "As I understand it," I continued, not as one of their supplicant number, but as parodist, "our consciousness detects signals from the neural network, but, like an old radio receiver, it also picks up a lot of static. Some of this noise comes from within the network itself, produced by the operation of the neurons and circuits of neurons, noise from within the brain. Other noises come from outside the brain, outside the self. The sources of some of these noises are familiar, homely—like a sidewalk gum blob in the shape of a familiar face, a phrase on a bus placard that echoes a phrase heard long ago and long forgotten, an odor from a bag of garbage that one is sure one has smelled before, but who knows where or when—while other noises reach us from sources that are more distant, exotic, and intriguing—from books, where noise hisses and pops along the page between the lines, from conversations with strangers, where noise crackles around the edges of the import of the talk, detected by the faculty of peripheral audition, from—"

"Okay, okay," said Sullivan. "That's enough. Time to wrap up the bull session and get down to the business of justice. Take a seat, everybody. I'm going to call a bunch of you for a voir dire."

"Have you ever thought of writing your memoirs, Chief Clerk Sullivan?" I asked, besotted by my little victory.

"Take your seat," he growled enthusiastically.

THIS TIME, I was among those called for the voir dire. I took my place in one of the two straight lines in the hallway and, along with the others who had been chosen, journeyed by antique elevator to an upper floor and filed into a courtroom, where I sat in the seat in the gallery to which I was directed by an officer of the court.

A judge presided. A prosecutor stood beside a table before the judge. At another table before the judge sat two defendants, two lawyers, and two interpreters.

"The defendants are charged with the sale of a controlled substance," the prosecutor began. Each of the interpreters bent to the ear of his assigned defendant and repeated the remark, one translating into Haitian French, the other into Dominican Spanish.

"You may have noticed the presence of translators in the court," the prosecutor continued.

Whisper, whisper, mumble, mumble in Haitian French and Dominican Spanish.

"They are here because neither of the defendants will admit to speaking English, the official language of the criminal justice system of the state of New York."

Murmurous translation.

The two defendants turned to look at the potential jurors, *their* potential jurors, the people who might decide their guilt or innocence, the people who might say the word that put them in jail or got them deported. Us.

They looked like frightened children.

"They've probably been coached by their lawyers," said BW. "They've been told to look like frightened children, shown how to look like frightened children."

"If so, it worked," I said. "They do look like frightened children."

"I'm sure they are," said Matthew. "They've probably turned to the sale of controlled substances because the systemic injustices of our government's social policies keep them and their families mired in poverty."

"Where did *that* come from?" asked BW.

"I'm not quite sure," said Matthew.

"I think you're channeling Effie, that sweet young thing with the adorable little breasts who was, once upon a time, determined to save the world, and all the people in it," said BW.

"Don't make her sound like a quitter," Matthew objected. "She's just a little tired. Everyone gets tired after a while, even Effie. She'll bounce back. She's resilient. She's got—"

"Grit?" asked BW. "Gumption? Backbone? Moxie?"

"You know what. She's got it. She does."

"Will you two please shut up?" I said. "Just observe. Make no comments."

A sobering sense of responsibility had settled on me, grave and heavy. I felt myself stiffen under its weight. I looked at my fellow potential jurors. A few of them seemed similarly sobered. Many did not. They still wore the various attitudes of boredom and preoccupation that serve as urban insulation.

Twelve of us were called from the gallery to take seats in the jury box, where we were questioned by the prosecuting and defense attorneys to determine whether we were worthy to sit in judgment of the two frightened boys. I began musing on my essential unworthiness, asking myself whether there was anything at all in my personal makeup that would justify my passing judgment on a fellow creature, and I had been lost in thought of that kind for some time when I realized that the questioning had progressed to the lanky and malodorous fellow to my immediate right.

"Is it going to bother you that there are translators in the court?" one of the defense attorneys asked him.

"Well, yeah, sure it's going to bother me," he said.

"Do you object to the use of languages other than English?"

"Hell, no, I don't object to languages other than English. The world got some five or six thousand languages. Ain't none of them better than any other, far as I'm concerned."

"Well, then—"

"Personally, I'm a real big fan of Frisian. Not that I speak it, but—"

"That is an admirable—"

"But a lot of languages are what they call endangered—they're being overwhelmed by the big boys—"

"We don't really have time—"

"There're actually dozens of languages today that only have one living speaker left—and when that one dies the language dies with him." The murmurous translation brought expressions of wonder and remorse to the faces of the defendants. "Makes you kind of ask yourself how those people make themselves understood, don't it? I mean—"

"Your honor—" said the attorney, throwing his hands in the air.

"Get off your hobbyhorse and answer the question," said the judge.

"Yes, sir," said the lanky fellow. "What was it again?"

"Given your enlightened attitude toward the world's many languages, why do you object to the translators?"

"They're drivin' me nuts."

The translation. Suppressed giggles from the frightened boys.

"And why is that?"

"Every time anybody says something, those two are mumbling it back in tongues, and it's like I got some schizophrenic voices mumbling at me in my brain."

"I see."

"I sit through a whole trial of that, you're gonna have to put me away."

"In that case—"

"Forward my mail to the funny farm, 'cause I'm gonna be gone from here."

"You're excused."

"All my wires be crossed by that babelic cacophony—"

"Silence!" bellowed the judge, and down came his gavel.

The defense attorney sat down. The prosecuting attorney rose and approached me.

"Please state your name."

"Peter Leroy."

"So far, so good," said BW.

"Have you ever been the victim of a crime?"

"No," I said, confidently, shaking my head to underscore how very certain I was of the veracity of the answer.

"Why did you say that?" said Matthew. "It's not true!"

He was right. As soon as I had said no, I recalled the times when I had been a victim of crimes.

"You've been robbed—" Matthew began, and I could practically see him holding the index finger of his left hand with the first three fingers of his right, beginning to tick off the items in the catalog of my victimization.

"Robbed?" scoffed BW. "When?"

"Robbed of lunch money," said Matthew, evidently beginning to tick off items in a subcategory, "third grade—"

"I think the statute of limitations on the theft of lunch money is about a week and a half," sneered BW.

"He's had cars stolen—two of them," Matthew announced.

"I'll give you that," said BW.

"And the woman at the delicatessen cheats him when he buys his coffee," claimed Matthew, pressing his advantage.

"What?" I said aloud.

"She does," said Matthew, sniffily. "She puts other people's coffee containers into a little bag, but yours—"

"I asked what you do," said the prosecuting attorney.

A complex question, that.

"I—"

"Darryl O'Farrell would not allow this opportunity to slip by," said Matthew.

"We are as one in that opinion," said BW.

"I assist people in writing their memoirs," I said.

"Sounds like interesting work," yawned the prosecuting attorney.

"It is," I lied. "Interesting and tremendously satisfying—personally." I allowed myself a glance at the potential jurors in the gallery. "It gives me great pleasure to help a client find the center—the essential meaning—in a life that may have seemed chaotic and insignificant as it was lived from day to day."

"I'm sure—"

"A memoir—writing a memoir—with my help—enables—empowers—my clients to take control of their lives—even after the fact—or facts—to rethink their lives—reconstruct their lives—to find the little victories that show the world that they have—um—lived."

An embarrassing silence lay upon the court. The translators didn't even bother murmuring a version of my pitch.

"Many people like to write the memoirs of their pets," I asserted in a voice that didn't sound too desperate, I think. "In some ways, it's a lot like taxidermy."

The prosecuting attorney drew a breath and glanced over his shoulder at the defense attorneys, who shook their heads as one and said, "No questions."

Chapter 25

I Am Shaken

"You see, the important thing is the rhythm. You always have rhythm in your shaking. With a Manhattan you shake to foxtrot time. A Bronx to two-step time. A dry martini you always shake to waltz time."

—Nick Charles (William Powell)
in Frances Goodrich and Albert Hackett's screenplay
for Dashiell Hammett's *The Thin Man*

"IT WENT WELL, I think," I claimed as I zipped a strip of peel from a lemon for Albertine's martini. "I managed to mention the pet memoirs." I chose a glass cocktail shaker, one that Albertine had found in a second-hand shop and bought for my birthday a couple of years earlier.

"Are you all right?" she asked. "You seem a little depressed."

"I am. I'm surprised that I am. I wasn't. I mean I wasn't until I got home."

"Thanks."

"Maybe I mean that I didn't know I was depressed until I got home."

"Thanks again."

"What I mean is that only here, in the comfort and security of home, in your embrace, here where I know that I am welcome and loved, where

I know that I can be honest, with you and with myself, am I able to allow myself to admit that I'm depressed."

"Just keep it coming. I love that sweet talk."

"How many shots of gin did I put in?"

"Five."

"You're sure?"

"I'm an eyewitness."

"We're almost out of vermouth."

"I feel your pain."

"You're a darling."

"I am. You're right. You haven't told me whether you were chosen for the jury."

"I wasn't."

"Disappointed?"

"In a way. I was curious." Should I shake or stir?

"Don't let it get you down."

"Oh, no. No. Certainly not. I don't consider it a defeat or anything like that. Not at all. Not at all." Shake, I decided.

"Of course not."

"I mean, it's not like not being chosen for a dodgeball side."

I began shaking the martinis.

"We have to talk a bit about the bills," said Albertine.

I stopped shaking the martinis.

"Oh," I said. I should have stirred. Shaking had somehow struck a jarring note, jolted us into the region of deficit finance.

"All of your clients have become dilatory in their remittance practices."

"They're not paying on time?"

"They're all behind."

"I'll make some calls."

"Oh, don't do that. Please. Don't do that."

"Why?"

"Must I remind you?"

"You mean the Eager Readers people?"

"I do."

"Well, I was properly annoyed. They were about a month behind, weren't they?"

"Yes, and what they owed us would have paid a month's expenses, even the health insurance."

"There's a but lurking in one of the dark corners."

"You alienated them when you called."

"I remember exactly what I said."

"You made that poor girl cry."

"I said, 'You owe me money for work that I have done for you.'"

"And it offended her, deeply, to have you say such a thing to her."

"I also said, and I know that this is exactly what I said, 'I worked ten and twelve hours a day, seven days a week to meet your deadline, and now you're thanking me by not paying me.'"

"That's when she burst into tears."

"You're right."

"And you hung up on her."

"I wouldn't say 'hung up on her.' I could think of no response to tears—so I said goodbye—and then I hung up."

"Your goodbye was rather—emphatic."

"I had to make myself heard—over the tears—precisely so that she wouldn't think that I was hanging up on her—without the customary civility of a goodbye."

"And what did all of that get us?"

"Well, it got me a sharp rebuke from the editor in chief, an e-mail scolding me for my 'disrespect,' and a demand that I apologize to the sensitive dear in accounting."

"And a check?"

"No."

"The checks, a series of small checks, came dribbling in, as I recall, at a pace that might be called glacial."

"True," I sighed.

"Don't call," she said. "I'll take another cash advance on a credit card tomorrow."

I returned to shaking the martinis, more vigorously, perhaps, than I ordinarily did. After a moment or two of my violent agitation, the repeated collision of ice against glass knocked a hole in the side of my birthday shaker. "Shit," I said, regarding the glass, ice, gin, and vermouth on my shoes.

Albertine said nothing, in the manner of long-suffering wives everywhere, and went to work to remove the evidence. I chose a metal shaker, sturdy stainless steel, and shook up another batch, without a hitch.

Chapter 26

I Paper the Town

When I see the posters that go up all over town announcing the impending appearance of an unknown singer or acting troupe, I ask myself, "Why not paper the town with similarly breathless announcements for my taxidermy business?" This is the kind of thinking that gets you somewhere. Keep your eyes open. Promotion is everywhere. Get with it. Get out there. Paper your town.

—Darryl O'Farrell, *Creative Self-Promotion for Taxidermists*

I LAY IN BED trying to think of a headline or slogan that would catch the eye and lure the quick-walking passersby into reading my posters. Perhaps I was blinded by the pattern I saw in the tear-off sheets around the neighborhood. They all took a direct approach. Dog Walker. Day Care. Lose Weight Fast. Work at Home. It seemed best to fit in, conform to the conventions of the genre. I could lead off with "Memoir Assistance."

"Make it 'Confidential Memoir Assistance,'" suggested Matthew. "People may be embarrassed to admit that they need assistance with their memoirs."

"Too many syllables," said BW. "Too hard to take in at a glance."

"'Write Your Memoirs,'" I suggested.

"That's direct," said Matthew. "I like it."

"Direct and dull," said BW. "It sounds like work."

"You're awfully quick with the criticism," scolded Matthew, "but I don't hear any ideas from you."

" 'Cheat Death,' " said BW.

"Wow," I said. "That's powerful."

"Or 'Make Big Money.' "

"Also very strong," I said.

"But, Peter, surely you recall that Darryl O'Farrell explicitly warned against such a crude, blunt, obvious—" said Matthew.

"Darryl O'Farrell is a taxidermist," said BW.

I slipped out of bed, got a sweatshirt and sweatpants from the wardrobe, and pulled them on in the dark.

"Where are we going?" asked BW.

"To the office," I whispered. "I don't want you two waking Albertine."

In the office, I sat at the computer and composed four letter-size posters with tear-off tabs: Confidential Memoir Assistance, Write Your Memoirs, Cheat Death, and Make Big Money.

"An excellent idea," said Matthew. "Put them to the test."

"I have to admit that I agree," said BW.

While the posters were printing, I stretched and thought of going back to bed, and the thought of the cozy warmth of bed and Albertine beside me made me realize that I needed one more poster in the mix.

"Worth a try," said BW when I had it laid out on the screen.

"A very long shot, I think," said Matthew.

WHILE RIDING the train downtown, and reading *Creative Self-Promotion,* as had become my habit, I was disappointed to come upon the passage that I have placed as headnote to this chapter. Of course, I had read it before. I must have read it before. I had read the whole book cover to cover several times. Nevertheless, I had honestly thought that the sheet-with-tear-offs idea was original with me. When I walked into that lamp pole, I didn't say to myself, "This reminds me of Darryl O'Farrell's exhortation to paper the town." I suppose I should have realized that the idea was derivative. After all, if every dog walker and personal trainer in the city was using it, how original could it be? I allowed myself to think that my application of the miniposter with tear-off contact information to the memoir-assistance industry was original, though. I thought that it wasn't unreasonable of me to give myself some credit there. Aren't inventors permitted to patent improvements? It's not as if they have to invent a replacement for the wheel to get a patent. They just have to come up with a significant improvement. I think that I am not deluding myself—or not deluding myself overmuch—to think that if there is or ever should be an organization such as the American Guild of Memoir Assistants, they would be willing to give me a dinner for the improvement.

"On the other hand," said Matthew, "if Albertine finds the whole idea laughable, you can blame it on Darryl O'Farrell."

WE, THE UNCHOSEN, SAT in our usual dullness in the Jury Assembly Room, thinking, I suppose, that we had seen it all by now, that the few days' experience we had had with the justice system had told us all there was to know. We were bored now, and ready to go on to something else.

Chief Clerk Sullivan took a deep breath and boomed, "Ladies and gentlemen—" and then he waited for silence. He had excellent technique. He did not boom a second time. He waited for the compliant among the assembled to spread his boom by word of mouth, and it rolled through the room like rumbling summer thunder, and when it reached the walls it rippled back as a shushing that rebounded until it subsided and all attention was turned toward the front of the room, where Sullivan smiled at his success. I could see in that smile the satisfaction of one who had seen the technique work many times before, a past master. He knew that it always worked. The man should write his memoirs.

"I'm going to call a hundred of you for a voir dire," he said. A hundred! If you had been there, you could have seen us stiffen. A hundred of us. Why a hundred? He had called a couple of dozen at a time for voir dires before. Why a hundred now? There weren't many more than a hundred of us in the Jury Assembly Room now, with so many at other voir dires or chosen for juries. We looked around. We looked at one another for the answer.

A woman beside me was nodding her head as if she had the answer. I caught her eye and raised an eyebrow questioningly.

"The delicatessen murders," she mouthed. If a silent gesture can have volume, this was as thunderous as Sullivan's boom. It was passed among us, and it chilled us. This was more than we had bargained for. This was life and death. We were, a hundred of us, about to be asked to think about guilt and innocence and truth at a level that silenced us.

Sullivan began calling names. As people were called, they rose. A new dignity had come over them. No one smiled, as some had when called for earlier voir dires. They wore the dignity of gravitas. Even those who wore casual clothes, jeans and windbreakers, straightened themselves and their clothing, cloaked themselves in their importance.

When a hundred had been chosen, Sullivan said, handing a stack of cards to the officer of the court who had stood beside him, impassively, silently waiting, "One hundred," and the officer took the cards and went out the double doors into the hall. About twenty of us remained. We wanted to feel relieved, but we'd been fooled before, or had been made to see the folly of assuming that we knew what would happen to us next. Justice moves in mysterious ways. We sat silently, apprehensively.

Sullivan was silent. He looked out at us. He began looking through our cards, slowly and deliberately, as if he were looking for one card, the card of one of us, to single out and—what? What would we be asked to do? Would it be something that we could do?

"The rest of you," he said softly, "are dismissed—"

We turned toward one another, we smiled at one another.

"—but—"

The smiles froze on our faces.

"—you can look forward to being called again after five years have elapsed."

There commenced among us, the sometime inhabitants of the Jury Assembly Room, a shuffling departure, but there was something about the look on Chief Clerk Sullivan's face that made me watch him while he watched us. The look told me that he really had seen it all before. What was that look? At first it seemed to be amusement, a wry detachment, a touch of condescension, perhaps, but the longer I watched him watching us, the better I could see it for what it was. The gathering of personal belongings, the leaving of newspapers for the cleanup crew, here and there an agreement to go somewhere for a drink, but in the main the stuttering movement of a crowd toward a single exit, all of it observed by Sullivan

Sullivan, whose manner of sitting on the desk where he held court, answering the occasional question with the answer he'd been giving to it for decades, acknowledging the occasional goodbye with a nod of his head, all said that he had seen it before, seen it all before. Would I ever find a better client?

I stopped on my way out and stood before his desk. I said nothing. I waited. Imitation is the sincerest form of flattery. He went on flipping the pages of the *Post*. I waited.

"Yes?" he said at last, without looking up.

"*Have* you ever considered writing your memoirs?" I asked.

"I think of it as a project for my retirement," he said. "Something to do in Florida instead of golf."

"Many people who put things off until retirement never get to do them at all," I said, with what I think was just the right note of regret for those missed opportunities.

He looked up at that. "What are you getting at?"

"Death comes when we least expect it—"

"Jesus, Mary, and Joseph!" he declared, crossing himself. "On your way with you!"

"But—"

He reached for the stack of cards.

"I'm going," I said, and I went.

IN THE ELEVATOR LOBBY, the other liberated potential jurors were congratulating one another on their good fortune while waiting for the ancient elevator.

"They are congratulating themselves, really, for having escaped their duty as citizens," snarled Matthew. "Effie would be revolted by this celebration of irresponsibility."

"They're relieved," said BW. "Peter is relieved. I'm relieved. It is enough to have to watch the folly, without having to pass judgment."

"They're like children released from school," sneered Matthew.

"And why shouldn't they be?" asked BW. "The weight is off their shoulders."

"The weight is never off anyone's shoulders," said Matthew. "The burden of the world's cares lies heavy on us every day—"

"Will you two stop bickering and help me find a client in this crowd?" I pleaded.

"You talking to me?" It was a burly fellow, good-natured for the moment, but the kind who can turn into a raging bull if he suspects that you vote the wrong way.

"No—I—I was—"

"Go to it," said BW. "Pitch him."

"I was—on my cell phone."

"Coward."

"Cell phone?" The bull looked me over. He saw no cell phone. His nostrils flared a bit.

I brought it out. "I made it myself," I said. "Assembled it myself. From broken bits and pieces."

"But you—how were you using it? I don't see any ear buds or mouthpiece, and you sure as hell weren't holding that thing in your hand when I turned around." He scraped a hoof on the encrusted floor.

"No," I said, chuckling. "You're right. I've got—"

"Yeah?" he sneered, in the manner of one who smells a liberal.

"Implants. Dental implants. Transducers in my teeth."

"No shit!" He squatted slightly and tilted his head to try to look into my mouth. "Any pain associated with that?"

The elevator arrived. All of us squeezed ourselves into it. No one was willing to be left behind, and the group, as a group, was for the time being so cohesive in its shared sense of release that none of its members was willing to let any other languish in the lobby while the rest made their descent. That cohesive sense of groupness made them insist that I squeeze in with them, though I lagged behind until the car was full and then shrugged to indicate that I guessed I would have to wait for the next one.

"Come on!" roared the bull. "We're not gonna leave you here! Sully might come out and grab you for a trial."

I squeezed in.

"This guy's got dental implants," he announced to the crowd. No response. "Cell-phone buds—right in his teeth. Hands-free all the time. No wires. No nothin'. And he made his own cell phone."

A buzz of admiration filled the car, and from somewhere in the compressed crowd came the question, "Who's your dentist?"

"Who's my dentist? Ah—gee—who remembers the name of his dentist? It's—ah—Darryl—Darryl O'Farrell."

"You've got the attention of the entire car," said BW. "Pitch 'em."

Did I have the nerve to approach anyone in such close quarters, where every word would be overheard?

"This really is a golden opportunity," said Matthew.

I began to think that perhaps I should be more selective in trying to employ the techniques of taxidermy promotion in the cause of memoir-assistance promotion. Taxidermists, as a group, might be much more forward than memoirists or memoir facilitators. We are not the sort to buttonhole potential clients in crowded elevators and pitch them hard. That might work for taxidermists, but it isn't the thing for memoirists. We are a more subtle breed. In general, some sort of print communication is more our sort of thing. It doesn't intrude on the mark's privacy in the way that even a whispered oral approach does.

"If you don't pitch these people now," said BW, "you ought to make yourself sleep on the couch tonight."

That threw my switch. I said, suddenly, "Darryl is—he's quite an interesting guy. He's had—an interesting life, too." I chuckled and shook my head as if remembering something amusing about Darryl the dentist. "You know, it's funny," I said. "He didn't think that he had led an interesting life until he began writing his memoirs. Before that, it seemed that he had followed a well-worn path into the comfortable oblivion of general dentistry on the Upper East Side, with hardly an outstanding moment since the heady days of dental school—but as we began to work together—I assist people in writing their memoirs—professionally—as a board-certified—ah—memorologist—and as we began to work together I helped him recall some of the things that really made his life remarkable—little things—the little successes that we tend to overlook—funny things—poignant things."

"You're not getting anywhere with this," said BW. "Do you mind if I give it one quick shot before the doors open?"

"I—uh—I've never allowed you to—"

"Now," he said aloud, without authorization, "we're getting inquiries about the screen rights."

"Do you have a card?" asked an invisible someone from the rear of the car.

"Yeah, let me have your card," said another.

"I'll take one."

I distributed all the cards I had.

THAT CERTAINLY WAS a success," said BW, in a tone so full of self-congratulation that "thanks to me" would have been entirely superfluous.

"It was," I admitted, "but it can't be considered a technique. It was a unique situation. I grant you that you did a fine job of seizing the moment, and I'm grateful to you for that, but I need a sustainable, ongoing promotional effort that does not depend on chance encounters in crowded elevators."

"Lamppost posters?"

"Yes," I said, defiantly. " 'Lampposters.' "

"That's good," said Matthew. "I like that."

Thanks to the early release, I had the whole afternoon to paper the town with posters for Memoirs While You Wait. I started right where I was, spent an hour or two downtown, then took the subway to Grand Central, and spent two hours in that area. When I started posting lampposters it had been my intention to finish the job uptown in the blocks around our apartment, but I changed my mind as I worked, deciding that it would be best if Albertine wasn't likely to see any of them when she was out shopping or taking her morning walk. She would find out about them when they had drawn customers. When we were prospering, I'd tell her the secret of my success. "It sounds foolish," I'd be able to say then, "but when you look at the results you've got to love it."

At about four o'clock, I took the subway home. I found that Darryl O'Farrell had made me a passionate spectator. In every assemblage of my species, now I looked for the one or two who seemed to think that they had a story to tell. The more I had begun to look, the more I had begun to see. Perhaps it was my state of mind, the little bit of self-confidence that posting my lampposters had given me, but I seemed to see in the car in which I was riding a particularly rich vein of potential clients.

Holding the pole that I was holding, standing directly opposite me, was the pale-skinned actress I had seen on this line before. She was reading a screenplay, rehearsing, I think. In a way, she was practicing a pitch.

She mouthed the words "I am convinced that the theme of life is loss," so perfectly enunciated, though without a sound, that I could tell exactly what the words were. Then she grinned, as if she were savoring the effect that the line would have on her audience, when she spoke it and long after she had spoken it, an audience dispersed now, at the moment of her smiling in the subway, in time and space, to be united temporarily in the future by their witnessing her delivery of the line and by its effect on them. She pleased herself. She did not seem to be aware of her present audience, not at all, though I wasn't her only spectator.

A man beside her, wearing a hat made from a newspaper page, smiled indulgently at her performance, as if she were his precocious niece. A big woman, seated between two other big women, began to croon. "Losing you," she sang softly, "I'm losing you." A subway preacher standing beside me turned toward the singer and held his Bible toward her. "Sister," he asked, "is there a pain in your heart?" A baby in a stroller found this suddenly funny, giggled in a baby's explosive way, and blew baby bubbles of spittle. "Oh, iddle baby, you don't got a pain in your heart, do you?" said a muscular young man with a shaved head. He leaned toward the stroller and tilted his head so that the baby could toy with the silver bangles that dangled from the piercings that ran up and around the rim of his ear. Then the door between cars burst open and two enterprising teenagers swaggered into our midst.

"Ladies and gentlemen, may I have your attention, please?" said the taller one, the first one through the door. "My name is Shawn and this is my friend Tyrone. We are selling candy to raise money for new uniforms for the tae kwon do team at our high school, the High School of Martial Arts. At the present time we only have licorice whips. These are the fine kind of licorice whips that your grandmama or granddaddy probably remember if they are still around and haven't passed over."

"Amen," said Tyrone.

"Mm, mm, mm," said the big woman, and "Mm, mm, mm," said the two big women on either side of her.

"They are long, black, and flexible."

"Oh, yes," said Tyrone. The big woman began digging in her purse.

"They can be used to tie your lover to the bedposts, for tickling, and of course for whipping—if you are into that sort of thing."

"Sell it," said Tyrone.

"While neither Tyrone nor I personally condone such use, I mention it so you see that they are a versatile candy," said Shawn.

"And they taste good," said Tyrone, coming into his own.

"Each package of licorice whips is one dollar," said Shawn, "and I hope you will help us out by buying some because otherwise Tyrone and I are going to have to employ the esoteric techniques we have learned at the High School of Martial Arts to whip your ass."

"Ooh, sign me up for that, Shawn!" said the muscular young man with the shaved head and the ornamented ears.

"He's kidding about that," said Tyrone, apologetically, I thought.

"Thank you," said Shawn, "and have a nice day."

Reaching into my pocket for a dollar, I asked myself whether I could bring myself to do what Shawn and Tyrone did. Could I? It wouldn't be that hard, not after my masterly performance in the elevator. All I would have to do was stand up in a crowded subway car and say, "Ladies and gentlemen, may I have your attention please? My name is Peter Leroy and these are my friends Matthew and BW, and I'm selling memoir-writing services." Nothing to it, really.

I watched the boys work their way down the car and go through the doors to the next car. My heart began to race. My palms began to sweat.

"Go ahead," said BW. "Give it a shot."

I took a breath. I swallowed.

"If Albertine were here," said Matthew, "she would say, 'Don't you dare.' Besides, this is your stop."

"Good point," I said. I got out of the car, walked up to the street, and walked home, without opening my mouth again.

Chapter 27

I Get to Say "Honey, I'm Home"

If all else fails, cross your fingers and put your faith in chance. You may console yourself with the thought that were it not for chance there would be no animals to stuff and mount and no taxidermists to stuff and mount them, for what is everything around us but the latest edition in the endless dance of adaptation through change and chance? I will offer you a personal anecdote. My assistant of many years announced one day that her husband had fallen gravely ill. She would have to leave my employ to care for him. When she saw my face fall, she offered to send her daughter to help me. She feared that the girl wouldn't be much use, but perhaps, if I was patient with her, I might at least teach her to sweep and dust. The girl arrived, and from the moment she stepped into the shop, she demonstrated a remarkable eye for the finest and most subtle effects of the taxidermist's art. She knew, without any introduction to the mysteries of the craft, why I had given a certain tilt to a collie's head, why I arranged a beloved corgi's ears just so. She understood my work, and admired my skill, and endorsed my devotion to it. Sweep and dust! Her proper work was to sit and watch, which I persuaded her to do. My work, which I now performed for her, was never better. Reader, I married her. She is lying here beside me, sweetly sleeping, while I compose this paragraph. In the morning, I will take up the tools of my trade again, and ply it under her approving eyes. You should be so lucky.

—Darryl O'Farrell, *Creative Self-Promotion for Taxidermists*

I STIRRED. It was a night for stirring. I felt that I had reached a state of clarity, and I wanted a world of clarity around me, a world centered on the clear, cold liquid in my glass.

"How did it go?" asked Albertine. Her bright eyes told me that she had something she wanted to say. However, I also had something I wanted to say, and I really wanted to say my piece first.

"Well, I have been released, and I made it home without incident." I thought it best not to say anything about my having come so very close to embarrassing myself in the subway.

"Bravo, my darling," she said, clapping her sweet hands.

"Thanks."

"I have good news—" she began.

I held up my hand. "Your bright eyes tell me that you have something you want to say," I said. "I also have something I want to say, though, and I really want to say my piece first, okay?"

"Before the good news?"

"Yes."

"Well—all right—but—"

"What I have to say is about—coming home," I said, feeling that by establishing my theme I would stake my claim to illustrating it fully.

"Are you sure you wouldn't like to hear my news first? It will only take a minute."

"I think I have to tell you this first, the story of my coming home."

"A whole story?"

"It begins with my observations of the people in the Jury Assembly Room over the several days I spent on jury duty—"

"You're stirring those poor drinks to death."

"Oh. Sorry." I poured. We clinked our glasses. "In the room," I continued, "day after day, the people came and went, continually shifting their seats. It would be interesting to study the dynamics of a crowd like that, perhaps by using time-lapse photography from above, something like that. The shifting and shuffling was what interested me. Some of it was caused by need—people going to the bathroom to use their cell phones, or just stretching their legs—and some of it was caused by shifting itself—people leaving their places and then finding on their return that their places had been filled by someone else, and so shuffling off to other places—but some of it was, I'm convinced, shifting and shuffling just to avoid the deadly stillness of a static state. You would find in any crowd primarily confined to a single room, inevitably, a lot of coming and going, not only occasioned by errands and displacements, but because people must be coming and going, the way a shark must keep swimming. I decided, from watching them come and go, that the mind must be like that, like a crowd confined primarily to a single room. The mind's elements cannot come and go, but they can bestir themselves, to avoid a static state, and they do, shifting and shuffling to keep the mind alive. We call that activity, a mental stretching of the legs, thinking—daydreaming—imagination—and it's from the restless shuffling and shifting in my populous mind that all my harebrained schemes arise."

"Peter—"

"Harebrained schemes, yes, harebrained schemes."

"Now let me tell you—"

"Not yet, my darling, not just yet. This is about coming home, remember?"

"I had lost track of that."

"You see how the mind is stimulated and distracted in such circumstances, left in relative isolation with little to stimulate or disturb it. You see the way one conceives the most fabulous and outlandish and impossible schemes. No outside stimulus is required, really, if the mind has a few memories to work with. Hermits must imagine the most complex conspiracies. You recall Balzac's saying that 'In the country, the lack of occupation and the monotony of life are apt to turn the active mind to cooking.' "

"I recall it whenever I find myself thinking that having a country house might be nice. It sends me right to my stack of take-out menus."

"The situation is quite similar in the jury room, where the lack of occupation and the monotony of life are apt to inspire a restless shuffling and shifting—"

"And so you shuffled on home! Now—"

"—*and* to inspire prospective jurors to the most surprising revelations, declarations made to complete strangers, *and* to turn the active mind to eavesdropping and the construction of fancies and tales built upon the smallest foundations, almost upon no foundation at all."

"What did you hear?"

"Many things."

"But there's something in particular, something that upset you."

"A young woman passing by said, to another young woman walking beside her, 'I may not go home tonight. I may never go home again.' Just that, and then they were out the door."

"I wonder, why—"

"I wonder, too, but at the moment I didn't wonder at all, I just wanted to be home, at once, without the necessity of a journey home, just to be at home again, and I wished for it."

"May I have a second martini, please."

"Sure," I said, and I took her glass. "A full one?"

"Just half."

"Wishing didn't make it so, of course," I said, "but here I am now, and I feel as glad to be here now as I would have felt at the moment when the desire was so fresh and urgent. I realized that the desire to be home and the satisfaction of the desire are emotions that I rarely feel. Ordinarily, filling my days as I do by writing my memoirs and tapping out whatever hackwork comes along, I am already at home when the day ends, never having left it in the first place, except, perhaps, to go to the delicatessen to get a container of coffee."

"Ahh, the Big Coffee."

"Yes. The Big Coffee. Because I am usually at home, working at home as well as living at home, and rarely away from home at all, I rarely experience that feeling, the warm flush that spreads so pleasantly throughout the corpus as one approaches home, having been away. Perhaps it was that feeling that kept Odysseus going, homeward, homeward, despite the difficulties and distractions, and perhaps, paradoxically, it was the anticipation of that pleasant feeling that sent explorers to the distant reaches of the planet and beyond, the anticipation that, when their discoveries had been made, when the exotic lands had been poked and probed and plundered, the voyager would turn, turn about, face toward home, and begin to go back. Then, with the turn toward home, the pleasant feeling would begin, the warm flush that suffuses us when we are homeward bound."

I delivered her drink.

"As the train drew nearer to my stop," I said, "I began to feel it, and I relished it."

"And now you're home."

"Yes. Home is the sailor."

"I'm glad. Now—"

"I'm not quite finished," I said. "Almost, but not quite. I don't know which was the stronger influence on this, the conviction that every scheme I've ever schemed has been a harebrained scheme or the pleasant flush of the homeward bound, but I've decided that it is time for me to abandon harebrained schemes forever and get a regular job of some kind, the kind that requires one to go somewhere away from home and do someone else's bidding for a few hours a day."

"You would hate that."

"I would. Yes. But I would get to feel that feeling every working day, when I set my burden down and turned toward home, and when I got here I would get to fling the door wide and shout, 'Honey, I'm home!' "

"Stop."

"I—"

"Stop," she insisted. "And listen to me. It's my turn."

"Okay."

"The phone has been ringing all day."

"Bill collectors?"

"Would-be memoirists."

"What?"

"It started just after noon. A woman called and said that she wanted to 'enroll.' 'Enroll in what?' I asked. 'The writing thing,' she said. 'Ahh, the writing thing,' said I. 'You want Peter Leroy to help you write your memoirs.' You see how quick and clever I am."

"I never doubted it."

" 'I saw the poster,' she said, and I thought I heard a catch in her voice. I said, gently, 'What poster?' She sniffled, cleared her throat, and said, 'Perpetuate Your Pet.' At once I understood all. You've been out taping posters to lampposts, haven't you, you plucky lad?"

"Well, you see, I—"

"You didn't tell me."

"No, I—"

"You wanted to see if they worked before you told me about your little scheme."

"Yeah."

"You figured I'd forbid it if you told me first."

I took a poster from my pack and handed it to her.

"I would definitely have forbidden it," she said. "You didn't put any of these up in our neighborhood, did you?"

"No. I didn't want to embarrass you."

"I'll put some up tomorrow. And I can put one in the laundry room here in the building. They'll probably let me put one up at the bank, too. And the rest rooms at Madeleine's."

"You think it's a good idea?"

"Peter, you've got eleven clients."

"Eleven! How can I possibly—"

"You're going to give seminars."

"I am?"

"Yes. When the calls kept coming in, I realized that you were going to be overburdened, so I began calling the callers back. 'Congratulations,' I said to them, 'you have been accepted into Mr. Leroy's memoir-writing seminar. I have openings on Monday and Tuesday.' I explained to the last caller that you keep the seminars strictly limited to five memoirists-in-training, so that you can give people the individual attention they need, but that I would put her on the waiting list for Wednesday's seminar."

"Seminars," I muttered, a bit dazed by the prospect.

"You don't mind my committing you to that—without asking?"

"Mind? It's brilliant."

"If the calls keep coming in, and I bet they will, I don't see why you couldn't hold one a day. Maybe even two a day."

"Did any of the—" I hesitated.

"What?" she asked.

"Did they all call because they want to memorialize their pets?"

"Ten out of eleven, including the bartender."

"The bartender called?"

"The bartender called."

"How did you know it was the bartender?"

"Because she said—with a sniffle—'Please tell him this is Mojito's mom.'"

"Ten out of eleven," I said. "And the eleventh?"

"She wants to lose weight fast. I don't know how you're going to deliver on that."

"Something will come to me." I said it, and I meant it. Something would come to me. I was sure it would. Inspiration is really just noise in the neural network—and there's a lot of noise in mine.

IN BED, we read for a while, then turned the lights off for our few hours of sleep before Albertine's midnight session at Madeleine's.

"Al?" I said after lying in the dark for a moment.

"Mm?"

"I won't get to say 'Honey, I'm home.' I won't get to make the journey homeward. I won't feel the warm flush."

"The Big Coffee," she murmured.

"The Big Coffee?"

"It's a journey. The journey to the delicatessen. It's a quest. The quest for the Big Coffee. And when you've found it, when you have the coffee in hand, you will turn, turn about, face toward home, and begin to return. Then, with the turn toward home, when you are homeward bound, the pleasant feeling will begin, the warm flush will suffuse you, and when you get here, you can fling the door wide—"

"And shout 'Honey, I'm home!'"

"Exactly."

"You are a treasure, my long-suffering darling."

I lay in the dark for a while longer.

"Al?" I said.

"Mm?"

"I'm going to be preserving people's pets."

"Mm."

"I'm going to be a taxidermist."

"My mother will be *so* proud," she said, and I could almost hear her smile.

Chapter 28

I Consider My Luck

Time and change are not optional, for the universe is a story and it is composed of processes. In such a world, time and causality are synonymous. There is no meaning to the past of an event except the set of events that caused it. And there is no meaning to the future of an event except the set of events it will influence.

—Lee Smolin, *Three Roads to Quantum Gravity*

I USED TO THINK that "Jack and the Beanstalk" was about luck, and dumb luck at that. As I remembered the tale, Jack was a dull boy, a sluggard, who complained when his mother sent him to town to sell the cow, their only remaining asset, so that they could buy some food. Whenever Jack came to mind, as he has from time to time over the years, I saw him trudging along a dusty country road, reluctantly, tugging the cow along behind him. He would rather be doing anything else; in fact, he would rather be doing nothing. That, I thought, was the essence of Jack, that he would rather be doing nothing. He had arrived at this state of mind, I had come to believe, because his past was a string of failures. Earlier, in the time before the tale that we are told, his agile mind had concocted one harebrained scheme after another, and he had thrown himself into each one with the headstrong verve of the plucky lad, and every time he had failed, because every scheme was foolish, a failure foreordained. Foolishness had made him feckless in the past, and he was feckless now for lack of trying, beaten, angry with himself, fate, the world. "I've failed so often," he moaned, "that it would be best to do nothing from now on, thereby reducing the risk of future failure to the absolute minimum." So. There he was, trudging along, sad and sullen. Why, oh why, had his mother charged him with taking the cow to market and selling it? Didn't she understand that the effort was as doomed to failure as Jack was fated to fail? He was sure to be swindled at the market, he just knew he was. The sharpers would see him coming. They'd make his head swim with their arguments and calculations, and he'd be lucky to leave with the value of a cow's tail in his pocket. The future is the name we give to our hopes and fears, and Jack felt certain that his future would be the flop his past had been.

As I understood Jack, his fear of a greater failure was what made him so willing to trade the cow for a handful of beans. A handful of beans! Not a bad bargain if you're convinced that you will lose the cow and your shirt if you go all the way to the market. Take the beans and head for home. Feel the warm flush. He did, and I imagined that he must have felt good about what he had done. He might have done so much worse.

As I understood "Jack and the Beanstalk," its essential message was that, sometimes, it's just dumb luck that gets you through. I saw it as a tale about chance, upon which so much in life, including life itself, depends. Even a gullible bumpkin can get by if he has a little luck, if the cards fall his way.

So I thought, or so I had come to think, over the years that had intervened between my last reading of the tale, as a child, and the time when I began this book, a time when I dearly wished that I had a cow to sell. However, my reading in bed in the time before Albertine and I turned the lights off at the end of the preceding chapter had been in the nature of research, or fact-checking. I had consulted the version of "Jack and the Beanstalk" that appears in *The Red Fairy Book,* edited by Andrew Lang, originally published in 1890. It had given me much to think about. Revisiting the source had shown me that I had been wrong about "Jack and the Beanstalk" and about Jack. I learned that Jack, far from being a sullen sluggard . . .

. . . was a giddy, thoughtless boy, but very kindhearted and affectionate.

A giddy, thoughtless boy? A boy, in short. Nothing wrong in that.
However, no evidence of the history of failure that I had come to think
preceded the opening scene. None of the brooding and sulking, none of
the guilt that I had imagined. He wasn't even reluctant and fearful when
he set out on the dusty road to the market:

Jack liked going to the market to sell the cow very much . . .

Ah, well. That's the trouble with checking the facts: so often it de-
stroys our illusions. However, if the work of memory has been particularly mischievous in distorting them, the facts may also bring some
pleasant surprises. I was surprised, for example, to discover on rereading
(or rediscover on rereading) that Jack was aided in his struggles by a
fairy. I picture her as long-tressed and pale, a fairy painted by John
William Waterhouse. Near the end of the tale we learn this:

Before her departure for fairyland, the Fairy explained to Jack that
she had sent the butcher to meet him with the beans . . .

Butcher! That I found surprising, too, though not so pleasantly as the
discovery of the beautiful fairy. The butcher gave me pause. The butcher
made me wonder. Why should the man whom Jack encountered along
the way to the market be a butcher? Why not a seed-vendor? I grant you
that it would be logical for Jack to be seeking a butcher when he had a
cow to sell, but this is a butcher who, when he makes his first appearance
on the road to the market, has "some beautiful beans in his hand." If he
is a butcher, why is he carrying beans? I've dealt with some butchers,
and experience has taught me that they do not, as a rule, have beans
about them. "Not my department," they say when asked—the polite
ones, that is. Why, oh why, would the lissome auburn-haired fairy send a
butcher to do the work of a beanmonger?

. . . in order to try what sort of lad he was.

Of course, of course, of course. It was a test. I was, in my rereading, beginning to see a message in the tale different from the one that I had supposed to be its burden. Life is a series of tests, the tale told me, making it, in that respect at least, very much like school, and making school, with all its tests and quizzes and exams, ideal training for life. A test, but what sort of test? Was the fairy trying to find out whether Jack knew a bogus butcher when he saw one? Did Jack even perceive that he was a butcher? Was he wearing a bloodstained apron? Carrying a cleaver? Tattooed with the secret sign of the Guild of Itinerant Butchers? Did Jack ask himself why a butcher would be walking along the market road bearing beans? Did Jack smell a rat? Did he detect at least a whiff of rat in the air? No. He was a gullible bumpkin, like me, but being gullible didn't count against him, because the butcher and his beans were merely the start of the test, the dusty-road-to-market equivalent of breaking the seal on the exam booklet. The beanstalk itself was the real test:

> "If you had looked at the gigantic Beanstalk and only stupidly wondered about it," she said, "I should have left you where misfortune had placed you, only restoring her cow to your mother."

Apparently, the world as run by fairies was a system not of reward and punishment but of reward and neglect. If one failed the test, one got—nothing. One was not punished. One was simply left to live as fortune's fool. (This is not to say that in Jack's world there were no imps and demons that administered other standardized tests and parceled out punishment aplenty for failure, only that fairy justice didn't work that way.)

> "But you showed an inquiring mind, and great courage and enterprise, therefore you deserve to rise . . ."

Aha! There it is! This is the real lesson of the tale. This is the bit of wisdom that storytelling grandparents intended to inculcate in their little lads and lasses when they told Jack's tale at hearthside on a wintry e'en. What does one need to succeed? An inquiring mind. Courage. Enterprise. These three shall see you through.

"... and when you mounted the Beanstalk you climbed the Ladder of Fortune."

Interesting. Only then? Not before then? Wasn't the entire path that Jack took from the time his mother asked him to take the cow to market a part of the ladder of fortune? Why not say that he had set his foot on the ladder when he agreed to take the cow in the first place? There was some courage in that, and a bit of enterprise. No sign of an inquiring mind, I suppose. How about the moment of accepting the beans? There was some evidence of an inquiring mind there, I think, since they seemed to be extraordinary beans. Some enterprise, too, since beans are seeds, and seeds encapsulate more future value than present value, making a barter for beans an investment in bean futures, and we must be counted enterprising when we make an investment, even if we invest badly while believing that we are investing well. I see no evidence of courage in that investment, though, since Jack was, I persist in believing, trading the cow for beans to avoid humiliating himself at the market. Well, then, how about that time at daybreak when he went out into the garden and planted the beans? That shows an inquiring mind, certainly. Planting seeds and raising crops are also evidence of enterprise, the very metaphor for it, as those CEOs who promise their stockholders that they will "grow" the business while they are surreptitiously plundering it know. No courage there, I suppose. Something like timidity, in fact, creeping out before mother was up to plant the seeds unseen. So. I understand. Jack had exhibited one or two of the essential qualities before the magic moment, but only when he mounted the beanstalk did he put all three to work at once, and only then did he set foot upon the ladder of fortune. Okay. It works for me.

After the fairy has revealed her part in Jack's rise . . .

She then took her leave of Jack and his mother.

The fairy, I take it, represents luck. Luck, in my book, is nothing more than the name we give after the fact to an unexpected agent that initiates a string of events that runs particularly well or particularly badly. A statement about luck is a statement about the mind, not about

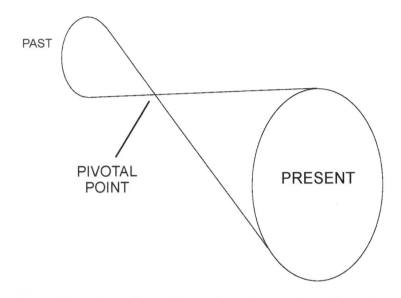

FIGURE 8: Looking backward, we seem to see a pivotal point—a single event, choice, or act—that has made all the difference, made our present circumstances what they are, even made us what we are.

the world. We recognize the agent of our luck only in retrospect, looking backward from a time when we feel that we have been lucky to find the moment that set off the cascade of events that brought us where we are. We expect to find a single moment, one event, a pivotal point in the history of our luck, and because that is what we expect to find, it is what we usually do find. We find what seems to have been the lucky break or the big mistake, and so we thank our lucky stars that we took the road less traveled or curse the fates that sent that little wavelet that flipped us on our backs. With hindsight, we seem to see that everything preceding the pivotal point was leading up to it, tending toward it, and that everything following it grew from it.

To any observer outside the lucky one himself, however, luck is simply chance. Chance is neutral. It is not the case that chance favors the prepared mind; it is, rather, that the prepared mind recognizes the main chance when—if—it comes. Like rain and sunlight, chance falls upon us equally, but sometimes opportunity knocks in such an outlandish fashion that only a gullible bumpkin would be likely to welcome it in. In that way, gullible-bumpkinhood was the secret to Jack's eventual success, the preparation that led him to seize the main chance when it came along. Without the beans, there would have been no beanstalk, and only a gullible bumpkin or credulous rube, like Jack, like me, would have traded the cow for a handful of beans. The fairy knew that Jack was gullible, and she took advantage of that gullibility to get him started on the path to the ladder of fortune. Has she left Jack forever? I think not. He is still a boy at the end of the tale. He still has a long way to go in life, and I would hate to think that he was going to have to make his way on his own. One's perch on the ladder of fortune is precarious. The rails are slippery, some of the rungs are missing, others are rotten. He will rise, but he will fall. Plucky lad that he is, he will scramble upward after each fall. That is, he will attempt to scramble upward after each fall. Some of his upward-scrambling schemes will be ridiculously harebrained and many of his pluckiest efforts will be feckless. Through it all, the fairy will stay with him. She will assume mortal form and become Jack's long-suffering wife. Ultimately, I think it's likely that he will settle down and write his memoirs: *The Personal History, Adventures, Experiences & Observations of Jack, the Beanstalk Boy.* Wherever he has arrived on the ladder of fortune, how high he has climbed, how far he has slipped, won't matter, then. We memoirists know that we do not make life's journey to get somewhere; we make the journey so that we can tell the tale. We assist as passionate spectators at the little drama of our own lives.

"That is the most self-serving interpretation I can imagine," sneered Matthew.

"I'm sorry," I said, "but I can't help seeing myself in Jack."

"He was a gullible bumpkin, like you, that's true," said BW.

"He was also kindhearted and affectionate, like me," I said.

"Also giddy and thoughtless, as I recall," said Matthew.

"Most of all, though," I said with some force, "he was plucky, and enterprising, and curious, like me—and of those three the greatest is curiosity. Curiosity may have led me down many a blind alley, but curiosity will ensure that I don't miss the main chance if it ever comes my way. Most people walk by the extraordinary. They don't want to know about it. They don't want to have to revise their lives to accommodate it. They don't want to have to realign their neural networks to fit it in. Not so the curious lad. He seizes the unusual. He knows it when he sees, it, too. He's as sensitive to it as the spider at the nerve center of its web. The odd thing, the unusual thing, or the extraordinary opportunity tickles the hair on the back of his neck. The curious lad leaps on the extraordinary thing, whether he finds it in the outstretched hand of a strolling butcher or lying at the center of a rickety card table or among the dusty whatnots on an upper floor of an old curiosity shop or nowhere in the world at all but within the noise inside his mind when he can't sleep. His passionate curiosity pushes him, leads him, commands him to find out more, plumb the mysterious depths of this thing, this idea, and—"

"It must be just about time to get up and go to Madeleine's," said Matthew.

"Oh, good. I could use a drink," said BW.

"No!" I insisted. "I'm not quite finished. Listen to me, if you ever want me to listen to you again."

"All right. All right."

"Calm down. Speak your piece."

"If you pursue anything—even a screwball idea or a harebrained scheme—to the point where you understand it, you will understand more of life than all but a very few people ever do, and if you are also bold and if you are also enterprising, you can turn your little understanding to your advantage—you can climb the ladder of fortune—and when you have done so, all the people who envy you your position on the ladder will regard the day when curiosity got the better of you and you traded the cow for the beans—or picked up the battered book on Henry's table—as a great stroke of luck, but I know, and knew the moment that it occurred, that the greatest stroke of luck in my life—"

Chapter 29

I Effect a Transformation

Duration is the transformation of a succession into a reversion. In other words: the becoming of a memory.

—Alfred Jarry, "How to Construct a Time Machine"

"PETER?" said a voice.

I was being shaken.

"Mm?" I said, not quite sure where I was.

"It's time to get up. We've got to get dressed and go."

"Mm?"

"Do you want to stay here?"

Stay here? Where? In the cardiac ward? In a corner room at the Albatross? Hidden in a cupboard in the giant's castle?

I opened my eyes. Here. Oh, yes. Here was New York, our bedroom, our bed. I could stay here, in this bed. That was the offer she was making. No. I couldn't stay here. I didn't want to stay here. I wanted to get out of bed and go to Madeleine's with Albertine. I began forcing my body to follow the plan.

"Don't get up," said Albertine. "You seem so tired."

"It's Matthew and BW," I said. "Those two guys are wearing me out."

"They've taken you for quite a ride."

"You don't know the half of it."

"But I will, someday, won't I?"

"Oh, yes. I'll write it all down. I'll read it to you. Right now, though, I wish they would agree to go."

"Why don't you stay here and try to come to some arrangement with them? See if they won't let me have you all to myself on the weekends, for example."

"I see the wisdom in that, but I'd rather go to Madeleine's with you."

"Then bring them along. They'll do to swell the crowd. Take a table in the back. Get this thing settled, and if you can—send them on their way."

It was a rainy night. We walked the short way to Madeleine's under our umbrellas, fighting to keep them turned against the wind, not talking. I was afraid that the weather would thin the house at Madeleine's, and I didn't want to say anything that might lead one or the other of us to mention that possibility.

BW, MATTHEW, AND I took seats at a table in the darkest corner and surveyed the room. Apparently the rain had had the opposite of the expected effect on people: it had made them leave the dull shelter of their apartments and seek the warmth of the presence of others, the solace of music at midnight. The room was full.

"If it weren't impossible," said BW, after glancing around the room, "I would say that I know that woman."

"Which one?" asked Matthew.

"The one in the very short dress."

"That's Sheila, the lover of crab cakes," I said.

"It can't be," said BW.

"It has to be," I said. "Of course it is. She must live in the neighborhood. That's how she made it into the Miami of my mind."

"In that case," said Matthew, "I suppose that it's not absolutely impossible that the fellow with the silver hair is the eminence from the Charlesbank cardiac ward."

"It is," I said, "and look who's with him."

"Sister Solace."

"Are they an item?"

"From the look of things, I'd say that they've been an item for many years."

"They're all here, aren't they?"

The three of us looked around the room, surreptitiously, with the impenetrable air of indifference assumed by the most polished of passionate spectators. Not quite everyone was there. Cerise was, and the entire family of vacationing Germans, and the orderly who had wheeled Matthew's gurney, and the Duke and Duchess of Kitsch, and most of the others, but—

"None of your people are here," BW noted. "No aerobicized bartender, no Sullivan Sullivan."

"That is because I actually was called for jury duty. I actually sat in the Jury Assembly Room. I really spoke to those people. My experiences with them were limited by their close proximity to reality."

"Effie's not here, either," said Matthew dourly.

"No," I said. "She's in Maine, in a cabin in the woods somewhere, away from it all, aloof from the world, and I think, Matthew, that you should go and join her there."

"You do?"

"I do."

"But—will she want me?"

"Matthew, she is pining for you."

"Do you really think so?"

"Believe me. I know. Go."

"Just a moment, please," said BW.

"You don't have to come," said Matthew.

"I don't?"

"No."

"I'm pleased—but—I'm also astonished. Are you sure?"

"Quite sure."

"Matthew—I—I'm not sure that you can get along without me. Forgive me for putting it this way, but you may be enterprising—let's say that you are enterprising—but curious and bold you are not. You need me, I think."

"Ah! The solipsism of the imaginary friend! The egotism of the alter ego! Of course I needed you. That's why I invented you. I needed you, and you have served me well. I've learned from you. I've benefited from all of your experiences. It was through you that I contemplated taking a sabbatical from the world's anger and pain; through you I've vacationed among the grasping rich on the famous Phantom Islands; I've learned to feel compassion for even the lowliest of creatures—the horseshoe crab, for instance—and to accept the fact that nature is absurd and essentially unjust; I've come to understand the details that underlie Effie's revulsion at the pernicious antics of our species; through you I've contemplated my most fantastic castle-in-the-air, that ideal engineered world—clean, logical, and neat—that I supposed Effie and I might someday build, and found that the simplest error in such a plan—the unexpected presence of a goose or the absence of a barbecue grill—might bring the whole thing crashing down; I've hobnobbed with artists and media personalities, swilled mojitos, and analyzed the evils of unchecked capitalism and the distribution of unintelligence among manunkind; I have ensconced in my imaginary seraglio all the women that I have never possessed; and I have learned to avoid crab cakes or anything else in life that wraps disappointment in a golden crust."

"I know," I said. "Me too."

"But now, my friend," said Matthew, with surprising regret, "it is time for you to go."

BW turned to me. "Where?" he asked.

"The friend of a friend is willing to rent you a furnished apartment in Barcelona at a very good rate," I said.

"I'm off," he said. He rose, stood straight, and with the barest suggestion of clicking his heels bowed slightly to each of us in turn, blew a kiss to Albertine, and left.

"Now you, Matthew," I said.

"Are you going to count the ways in which I have been useful to you?"

"No. I think you know most of them. I will thank you for allowing me to contemplate my mortality from a distance, though."

"My pleasure," he said, wincing.

"I apologize for inflicting that on you."

"No need. You really only asked me to play my part—and you brought me through. All in all, I've enjoyed being one of the musketeers."

"Now—go—go to Effie."

"I will," he said. "There is one thing I'd like to say, though."

"One thing."

"You may be making a mistake."

"A mistake."

"Yes. Each of us has the three essential qualities in varying degrees. Have you thought about that? Curiosity, courage, and enterprise. Together we were a whole man. Without us, you—"

"Matthew, look around this room and tell me what you see."

"Chairs, tables, people, a piano, drinks—"

"Yes. Very good. Now turn to your left and tell me what you see."

"A wall, a sconce, a mirror—"

"And in the mirror?"

"You."

"A man alone. A man of parts, but a man alone."

"You're putting me in my place."

"I'm sorry, but I am."

"You're not asking me to go. You're sending me away."

"I am pointing out to you that in the part of my mind that I call Maine, there is a cozy cabin in the woods, and there waits a woman who loves you."

"Goodnight, then," he said, rising.

"Goodnight, and goodbye," I said. I didn't watch him leave. I hope he'll be happy. I do. I hope he remembers to pack his mittens.

I sat still, listening to Albertine play, but scanning my mind as well, to see whether they were still there. They were, of course, but not as presences, only as memories, matter for a memoir.

Chapter 30

I Am at Home

The word *Bohemia* tells you everything. Bohemia has nothing and lives upon what it has. Hope is its religion; faith (in oneself) its creed; and charity is supposed to be its budget. All these young men are greater than their misfortune; they are under the feet of Fortune, yet more than equal to Fate. Always ready to mount and ride an if, witty as a feuilleton, blithe as only those can be who are deep in debt and drink deep to match, and finally—for here I come to my point—hot lovers, and what lovers!

—Honoré de Balzac, *A Prince of Bohemia*

ALBERTINE AND I WALKED HOME arm in arm, singing in the rain. She was lighthearted and light on her feet, pleased by the turnout, her performance, and its reception. After we let ourselves into the apartment, when we were behind the door and out of sight, she held me by the shoulders and looked at me intensely, scrutinizing my face, delving the depths of my eyes, and then she drew me to her suddenly and hugged me tight.

"Honey, you're home," she whispered in my ear, "and I am very glad. You have been far, far away at times, for days and days now, but I think you're back now, home again. There is a clarity in your eyes that I haven't seen for quite a while."

"Yes," I said. "I'm home, and we're alone."

"Alone at last!"

"You didn't know when you married me that you would be living with such a crowd," I said. "Neither did I, for that matter."

"I knew that there was a lot going on behind those eyes. I knew it when you spoke to me in the hall that day when we took the college entrance exams."

"I was in awe of you."

"You didn't impress me at first."

"Just another awestruck boy ready to fall at your feet."

"Something like that, but then you spoke."

"I knew, somehow, that I had one chance—"

"At best. There was the possibility, in those days, that I would have walked on by, without giving you even that one chance."

"I understood that your pausing, and your small smile, represented an opportunity not to be missed."

"And you seized it, boldly—"

"I just started speaking. It was that or stand there staring stupidly and wondering about you."

"If you had stood there staring and only stupidly wondering about me, I would have left you where you stood so stupidly staring, or would have cut you with a sharp remark and sent you whimpering home to your mother, but you took me quite by surprise—"

"I did, didn't I?"

"Oh, yes, you certainly did. I wonder if you have any idea how brilliantly you made yourself stand out against the gray ground of those other suitors."

" 'As brilliantly as a wart on a bald head'? I asked, in my best bumpkin manner.

" 'You have given my life its pivot and purpose,' you said to me."

" 'Pivot and purpose?' you asked."

" 'Pivot,' you said, 'because my life will balance on the moment of this meeting.' "

"Life, of course, is just the first draft of our memoirs."

" 'Purpose, because I know now that the point of everything I have ever done was to prepare me for this moment—' "

"I hadn't done much, really—though I had had some success with that airplane I built from parts of old motorcycles—"

" '—and that henceforth everything I will ever do—' "

"I can't have said 'henceforth.' "

" '—will be to woo and win you.' "

"I meant it."

"I knew that, and I know it now."

"You did? You do?"

"I did. I do."

"How?"

"I looked into your eyes—"

"Where you saw evidence that I had an inquiring mind, great courage, and enterprise, and therefore deserved to rise?"

"I looked into your eyes and saw what I see in your eyes now, and what I seek in them on days when I feel tired—when I feel the passage of time—when I don't want to look in a mirror. Through all the years since that encounter, I have always been able to look into your eyes and see that you look back at me with the same full measure of passion that I saw there that afternoon."

"I am your passionate spectator."

"You are," she said, with a promise in her smile, "and therefore you deserve your prize."